COUNTRYMEN
OF BONES

COUNTRYMEN OF BONES

◇

A NOVEL BY
Robert Olen Butler

Henry Holt and Company
New York

For Allen H. Peacock

Henry Holt and Company, Inc.
Publishers since 1866
115 West 18th Street
New York, New York 10011

Henry Holt® is a registered trademark
of Henry Holt and Company, Inc.

Published in Canada by Fitzhenry & Whiteside Ltd.,
195 Allstate Parkway, Markham, Ontario L3R 4T8.
Originally published in hardcover in 1983 by Horizon Press.
Reissued in cloth and paper in 1994 by Henry Holt and Company.

Library of Congress Cataloging-in-Publication Data
Butler, Robert Olen.
Countrymen of bones / Robert Olen Butler.—1st Owl book ed.
p.   cm.
1. Indians of North America—New Mexico—Antiquities—Fiction.
2. Atomic bomb—New Mexico—Los Alamos—History—Fiction.   3. Man
—woman relationships—New Mexico—Fiction.   4. Archaeologists—New
Mexico—Fiction.   5. Physicists—New Mexico—Fiction.   I. Title.
PS3552.U8278C6   1994   93-37099
813'.54—dc20   CIP

ISBN 0-8050-3202-9
ISBN 0-8050-3142-1 (An Owl Book: pbk.)

Henry Holt books are available for special promotions and
premiums. For details contact: Director, Special Markets.

Printed in the United States of America
All first editions are printed on acid-free paper.∞

1   3   5   7   9   10   8   6   4   2
1   3   5   7   9   10   8   6   4   2
pbk.

I wonder, have I lived a skeleton's life,
As a questioner about reality,
A countryman of all the bones of the world?
                                    —Wallace Stevens

DARRELL REEVES LOOKED TO the south when he heard the bombs falling, south down the trackless Jornada del Muerto, the journey of the dead, where the mesquite sucked deep into the desert soil. The mesquite was stunted and hard, like the souls of the men making this war, Darrell thought, and no shadow touched another. Far off, a sand devil rose up; silent from this distance, the swirl of wind climbed, taking on its body of dust and sand, broadening and flexing and then sliding away.

Darrell waited for the bombs again, the B-29's making their practice runs in the Alamogordo Range. But the only sounds, now that he had turned, were the bellows-pop of a tent in the wind and Betty beginning to titter, holding it in but the sound shaping into an explicit giggle. Darrell's hands jumped up, the blade of his trowel flashed in the sun, he turned and wanted to gouge out the foolishness in her and in Thomas who sat beside her in the mouth of the equipment tent. Their faces turned to him—they looked very young—and their levity vanished. They knew Darrell's disappointment over the excavation. Thomas said, "We're sorry, Dr. Reeves."

Darrell nodded but he could not say to them, it's all right, even though he wanted to. He crossed the fifty yards to his tent, not looking at the space that had held the mound of earth, the mound gone now, every particle sifted through the rocking screens and piled as back dirt in a long, professional hedgerow nearby.

He entered the tent and sat on the rattan chair and he would not think about the chances of the mound being empty but the earth beneath it being full. The whole idea of an ancient Indian burial out here in the middle of the desert was a very long shot anyway, he thought. "Foolish," he said aloud. It had been no mound at all. And his thoughts drooped to his hands and he looked at the trowel. He took out his handkerchief, soaked with his sweat, and he wiped the trowel clean. It was a long-bladed trowel. He'd had it ground down from a ten-inch trowel used by a brickmason. The blade was as strong and flexible as a Toledo sword. Darrell held it in a shaft of sunlight and turned in in his hands and the blade flashed, faded, and flashed again. A quick gust of memory: his wife, angry, had challenged him, Do you expect to excavate your way to God with your tweezers and brushes? No, he'd answered, those are only for when I draw near; most of the work would be done with my mason's trowel. His head jerked up. He was thirty-seven and his wife had left his life a decade ago. He challenged his mind for letting her in now. He decided it was the disappointment that brought the intrusion, and it was the heat, though the sun would be down in three hours and the desert would turn cold. And as for the disappointment: he'd draw up the grid of a digging plan and they'd see what might be in the earth. His two workers would not graduate for three months and he could have them longer than that, if Betty didn't join the Red Cross and if Thomas's punctured eardrum kept him out of the war for good.

The lolloping thump of an approaching horse turned Darrell's face to the tent door and the sound drew near and scuffled to a stop. A long moment passed but there were no voices. The silence persisted and Darrell rose and stepped out into the sunlight. Thomas and Betty were standing facing the horseman, but they were held motionless. The horseman had stopped just out of easy talking range. He was a man with a wide-brimmed, flat-topped hat, the shadow of which obscured his face. He sat stiff-backed on a chestnut Arabian and he seemed to Darrell to be taking the site in, though he moved not at all. Darrell walked toward the man and only the horse moved, dipping its head briefly. The man was compact, hard, a short-handled ax; and his face, that grew clear in the shadow of the hat as Darrell approached, had the same hardness to it, with the eyes deep-cut and the mouth wide and sharp-edged, like the break of a potsherd.

Before Darrell could speak, the man said, "You with them others, are you?"

"What others?" Darrell said.

The man did not reply at once; the face did not change; not a flicker of feeling crossed it; but Darrell sensed the man was making a crucial judgment.

Finally the man said, "The others ten mile down south of here."

"We're from the University of Santa Fe. We're alone here, doing an archaeological dig."

"The others down there who are trying to force all the ranchers out," the man said as if he hadn't heard Darrell.

"We're associated with no one else."

"What do you want with this god-forsaken place, anyway?"

"We suspect there might be . . ."

"If you think your hints about my cattle are gonna scare me just because you got some goons with uniforms, you better think again."

"We threatened no one," Darrell said and he felt his chest pumping up now. He could accept only so much irrationality. But even as Darrell's anger rose, the horseman's left hand moved from the horn of the saddle to his hip, and the movement drew Darrell's eyes to a rifle in a saddle holster and he kept his anger in. "We're associated with no one else. No one. I have no idea who that is, ten miles to the south."

The man sat unmoving, his left arm akimbo, and the silence

13

stretched on until a faint rumbling came from far to the south-east, beyond the mountains. The horseman looked back over his shoulder and then abruptly jerked at the reins and galloped off.

TWO HUNDRED MILES TO the north, below the rim of the caldera of an ancient volcano, lay Los Alamos. Gripped in canyons between thick fingers of piñon and juniper were the clusters of hasty buildings—barracks and dormitories and laboratories swirled in eddies shaped by the impulses of the minds there.

In the back of a hall, Lloyd Coulter listened to the voices beginning to rise, beginning to bloat with passion, and he knew they were afraid; he knew he was himself afraid. Neddermeyer was at the chalk board, making one of his characteristic leaps of intuition, bypassing the steps of logic, sensing the rightness of his vision. Implosion.

Lloyd closed his eyes. Neddermeyer was crying out again, This gadget must be different fundamentally. Of course, said a voice from the ones who slouched on their canvas chairs pulled together as haphazardly as the buildings outside. Of course, another voice repeated. The plutonium gun is dead.

Lloyd tested that assertion. But in images, this time. Maybe that was how Neddermeyer's mind worked, like Lloyd's own, in images. Inside the bomb, the gun firing one bit of critical mass into another and then the lovely blooming. Lloyd could see that part clearly: a vast, starry mass, infinite numbers of particles one splitting another splitting another, faster, the bloom, the light, the letting go. But the chain suddenly broke. The bursting stars vanished. The gun was too slow, there were too many free particles as it was, the mass would not hold, they glanced off each other, exploded on their own, self-contained, leading nowhere.

Then Lloyd heard the only voice that mattered and he opened his eyes. The others had stopped speaking and they were all listening to J. Robert Oppenheimer. Oppenheimer. Lloyd smiled faintly. Oppie. That's how Lloyd knew this man who held all the others in thrall. Oppie. And Oppie would take away the fear in this room. He had risen, his head thrust forward on his thin stalk of a neck like a sharp-petaled flower in a steady wind. Oppie was talking about the betatron, the cloud chamber, about how they'd test Neddermeyer's vision of implosion. High explosives, their blast caught by a molded lens, pressed into a center where the plutonium waited like a bride. And Lloyd was helping set it up. The betatron was almost ready out at K-site, out where Lloyd could get away from the trailers and quonsets and pre-fabs, where he could slip into a stand of juniper and think what to do next about Anna.

He stepped outside. He stood on the porch of the lodge, one of the timbered buildings left over from the Los Alamos Ranch School the Army had taken over two years ago, in early 1943. More than two years. Time was running out. Oppie would win, Lloyd thought. Oppie would move the betatron experiments forward. Oppie had to make implosion work. Because there wasn't much time left.

Lloyd felt queasy. He wanted to shake the worries out of his head. He crossed the lawn of the lodge and entered the dusty street leading to his room in a quonset hut down by the central warehouse. He passed rows of expansible trailers with bed sheets flapping on clotheslines in between and children squalling and the air smelling of sour milk. They shouldn't have let the families in, Lloyd thought. There were more than five thousand people stuffed onto this little island floating in the Jemez Mountains. They shouldn't have let the families in. But he felt like a hypocrite at once. He envied his colleagues who had wives to sit with, to touch in this high thin air when it was dark. He chided himself for his hypocrisy and he thought of Anna and he turned into a sidestreet and walked down to the quartermaster building. It was a large building, clapboard, one of the structures they'd taken a little more time with, and he went in a side door with a military stencil on it: Technical Supplies, Standard Issue.

Anna Brown was standing by her desk, bent over slightly at the waist, her dark hair—sleek and curved at its front vertical

15

edge—fell down and hid her face. Anna's hair reminded Lloyd of an industrial design of Raymond Loewy, a bullet train or a Hupmobile, streamlined, the vision of a new age. He let the door slam shut and Anna straightened sharply, startled, and Lloyd felt bad, he wanted to go to her and put his arms around her, he yearned, his hands wanted to rise, but he could not move and he said, "I'm sorry, Miss Brown. I didn't mean to startle you."

Her face was on him now. He tried not to gasp, not to stammer. He knew he came off as slightly befuddled, a bit absentminded, in these encounters, but that was all right for now. He wasn't so much older than she. Maybe eight years, ten at the most. She was no less than twenty-six, he decided. He crossed to the wooden counter between them. She was rolling her eyes in relief and it was her eyes—very large, very dark—that dominated him. Her nose was a little too big, faintly aquiline; her mouth was a little too small; but her eyes filled him up. She was in her Army uniform, the color of leaf mold.

"You gave me a fright, Dr. Coulter," Anna said.

Lloyd had no answer. He hated this. He shouldn't have come impulsively. He should have gone out in the junipers first and thought it out, thought what to say. Then there was the clear, hard report of an explosion outside, far away. A commonplace sound at Los Alamos, but Anna's eyes shifted at the blast and Lloyd had a way out.

Words poured from him, rushed: "That's the X-ray Group. They're X-raying controlled spherical charges, trying to follow the pattern of the implosion by measuring the X-rays as a function of time by using a grid of Geiger counters."

Anna was looking at Lloyd again and a trace of the expression she'd had when he'd startled her had come back into her face. Lloyd added, "It's not working, those studies. That blast you just heard may well be the last test they conduct with the X-rays . . . The betatron will replace these . . . ." Lloyd had a vision of his own foolishness and his fists jumped up onto the wooden counter. He felt his anger pushing out, stretching his skin.

16

"Is there something you need, Dr. Coulter?"

"Yes," Lloyd said. "Yes." His mind thrashed around. "Twenty yards of connector cable."

"Didn't you get some of that just last week?"

"I need more."

Anna whisked a form off her desk and with a continuing swoop of her arm stepped forward and put the form in front of Lloyd. "You know what you've got to fill in, Dr. Coulter." Now she paused. She was standing near him and he looked at her and she smiled and her mouth widened and she was very pretty.

Lloyd could say no more. He lowered his face and took up a pen from the counter and dipped it in the well. There was a spot of ink by the well and he wondered if he'd done that when he'd grown angry a few moments ago. He felt angry now. Like an experiment predetonating. The loose neutrons kicking around in his head set him off too soon and in the wrong way. He noticed the tip of his pen spreading under the pressure of his hand. There was a blot of ink on the form. But Anna didn't seem to notice. She was speaking.

"You always explain your work to me," she said. He felt her lean near to him but he did not raise his face. "Like I was understanding it," she said.

He listened for a trace of ridicule in her voice but he could not hear any. "I'm sorry," he said.

"No," Anna said and her voice was so firm it raised his head to her. Her eyes fixed him. "I like it," she said. "I can follow a lot of it."

Lloyd nodded faintly.

"You must be very good," she said. "At your work. You're young, aren't you?"

"Comparatively . . . Compared to the others with my . . . level of responsibility."

"I know you're pretty important. You've got sign-off power."

"Sign-off power?"

"You can sign off for this stuff." She tapped the form. "Lots of it."

"Yes," he said.

"How old are you?" she asked.

"I'm thirty-six."

"You look younger . . . Didn't they take you?"

"The Army?"

"Yes."

"They took me here."

"From where?"

"The University of Chicago."

"Chicago?" Anna's shoulders rose and fell wistfully. "I love a big city."

Lloyd wanted to talk to her longer, ask her where she was from, let her ask more about him, but he was still in control, things had gone well and he didn't want to push it. He lowered his face and took up the pen. He felt Anna move away and he did not look up until the form was complete. When he finally did, he saw Anna sitting on the edge of her desk, her face turned to the window. He knew at once she was thinking about some big city. He knew this for certain, though he had no proof. Maybe this was how Neddermeyer got his ideas.

As soon as he thought of Neddermeyer, Lloyd grew conscious of the silence beyond the room, the vast silence that hung over Los Alamos like a rebuke—they had not yet filled the silence with the cry of their bomb. He backed away without a word and Anna did not move, her thoughts seeming to hold her there. It did not even occur to Lloyd to tell her good-bye as he slipped out the door and into the silent street.

FROM BEYOND THE TENT-OPENING Darrell heard the sound of a shovel digging, the intermittent chuff of its blade into the earth. He stretched his legs slowly, the pain in his knees sharp, his wrists aching too, but more dully. Even after his coffee and his breakfast, the pain lingered from the immobility of the night's sleep. He needed to go out and dig for awhile. The morning was growing very warm and he needed to move. He did not dwell on his rheumatism. It was the disease of his Indians. He'd picked it up at his age the same way they had— exposure to the damp, cold Midwestern earth, hunched down in the places they'd lived centuries before and where they'd commonly suffered these same aches. And it had kept him out of the Army, that and his brother Frank's good efforts. If it weren't for this little legacy of pain from his Indians, he'd be out somewhere in the Pacific killing Japanese. Or dead himself. Probably dead, he decided.

Darrell rose from his chair and put on his slouch hat and picked up his packet of tools. He stepped out into the desert glare. Thomas and Betty were side by side in the center five-foot square of the grid. Thomas was digging and Betty was sifting. The backs of the two were turned to Darrell and both were on their knees. Betty completed sifting a measure of the desert-gray soil through the rocking screen beside her while Thomas watched, holding a short-handled round-point shovel. Then they both bent over, their torsos disappeared from Darrell's view, their tails rose and waggled together and as Darrell smiled, Thomas and Betty straightened up fast, as if stung.

Darrell knew they'd found something. He strode toward them as they lunged back down. Thomas was taking his trowel out of his belt clip. "I'll take care of it," Darrell said and Thomas gave way at once, rotating around the foot-square test hole and letting Darrell crouch down, his knees hurting but the pain going almost completely without notice now. Even before he could see what was there, he'd drawn the mason's trowel from the packet, taking his lead from Thomas. There was a tiny patch of white at the dim bottom of the hole and he bent near. He extended his hand slowly into the shadows. His fingers touched something hard and shifted slightly. He began to crumble the earth away from the patch of white and it grew, curved, and Darrell's hand drew back, trembling. He could see the sutures of a skull.

Suddenly all the speculation that he'd put in abeyance garbled into his mind. It had been a burial after all. A geologist colleague at the univesity had told him about the mound of dirt out here—odd, geologically. Odd archaeologically, too. But worth exploring. And now there was a skull, a burial. But whose? As Darrell's mind worked, his fingers worked too and from the packet he took a delicate blade with a metal handle—a grapefruit knife—and he began to move the dirt away from the skull, following the coronal suture, exposing the frontal bone, the glabella, the parietal bone, and then the gape of the eyes, filled with the gray dirt; his mind had stopped, his abstraction had vanished: these were not the optic foramens but the eyes. A man. Darrell could not draw a breath; the wide, empty eyes stared at him from some moment in pre-history. Who are you? Darrell said softly in his mind. The Hohokam cremated their dead; the Mimbres buried their dead in the floor of their houses; the Athapascan, forefathers of the Apache, were nomads, brutal, a burial mound would fill them with contempt. Then whose face was this? The ridges above the eyes were prominent; Darrell's first guess was that it was a man. Beneath the center of the mound, he was a man of power. But out here in the desert? Darrell straightened up and looked across the flat land, the stubs of mesquite, a shrike falling, calling out, the jagged rim of mountains.

"Who is it?" Betty said, her voice tight.

Darrell looked at her and her face—pudgy, rubbery, her brow very prominent, her eyebrows plucked into thin lines—confused him. She was young; he could not read anything in her; the face at the bottom of the hole drew him down again and his hand went out and his fingers drew lightly across the man's brow.

LLOYD WAS SWEATING; HE felt the water bursting from his pores and he wanted to wipe it away but he feared for the vacuum tube. The three men—one an Army sergeant in uniform—were straining at the cable, the pulley whined, and the upper magnet came down slowly over the circular tube of the betatron. That was where the particles would be generated for the tests, accelerated up to a hundred million electron volts and shot out the opening in the concrete building and through the coordinated explosive charge and then, given the same impetus they would have inside the core of the bomb, they would rush into the cloud chamber that was bunkered on the other side of the charge, where the particles' energy would be measured.

The men were moving around now, abruptly moving. Lloyd blinked away his vision of the particles, stepped forward to where the men were securing the clamps on the magnet. The building squeezed in on Lloyd. He was anxious for all this to be done. A shadow appeared in the doorway and Lloyd turned to find Oppenheimer standing there. The doorway was short and Oppie's head was thrust forward. An explosion barked outside and Oppie angled his face just a bit. Practice charges a hundred yards off, testing the set-up for this site.

"Can we talk, Lloyd?"

"Certainly. Yes. Certainly."

Lloyd stepped outside with Oppie, who lit a cigarette, turning his torso away from the breeze, though it was faint.

"Let's walk," Oppenheimer said.

Lloyd nodded and they moved off, toward the stand of juniper. Lloyd preferred to keep the juniper strictly for his own purposes; but he also felt strongly that Oppie could do whatever he wanted and Lloyd did not even try to steer them anywhere else. Beyond the juniper a slope rose quickly to the top of the caldera and Lloyd kept his eyes up high there while they drew nearer the trees and he waited for Oppie to speak.

"How's the betatron coming along?" Oppenheimer finally said.

"All right. The guy from the University of Illinois is walking through this for the first time himself. But it's all right. From here on it's reasonably simple."

"That's what I wanted to know," Oppie said, stopping.

Lloyd looked at the man as he drew smoke deep into his lungs and held it there for a moment, as if he were studying it inside his body. The shadow of Oppie's felt hat darkened his face, made him look even sadder than usual. He exhaled the smoke and said, "The others can handle it from here?"

"Up to the final coordination. Yes."

"How long till then?"

"From four to five days."

"I have to go down to look over our site."

"Yes?"

"Trinity site."

Lloyd felt a prickling sweep down his chest and out along his arms. The test site for their first bomb. The atoms rushing into life.

"I want you to go down and help me, Lloyd. Just a couple of days."

"Of course," Lloyd said.

"You're organized. You've got a feel for things."

Lloyd felt his head duck down a bit. His eyes felt warm and his fists clenched hard. He wanted to say thank you but he could not speak.

"So you'll go?"

"Yes."

"Good. We leave in an hour." Oppie smiled at him and nodded and moved away in his jarring, flat-footed stride that looked as if he were walking fast down a steep incline.

Lloyd felt light-headed. He turned. And they'd even stopped short of the junipers.

BENEATH THE SKULL WERE shells and they made Darrell suck in a quick gasp of air, full of dust, but he could not exhale it. Shells. He brushed away the soil carefully. The shells fanned behind the skull. Each shell had been pierced to make a bead. Darrell's hands trembled and Thomas's thick hands were near-

22

by, brushing too, and the layer of shells was rising from the earth, carrying the skull.

Darrell let his mind come near, now that he was breathing calmly again. But he was still excited. These shells—thousands, Darrell knew; the man would be laid out on a cape of shell beads—these shells were not from the desert. They'd been brought, in an ancient commerce, from far away. They carried with them a clear image to Darrell of Cahokia, the ancient city that he had helped excavate outside Wabash, Illinois. At the center of Cahokia was Sun Mound, the largest prehistoric earthen construction in the world, a hundred feet high, its base covering fourteen acres. And Cahokia itself was at the center of a vast ancient Indian civilization. The city was larger in the twelfth century than any contemporary city in Europe, larger than Rome, larger than London. Its empire stretched over all the Midwest—up to what is now Wisconsin, out west to Oklahoma, down to the Gulf. And it was the Gulf that gave the city its shells for beads for the capes of the Sun King. Darrell had been a part of that discovery: the grave of one of the great Sun Kings. And the King had lain, like this man now, beneath Darrell's hands on a cape of shells. Darrell looked back down at the skull, exposed entirely, its chin resting on the balk of earth, the arc of shells behind it like a halo. Darrell closed his eyes and he felt something very complicated: this man—was he a King?—this King was coming back, emerging from the earth—what Kingdom did he rule?—Darrell wanted to hear him, to know the thoughts that had filled this head—but he felt a regret, too. He opened his eyes to the far mountains; he heard the rumbling of bombs beyond them; a distant sand devil swirled up, sucking at the desert and Darrell regretted exposing this ancient King to the race of men who lived the earth in this age. Then Darrell snapped his head down, squeezed his mind, his heart, shut. He was a scientist. He had bones, artifacts, to uncover. These speculations were inappropriate for now.

Later, though, that night, his kerosene lamp trimmed low,

his feelings—the impulsive, foolish, unscientific feelings—muted by his weariness and his aching knees, Darrell let himself begin to hypothesize. It seemed very unlikely that this desert was ever the site of an Indian city, not one with the power to provide the wealth of these shells. The mound had been relatively small. The developed cultures of the Southwest's prehistory were isolated, self-consciously isolated; their artifacts were indigenous. And mound-building was unheard of. How did this King—Darrell could think of him as nothing else now—how did this King find his way to the middle of the Jornada del Muerto, a place that God himself had turned his face from?

Darrell stepped out into the night to watch the sky and think. But once outside he heard a faint giggling, a scuffling sound. He looked to his left, to the tent where Thomas slept. It was dark. But he heard the sound again and it came from farther away. Darrell scanned past the dig-site, where the tarpaulin covered the King's skull, and as his eyes crossed the site his anger rose at the giggling sound. He looked at Betty's tent. A light shone around the edges of the closed flap.

Darrell strode across to the tent, his breath growing shorter with each step, and he ripped open the flap to find Thomas sitting on a canvas chair in the center of the tent and Betty sitting on his lap, her arms around his neck. Their round faces turned on him—twin moons—as round and as guileless as moons, Darrell felt, but he still could not hold back his anger. "Out," he growled.

Thomas tried to jump up and Betty staggered off his lap, brushing at her work trousers as if she were straightening a skirt.

Darrell felt the King's eyes gazing up into the night sky and these two children had no sense of what was happening. "Get back to your tent, Thomas."

"Yessir. Yessir." He was circling away from the chair, edging toward the opening that Darrell was blocking.

"We didn't do anything," Betty said. "Not really anything."

"I don't want you two . . ." Darrell began, but his anger suddenly drained away, leaving only a residue of annoyance. "No temptations," he said and then he felt a trembling begin to grow in himself that took him totally by surprise. "You're under university rules here," he said and he felt a stirring and his mind scrambled away but he could not detach himself enough to stop it; he felt a trembling and he wanted to touch a woman—not Betty necessarily; not Betty at all, he asserted—but he yearned and he turned abruptly and plunged back into the night.

A LOW FIELDSTONE FENCE surrounded the ranch house and Lloyd paused a moment at the gate, letting Oppie go on ahead. Lloyd turned and looked out across the desert. To the southwest he could see only flat, barren land that dashed out to the horizon as straight as the track of a gamma particle. And out at the farthest point, the rim of the earth simply rippled slightly and ended. He had a vision of a large city—Berlin, Tokyo—wiped as clean as this desert by the bomb. With a start, Lloyd turned back to the ranch house. The heat sucked at his skin and he opened the collar of his shirt. He'd already left his tie and coat in the car but Oppie still had on his tweed jacket. He was disappearing into the ranch house and Lloyd hurried to catch up.

Inside the ranch house two soldiers were carrying furniture out the back door. A long wooden laboratory table had already been set up in the center of the room and Oppie perched tentatively there. A captain came to him and Lloyd drew near to listen.

"There's still some problems with the ranchers," the captain said.

"How bad?" Oppenheimer said.

"We've had to get a little tough . . ."

Oppenheimer waved his hand at the captain, a gesture for the man to stop, although Lloyd didn't know if it meant stop getting tough or simply stop talking about it. Lloyd looked at the captain's face, which had suddenly gone blank. Did the captain understand the gesture? Lloyd wondered. There was a familiarity between the soldier and Oppie.

"One other little problem," the captain said. "An unusual one. There's some sort of . . . an excavation going on."

Oppie's head thrust forward, like a time-lapse photo of a flower seeking a light, and he said, "An excavation?"

"We haven't approached him yet, though we've checked up on him. His name is Dr. Darrell Reeves. He's an archaeologist from the University of Santa Fe. He and two student-assistants are doing some sort of an excavation about ten miles north of here."

Oppie's head drew back and extended again, his right hand played at the pocket flap on his tweed coat, he angled his face upwards—the sequence of gestures Lloyd associated with Oppie and the meetings, as the man struggled with technical problems.

The captain said, "He's thirty-seven, a doctorate from the University of Wisconsin, 4-F, no criminal record, and he's right out in the middle of our desert."

"I see," Oppie said.

"One other thing. His brother is highly placed in the Department of War." The captain paused and watched Oppenheimer closely, as if trying to read him. Oppie said nothing and the captain added, "But it's not going to be a problem. We can remove the archaeologist."

"I think we should go up there and see what he's doing," Oppenheimer said.

"Yessir . . . I'll get you a driver."

"That's all right, captain." Oppie turned to Lloyd. "Dr. Coulter can drive me out there."

Lloyd wondered at Oppie's mind. Lloyd himself would have just had the captain and his men remove the interlopers from the desert. But Oppie seemed intrigued by the archaeologist, open to him, and Lloyd chided himself. Yes, he thought. That was the responsibility of a scientist, to remain open. He followed Oppie out the door.

AT FIRST DARRELL THOUGHT the plume of dust was a sand devil, but he realized that he had raised his head at a sound; it was the drone of an engine and he knew someone was coming. He turned back to the King whose head and cervical vertebrae were exposed on the fan of shells. Darrell had a moment of protective fear. He felt the impulse to cover the skull, quickly, to hide it from these intruders roaring closer now. But he simply rose to his feet; his right hand holding the trowel fell loosely at his side; an Army jeep approached and stopped. Betty was emerging from behind her tent, her canteen in her hand.

Lloyd first saw the young woman, among the tents, a young woman who turned her face to him and he glanced away with a vague ripple of shyness; and standing in the center of a clearing, a long row of dirt beyond him, a hole at his feet, was a man with a slouch hat. He was a slender man, a little like Oppenheimer, but giving off a clear sense of strength, his arms and legs thin but hard like the brass mounting clamps on the gas-cylinders, and his skin was the color of brass, too, from the sun. Dismounting from the jeep, drawing nearer, Lloyd could see the man's eyes, pale blue, grey-blue, a surprising color, for some reason, a color that Lloyd could not fit into the spectrum.

"Are you Dr. Darrell Reeves?" Oppie said.

"Yes," Darrell said to the gangly man who approached. But Darrell's attention was drawn past the speaker to the man following behind. This second man was rather short and his forearms were large and powerful, thickly matted with black hair; his face was square and his eyes were wide-set and deep; there was a stiff solidity about him that reminded Darrell of a baked clay effigy.

"I'm Robert Oppenheimer," the gangly man said.

"Yes?"

27

"And this is my assistant, Dr. Lloyd Coulter."

Lloyd drew up beside Oppie and Darrell stepped forward, shifting the trowel to his left hand and putting out his right. Oppenheimer shook hands first and then Lloyd; Darrell noticed the power and the sweat in Lloyd's hand, Lloyd noticed the wiry strength and the dust in Darrell's.

Darrell said, "Won't you come in out of the sun, gentlemen? We can talk in my tent."

He led the two visitors toward his tent. He saw Betty still standing where she'd paused, canteen in hand. He felt a brief twinge of shame at his having been severe with her and Thomas last night. He decided to apologize to them at the first opportunity.

Inside the tent he set his guests in the two chairs—Oppenheimer in the rattan and Coulter—the solid little man still commanded Darrell's attention—in the canvas chair. Darrell offered them coffee, which they declined, and he sat on his bunk.

"May I smoke?" Oppenheimer said.

"Of course."

Oppenheimer lit his cigarette, shielding the match-flame as if he were outdoors, and then he said, "Dr. Coulter and I are part of some research being done by the Army on explosives."

"Explosives?" Darrell sensed a variance between the flatness with which Oppenheimer had said the word and the air of specialness about this little visit.

"Yes. High-yield explosives. The usual progress in bomb-making . . . This is part of the Alamogordo Range here, you know."

"I know. My brother works in the Department of War. He helped me get a special . . . dispensation to dig out here."

"I understand," Oppenheimer said. "What is it you're uncovering in your dig?"

Darrell heard a throb of sincere interest in the man's voice that surprised him. He glanced at Coulter whose eyes were fixed on Oppenheimer and whose expressionless face and stiff erectness in the chair made Darrell think again of the clay figures of Cahokia. Then Darrell began to explain the dig. He talked of the discovery of the mound, its incongruity, the slim odds of there being anything here. Then he described the discovery of the skull, the shells, the mystery of all this. "Just the last things those eyes saw, the last few minutes of the man's conversation," Darrell said. "Even if I had just that."

Oppenheimer raised his face to blow a plume of cigarette smoke into the air and he smiled. " 'I would thou hadst my bones, and I thy news,' " he said.

Darrell laughed, though the aptness of the quote seemed complex. "Is that . . . "

"I've been rereading Shakespeare in the past few weeks. That was Romeo and Juliet."

Darrell ventured an interpretation. "But *I* have *his* bones and none of his news . . . Not yet."

"How long will it take you to excavate your King?"

"I don't know how much there is."

"Could you finish in . . . say . . . fifteen weeks?"

"Perhaps . . ." In spite of Oppenheimer's deference, Darrell began to feel an implicit threat in the man. Fifteen weeks was not very long. He also sensed an ease in Oppenheimer, underneath the bony fretfulness of his exterior, that suggested the man had considerable resources at his command. On an impulse, Darrell said, "I'm short of help."

At once Oppenheimer said, "Does it need to be trained help?"

"No. Not necessarily." Darrell shifted his eyes slightly and Coulter's gaze was fixed now on him and Darrell started visibly.

Lloyd watched the faint recoil of the archaeologist's head and he wondered why the man was frightened of him and even as he wondered this, Lloyd felt a pulse of anger at him, his hands tightened and he felt a motiveless anger at this man whom he'd startled. The anger came from something outside himself, he felt, a scent in the air, an electron charge, pheromones, something; he felt angry.

Oppie said, "Perhaps we can help you a bit . . . Expedite your work . . ."

Lloyd watched the archaeologist's pale blue eyes—they'd dilated wide now—they were open and there was still a tiny trace of fear, Lloyd sensed, and he grew fretful at all of this, he grew irritated even at Oppie for carrying them this far from their real work. Lloyd wondered how the fire that was coming to this desert would touch the archaeologist's eyes, what fear would roil then in those pale eyes.

The archaeologist was speaking to Oppenheimer, though the eyes did not shift away from Lloyd for a moment more. "If you can spare a worker or two—even part-time—I can be out of your way sooner."

"Can I see what you've done so far?" Oppenheimer said. "This is enormously interesting to me."

The archaeologist rose up quickly. "Of course."

Lloyd followed the two men out of the tent. The young woman who had looked at him earlier was crouched near the hole in the ground. A young man was beside her and they both rose and retreated as the archaeologist approached. Lloyd resented this man's command over them.

At the hole Oppenheimer fell, as if in a faint, and Lloyd's hand went out instinctively before he realized that Oppie had thrown himself down to examine the excavation. Reeves hunched beside him and Lloyd looked at the woman. Her face was round and she was sweating, her forehead was profusely beaded and there were moon-stains of sweat beneath her arms. Lloyd thought of Anna, her face turned to the window, dreaming of some great city. Lloyd knew he had to do something decisive, bring her closer to him somehow.

Oppie and Reeves were talking in low, intense tones and then Oppie abruptly turned and said, "Come look at this, Lloyd."

Lloyd stepped forward and the two men parted for him. He remained on his feet and leaned over the rim of the hole. He pulled back at once. He knew the skull would look familiar,

30

the wide eyes, the broad mouth. It could be anyone. You always think you know a skull, he thought, trying to keep his balance by the hole. But he waited until the final good-byes were said and Oppie talked again about the fifteen weeks, about sending help, and Lloyd waited till Oppie and the archaeologist began to move toward the jeep, the archaeologist's two assistants tagging after. Then Lloyd stepped to the hole and spat on the skull.

ONLY HALF A MILE from the excavation site, Oppie told Lloyd to stop the jeep. Lloyd braked gradually and finally they sat, the engine idling, in the center of the desert, the sun high in the sky, pressing at them. Lloyd turned off the engine and the only sound was the soughing of the wind. Oppie rose up from where he sat beside Lloyd. He looked about him, peering off into the distance before the jeep, then to each side, and then back toward the excavation.

"This will do," Oppie said softly. "This is where it will happen."

Lloyd knew he meant the first bomb. Lloyd closed his eyes and wondered how it would be at that moment, what would be left here on this spot, how far the bloom would reach. He opened his eyes and looked back to the distant cluster of tents.

"You were frightened of the skull," Oppie said and Lloyd looked up into the man's gaze that seemed as pitiless as the sun that hung just behind his head.

"No."

"It's all right to be afraid . . ." Oppie turned his face to the desert. He looked around and said, very low, " 'I am unable to keep the balance of my mind. Seeing your radiant color filling the sky and seeing your mouths and eyes, I am afraid.' "

Lloyd knew Oppie had shifted his thoughts from the skull to the bomb. He'd heard Oppie quote Hindu philosophy before and it always irritated him. Lloyd did not fear the bomb. More than once he'd heard Oppie trying to justify himself and control

31

his fears of what he was doing by talking of the Nazi menace, the danger to western civiclization. But Lloyd knew that the Nazis had nothing to do with their work. Not anymore. The bomb had been conceived now. The bomb—its possibility—was part of their minds—part of their hearts—and so it already existed, it only had to find its outward shape, its moment; it was part of their natures now, his own, Oppie's, all the rest of them on their little island in the Jemez Mountains; part of Anna, even. At the thought of her, Lloyd felt something forming inside him. He said, "Do you want me to come down here and see to things?"

Oppie's face swung around. Lloyd was blinded by the sun and he put himself in Oppie's shadow. "Yes," Oppie said. "There are a few things I'd like you to oversee down here."

"I'd like to bring someone to help me. Administratively," Lloyd said and he knew he'd had an insight, a sudden leap.

"You'll be going back and forth. I still want your help on the implosion tests."

"That's all right. Can I take a low-level person? To help?"

"Yes."

"I have a person in mind. Excellent at details . . . May I have this person?"

"Anyone you want, who's non-scientific," Oppie said.

Anna Brown. Lloyd spoke her name in his mind but not aloud. He just moved his head, letting the sun fall on him once more, and he turned his face and closed his eyes and took in the sun and he felt as calm as a lizard on a rock.

JUST EAST OF THE center of the city, on Canyon Road, was the campus of the University of Santa Fe. Darrell parked his pre-war Plymouth on the street and he walked through an archway into the main courtyard, which was bounded by two-story co-lonnaded adobe buildings with upper balconies dark in shade despite the mid-day sun.

A door beyond an apricot tree led Darrell into the dean's

outer office. The secretary's desk was empty but the inner door was open and he saw Dean Felker, massive-seeming even behind his wide oak desk. Felker motioned for him to come in and he rose as Darrell approached. They shook hands and Felker said, "My secretary's gone off to work in a pilot-goggle plant or some such damn place."

Darrell muttered sympathetically and sat in a chair before the desk. The room was very plain; the smooth adobe walls were painted white; the ceiling was wood-plank with the beams exposed and squared. Against one wall was a tall, cherrywood Crosley console radio.

"I'm keeping up on the war news," Felker said, as Darrell looked at the radio.

"Of course."

"Things are . . . ah . . . going very well now. But I worry about the chief."

The word focused Darrell on the reason for this visit, though he knew Felker was referring to Roosevelt.

"He seems frail, from the sound of him lately," Felker said.

Darrell nodded and tried to think of something to say to gracefully bring this meeting to its purpose. He had to report officially to Felker on the progress of the excavation and obtain his permission to carry forward with it. There were some basic financial needs that required his approval.

"The toll we're paying with this war hasn't even begun to be counted," Felker said. "By the way, do you remember Hendricks?"

"Hendricks?"

"He taught chemistry until . . . let's see, he enlisted in early 1942. You were here then?"

"Yes. But I don't think I remember Hendricks."

"He's back. In Santa Fe, that is. I wish we had a post for him. He's been discharged. He lost a leg in Germany. Or perhaps France. I wish there was something to do for him, but I just don't have anything available."

The dean was growing more intense. He was explaining this

matter to Darrell as if to Hendricks himself. Darrell felt detached. The one-legged man was a stranger to him and he wanted to explain the discovery in the desert and leave. He would stop at his house and check his mail and go on back to the site yet this evening.

"It's a terrible toll," Felker was saying and his jowls quaked and Darrell wished he had some strong feeling for this man Hendricks but he didn't.

Then Felker touched his pocket watch, which lay on the desk top. He touched it once, lightly, with the tip of his forefinger, and the intensity vanished. Felker said, "I have . . . ah . . . someone coming in soon. What's the story on your expedition?"

Felker's abrupt turn made Darrell fumble about at first, but soon he began to describe the discovery step by step, clearly, smoothly, in almost the same words he'd used with the two scientists the day before.

"I'm sure it will all be made clear under your direction," the dean said.

Darrell knew that this was not rhetorical—the man meant just what he said. Felker's own discipline had been physics and they'd talked often before about the scientific method. Felker had great faith in it and so did Darrell and he said, "Thank you. Yes. My science sometimes can't answer things with quite the precision of your science, but we'll have a reasonable fix on the basics."

"Yes," Felker said with thoughtful sincerity. Then he glanced at his watch again and he repeated, "Yes," but this time it was to wrap things up.

Darrell rose and shook the dean's hand and he walked out of the office. As he passed under the apricot tree, he stopped. Something still nagged at him. His detachment over the former chemistry teacher's plight. He even had to squeeze hard at his mind to call back the name spoken just a few minutes ago. Hendricks. Darrell thought to get this man Hendricks's address in Santa Fe. There was nothing Darrell could do right away, he knew. He had to get back to the excavation. But maybe later on. Maybe in fifteen weeks he could look him up. Just having the address would be sufficient for now. He turned back to the dean's office.

The dean's inner door was closed. A man's voice came from inside—not the dean's. Darrell wondered how the man had gotten into the office without being seen. Darrell didn't want to interrupt, but he did draw nearer the door. Leaning close, he could hear the words and then he knew what the dean had been in a hurry about. The voice was a radio announcer reviewing yesterday's episode of "Ma Perkins." The dean was listening to a soap opera on his radio.

Darrell slipped out quietly; he didn't want to embarrass the dean; Hendricks's address would have to wait, he thought. But out on the street he saw a one-legged man approaching on crutches, awkward and breathing heavily. The man's blunt arrowhead of a jaw and cleft chin were familiar. He had seen the chemistry professor around campus before 1942.

Darrell approached the man, though he was conscious of its being an act of the will. The man's right pants leg was neatly folded and pinned up; it troubled Darrell but did not move him in a personal way.

"You're Hendricks, aren't you?' Darrell said.

The man cocked his head. His face looked young in spite of the deep furrows in his brow. The furrows were from pain, Darrell sensed. "Yes," Hendricks said.

"I remember you," Darrell said. "I'm Darrell Reeves. I teach archaeology."

"I don't remember you." The man's voice was flat, hard.

Darrell shrugged. "It's not important." He thought to say welcome back, but Hendricks seemed to have a bitter frankness to him and the welcome would only incite him.

The man's eyes were lookng hard at Darrell's face and just before Darrell had worked up enough resolve to turn around and get into his car without any more words, the man said, "Maybe I do remember you a little."

"Yes. Good."

"Were we friends?"

"No. I can't say that. We . . . didn't know each other, really."

"I didn't think so."

"You were right." Darrell felt vaguely irritated and he wanted desperately to bolt, to race off in his car, to return to his King as fast as he possibly could.

Suddenly the man closed his eyes tightly and opened them again. Darrell thought it must be a surge of pain, but Hendricks seemed suddenly calm; his voice softened and he said, "I'm sorry. So much has happened in between."

"I understand," Darrell said. "Look, I have some things to do. But that's my car there. Can I give you a lift somewhere?"

Hendricks glanced away, toward the arch into the university's courtyard. "Yes," Hendricks said. "You might as well. Yes."

In the car, Darrell said, "Dean Felker really wants to find a spot for you, I'm sure. He spoke of your situation with great . . . concern."

"You can drop me in The Plaza," Hendricks said. Then, after a pause, he added, "That's tangible help."

Darrell resolved not to initiate any more talk. After a moment Hendricks said, "That's help you can make plans around."

They crossed the Santa Fe River on the Castillo Street Bridge and passed the Cathedral of St. Francis, a massive block-stone church with its belfries tapering up to spires that weren't there, the tops seemingly snipped off, pruned back like a pragmatist's vision of religion. As they passed the church, Hendricks leaned slightly toward Darrell and said, "No one over here has heard the truth."

"What truth is that?"

"About what they're doing to the Jews."

"The Jews?"

"What's happening to them."

"You mean the slave labor?"

Hendricks lurched away from Darrell and he made a pinched,

hacking sound of contempt in his throat. "I didn't have to go through all this to find *that* out. I knew that before I even enlisted."

"I understand there've been some horrible incidents."

"Not incidents. No. Not just a little town here and there lined up and shot . . . I guess the movement of troops is too distracting for all these goddam journalists. Nobody seems to know . . . Look, almost as soon as we got to France I started hearing the stories. There was an ordnance major I knew. Rosenthal. A Jew from Brooklyn. He knew all the rumors. He said there were camps out there, still beyond the front, where they were murdering the Jews on a regular, planned schedule. Massive. Old and young. Sick and able-bodied. All of them."

Hendricks paused and Darrell had no words. He felt blank. He could shape no realistic image in his mind of what Hendricks was saying. He had no points of reference. He pressed his imagination, but like a tired child it flopped in a direction of its own and all Darrell could see was Cahokia, the enormous Sun Mound, thirty thousand Indians gathered in the plaza as the Sun King—his cape of shells flashing—raised his arms at the very highest point on the mound.

"I know the chemical," Hendricks said.

Darrell heard the man's words from far off.

"Rosenthal had been a high school chemistry teacher," Hendricks said. "His information was that the Nazis use Zyklon B. It's basically hydrogen cyanide. A very deadly gas, very effective—do you understand?"

"Yes. Of course." Darrell's voice sounded remote, faint to his own ears. He passed the Palace of Governors, a one-story adobe building with a portico running the length of its facade, making it look like an arcade of shops. He turned and drew up to the curb and stopped the car.

Hendricks said, "No one here seems to know what's going on."

"These rumors . . ." Darrell began, using the word firmly to try to put all this into some perspective he could understand.

"I'm no fool," Hendricks said. "I understand why you're

all so stupid about this . . . Even I don't dream about it. I know as much as anybody and all I dream about is some guy from my first goddam week in France. We bivouacked together and he and I shared a tent. We blew up our inflatable mattresses the night we camped and we both got light-headed from it, huffing and puffing. That night he went off to mess and got blown to bits by a mortar shell. I wasn't there at the time. I never saw his body. Not a drop of his blood. The Krauts dropped a mortar shell on him and he just vanished. But I put his things together to be shipped back home and I came to the inflatable mattress. I pulled the plug and there was his breath sighing out of there. He just sighed and sighed, his breath on my hands, and it was like he died right in front of me.'' Hendricks bent very near to Darrell. ''That's what I dream about. Just that.''

''I can understand,'' Darrell said and he knew he sounded like a damn fool. He wanted to leap out of the car and dash across the plaza, escape down a dusty alley.

But Hendricks suddenly sat upright and opened the door and he swung around, putting his foot on the running board. He pulled his crutches from the back seat.

''You need some help?'' Darrell said.

''No.'' And Hendricks staggered up onto his leg and crutches outside and slammed the door. He turned without a word or a nod and he lurched away, circling the rear of the car—Darrell watched in the rearview mirror—and he moved off into the plaza.

Darrell started his car but sat gripping the steering wheel for a time, listening to the engine muttering, letting his mind regain control, dismissing Hendricks as an enigma, a man who himself was as remote and half-real as a rumor. Darrell focused on doing what he had to do to leave town, to return to the dig.

He drove east on Canyon Road, past the university, and he thought of the Indian trail that once ran along this road, following the Santa Fe River and then out over the Sangre de Cristo Mountains to the pueblos of Pecos. Darrell felt himself moving among the ghosts of the generations of Indians, heading east, over the mountains, and of those who came later, the woodcutters coming and going on their burros, their ghosts moving now along this hard-packed dirt road, bound tightly by stone fences and adobe houses and the pin oaks and chestnuts. Even though there were no bones he felt the presence of these past generations and he was comforted at last; at last the one-legged man faded from his mind.

He turned down his narrow, rutted street and parked before his tiny house, a doorway in a plain adobe facade. When he got out of the car he heard from behind a wall next door the rasp of a phonograph record, a woman singing, "I had the craziest dream . . ."

Darrell entered his house and shut the door behind him and he began at once to sweat. He crouched down and mechanically began to pick up the mail on the floor under the door slot. He knew he would be troubled again. The newspapers were folded in half and held by rubber bands. The lead-story headlines flashed into him as he stacked the papers on the floor.He did not read them, but phrases stuck. Cobenz Falls; Carrier *Franklin* Lost, 800 Die; Russians Reach Baltic; A Thousand Dead; 500 Dead; Civilian Dead; Dead; Die; Fall. Darrell stopped. He turned his head away as he put the last two papers on the stack. Then he set the stack as far away as his arms would stretch. The rest of the mail consisted of fliers and professional journals. One of the journals had an article on sexing skeletons by the sciatic notch, a subject of particular interest to Darrell, but he did not pause to look at it. He felt suddenly angry. The world had gone mad and the madness was all being chronicled in carefully set type, each line justified, each jump column carefully referenced. Only those who were alive filled Darrell's head for a moment. Only the living, the madmen, running governments, armies, Darrell's arm shot out, he hit the stack of newspapers with his open hand and they scattered across the floor. But each paper remained neatly folded, the rubber bands held the papers together as they flipped across the floor

39

and came to a stop. Darrell's anger still roiled in him. But he leaned back against the door and waited. He emptied his head and he grew calm after a time.

He found a letter from his brother. He opened it and Frank wrote—as he always wrote—in vague, unimpassioned tones. Mary was fine. So were the kids. He worked late many nights. The cherry blossoms were just coming into bloom. He hoped Darrell was well.

Darrell rose up and crossed to the phone. He switched on the bridge lamp that stood nearby and lifted up the receiver, his intent only vaguely formed. He told the operator he wanted to phone Washington, D.C., and he looked at his watch. He gave the operator Frank's War Office phone number and waited for the patch into long distance and then, at last, into the office. As the phone rang, Darrell sat down in the roll-back chair and laid the fingers of his left hand in the indents of the chair's knuckle arm. This calmed him a bit and he passed through Frank's secretary and finally heard his brother's voice.

"Reeves," the voice said, firm, noncommital.

"Frank. It's Darrell."

"Why . . . How good to hear from you." The voice was still noncommital, and at the very moment Darrell fully understood why he'd placed the call—to find out if Hendricks was right—he realized it had been a mistake.

"Is somebody there with you?" Darrell said, though he knew it was just his brother's crust. "You can't talk freely?"

"I can talk . . . Did everything work out all right at Alamogordo? They didn't give you any trouble?"

"No. No trouble at all. Thanks for your help." Darrell considered simply saying he was fine and remarking on how beautiful the cherry blossoms must be and hanging up.

"How's it all going?" Frank said.

"Fine. Just fine."

"Glad to hear it."

"Frank."

"Yes?"

"What are they doing to the Jews over there?"

"The Jews?"

"What are the Nazis doing to them?"

"Are you all right, Darrell?"

"Yes. I've heard some stories . . ."

"Stories?"

"Things I've never seen in the newspapers . . . Never heard about . . . You should know . . ."

"Stories about the Jews?" Frank's questions were flat repetition. Darrell heard no piquing of interest in them, no concern.

"Frank . . ." Darrell suddenly despaired of learning anything this way, despaired even of getting his brother's voice to soften. Darrell felt their father slip into the room, his ghost, very clear in this room, as reasonable a father as had ever lived in all the history or prehistory of the world, a reasonable man, and Darrell struggled to keep his voice calm, to keep from yanking the phone out of the wall. "Frank," he said, "I've heard the Jews are being systematically murdered in camps with hydrogen cyanide . . ." He could say no more.

Frank did not reply. The line echoed and crackled but no words came at all.

"Frank," Darrell said sharply. "I want to know what's happening. Talk to me, Frank."

"Hydrogen cyanide, you say?" The brother's voice was brittle, patronizing.

"Are they killing the Jews in camps, Frank? What's happening to the Jews?" Darrell heard himself panting into the phone. But part of him felt detached. He wondered at his own intensity. He decided he was as angry at his brother as he was at the Nazis.

"Are you sure you're all right out there?" Frank said and Darrell hung up the phone.

THE TRACKS WERE PITIFUL and Lloyd's hands began to tremble in anger. The tracks were pitiful, the thin white tracks in the photograph, the spoor of charged atoms left by the gamma particle passing through the cloud chamber. The formulas hadn't been applied yet. That was a simple matter—old man Geiger's formula and the measurement of this particle's range would give them the energy of the particle, its potential impact on the plutonium in the core of a bomb. But Lloyd could see the reality, even without the formula. It wasn't nearly enough. The glossy photo, still smelling of fixer, was black—the backdrop; the track of the particle entered from the left, a thin white line, and it moved not even halfway across the blackness before curling slightly and ceasing. Pitiful. He barked to his assitants to check the timing coils on the betatron, check the size of the charge, check the bunkers that protected the betatron on one side and the cloud chamber on the other to see if they could bear a greater blast. He dropped the photo onto the desk and strode out of the room and into the street.

Though he quaked inside from the photo, though he feared the bomb would be set back, he felt a thin track of pleasure moving in him, thin but with great force, moving across the frame of his mind and not tailing off, keeping its force: he would tell Anna now. A week had passed since he'd gotten Oppie to agree and now the paperwork was through; it was official and Oppie was letting Lloyd tell Anna himself. She could go down to Trinity site with him. He'd had an intuition and now he would test it.

At Anna's supply office, Lloyd paused at the door. He heard a sound and he leaned near to listen. Anna was humming a tune to herself and Lloyd gently laid his head and the fingertips of his right hand on the door and listened. He didn't follow the tune; he couldn't place it; he just listened to the rise and fall of her wordless voice and he slowly grew frightened. He had never thought to doubt his intuition until now, until he heard her humming to herself, a tune strange to him, following an emotional track of her own, separate. She sang a few words, "I had the craziest dream . . ." and Lloyd knew he was on the verge of losing his nerve, losing his only chance. He opened the door.

Her eyes seemed as wide as a skull's. She looked at

him. Her humming had stopped but the sound hung in the air like a track in the cloud chamber; the air had been charged by it.

"Hello, Dr. Coulter," Anna said.

Lloyd crossed to the wooden counter and she approached him, her brow furrowed slightly in inquiry. He forced a smile. He was suddenly conscious of a danger—he could alarm her. He sensed that he could alarm her and he said, "Hello, Miss Brown."

"You want some more connector cable?" she said, laughing, laying one arm along the counter.

"No. Thanks . . . Miss Brown, I've admired your . . . organization in your department here."

"That so? Thanks. I do my best."

"But I have the feeling it's not too interesting here for you." Lloyd felt light-headed. Words were coming more easily than ever before. Another leap of intuition. He'd gotten his original idea this way and now these words came, corollaries of his idea, logical elaborations. "I have a clear feeling that it's not interesting," he repeated—he'd suddenly gotten too self-conscious and the words threatened to stop.

"You're sure right about that," Anna replied and it lifted Lloyd, wiped away his doubts, gave him more words.

"Your interest in my work—the real work of this place," he said. "Your interest in other places . . . All these things made me think you could use a change from this job."

Anna cocked her head. "Yes?"

"Dr. Oppenheimer—you know of Dr. Oppenheimer?"

"Of course," Anna said, solemnly. "He's the big cookie."

The phrase stopped Lloyd. He opened his mouth but nothing came out. Then he reset his mind, fixed on his idea and he said, "Dr. Oppenheimer himself has asked me to go down to our . . . special test site. Downstate. And he told me I should find someone to go down there and work as an assistant . . ." He wanted to add "to me" but his shyness wrenched at him and he knew he didn't have much more time to get all this out. "He said I should find someone who has a good . . .

organizational ability . . . It's a very important task . . . that we have to do. I don't know of very many people . . . That is, I've admired your ability . . . So I told Dr. Oppenheimer and he's gotten you transferred.'' Lloyd was out of breath. He could say no more. He had to wait for her response. Her face had gone blank and he felt a chasm open inside him, splitting down the center of his chest. She was angry at his presumption. She didn't want to go. She liked it here. She despised him. The chasm must fill up, he knew. He felt his hands clench into fists, he could not breathe, he wondered what would fill the chasm.

But then she smiled. "You mean I'm going to be transferred?''

Lloyd nodded.

"Down to the main test site?''

"Yes.''

Anna laughed once, hard, clear, a bark of a laugh and she said, ''That's terrific, Dr. Coulter. That's not bad at all.''

Lloyd gasped. He heard himself gasp and his arms went limp. He lifted his hands—they were very heavy—but at this moment he had to look at his hands. He looked at them as if they knew a terrible secret.

THE KING'S SKELETON LAY extended on a vast cape of shell-beads, his arms at his sides, his legs together, entering the earth just below his knees. Darrell stood by the rim of the hole as the sunlight turned buttery at the end of the day and he felt quiet at last, he felt completely focused on his King after a day of digging and scraping and sifting. They'd dug a deep trench all around the King, squaring and smoothing the corners and balks of earth, fashioning a platform for the King, almost finishing off the five-foot square, the basic unit of the dig. All that remained was to free the King's feet.

Darrell crouched and jumped down into the hole. The King lay on his platform at the level of Darrell's waist and Darrell bent to him. He looked again at the signs of the skeleton's sex. He had not yet made formal measurements to compare to the male-female standards, but he could tell the answer already; he knew by sight, though many of the differences were subtle. On the skull: the ridge above the eyes was prominent; the knob on the temporal bone behind the ear, the frontal sinuses, the palate, the teeth, all were large. Darrell drew his face close to the King's. The brow was very prominent indeed and he saw the man with thick eyebrows, with deep-set dark eyes, the eyes that floated once, right there. Darrell resisted the impulse to touch the skull. He drew back slightly and followed the spine. All along the vertebrae, Darrell could see the obvious markings for muscle and ligament attachments, signs of a man. The lumbar and atlas vertebrae were large, the sacrum was longer and narrower. He reached the pelvis and it was here, of course, that the man had asserted his sexuality. But the signs that remained after the flesh was gone were surprisingly subtle. Subtle, but clear. On the surface of the pelvis was a notch, the sciatic notch that let the nerve ride through, and the notch in the King was narrow and deep. A woman's would be wider, open just a bit wider as if there were a vague hunger in this notch in the woman's bone. The King's was closed slightly, reticent. Darrell bent nearer. He wondered at all the women this man might have had, his Kingly privilege extending through his tribe, this wide, flared bone moving slowly, the King planting his successor, his young son and his daughters, this King taking his quiet pleasure with the dark-eyed women who waited on him.

Darrell drew back. He felt a trill of pity for the man, buried out here in the desert, far from home. Surely far from home. Far from the ease he'd known, the cool nights in the Mississippi River bottoms as he lay with his women.

Darrell straightened up. He looked toward the tents and then to the south and he saw, far off, Betty and Thomas out on the desert, shoulder to shoulder, turned slightly to the east, watching, standing as motionless as the mountains they faced. Darrell's pity for the King sharpened. That this boy Thomas should be touching a woman now and the King must lie here alone: Darrell turned away. He sat down in the trench and leaned back against the balk-face, out of sight, deep in the earth.

But he didn't sit for long before he heard the sound of a car's engine approaching rapidly. When he stood up his bones ached with rheumatism and so he was distracted, easing his limbs into place, flexing the pain away, and when he finally turned his attention to the arrival, an Army captain was striding toward him from an olive-drab Chevrolet sedan. The man had left his front door open.

"Are you Reeves?" the captain said.

"Yes," Darrell said and he climbed out of the hole, keeping his face blank against the pain, determined not to show any weakness before this Army man.

With his hands clasped behind him, the captain waited for Darrell to gain his feet. The man's eyes were as gray and flat as shale. Darrell didn't like him and he said sharply, "What is it you want here, captain?"

"I want to warn you."

"Yes?"

The captain paused a moment, as if deciding whether to speak. He tilted his head and studied Darrell and then he said, in a voice that was quieter, more intimate, but no less arrogant, "I don't think it's a good idea for you to be out here. For your own good."

"Dr. Oppenheimer . . ."

"Yes, I know. This is just a private opinion."

"Captain," Darrell said and he tightened until his voice was steady, "I don't give a damn what your private opinion is."

The man's eyes widened briefly, though with a trace of amusement. He said, "Officially then. I must warn you that there's a dangerous man roaming across the desert."

"Dangerous?"

"A man who thinks he has some sort of claim against the government."

"Is this man a rancher?"

"Yes. Have you encountered him?" The captain's arrogance had vanished at once and he had become intently professional. Darrell decided he was probably an effective soldier.

"I don't know for sure. Perhaps ten days ago a man rode up on a horse. A very odd man. He didn't say much but he did seem very angry at your people down south of here."

"Short man? Dark?"

"Yes."

"I'm sure it was the same man. Did he say anything else?"

"No."

The captain pursed his lips and nodded his head in thought. Then he said, "If he comes back you should be very careful. He's shot and wounded one of our men and we think he's off now in the San Andres Mountains. There's no telling what he might decide to do next and I'm not sure he'll make a distinction between us down south and you and those two assistants of yours." At this, the captain angled his head back over his left shoulder while keeping his eyes on Darrell and Darrell followed the gesture to find Thomas and Betty still beyond the car but approaching from that very direction. The captain must have seen the two out on the desert as he'd driven in and the gesture was precise only by coincidence. But it gave the captain a presence, an aura of power, and Darrell felt more frightened of him than of the rancher.

"You've done your duty now, Captain," Darrell said.

The captain spun on his heel and strode to his car, slammed the door and raced off. The dust settled and the round faces of Betty and Thomas remained, the two faces close together, the eyes wide in their puzzlement. Darrell's fear shifted now, as the captain had desired, to the rancher in the mountains.

LLOYD AND ANNA WERE given strict instructions along with the Army sedan: under no condition were they to stop on the route from Los Alamos to Trinity except for food and gas at Roys in Belen, just south of Albuquerque. It was the standard instruction for anyone from the Los Alamos community and out on the road Lloyd could sense Anna's excitement. But they did not speak. Lloyd was unremittingly stolid behind the wheel and when, in the periphery of his vision, he saw Anna turning to him as if to talk, he only tightened his grip on the wheel. Facing the prospect of six hours with Anna, the burden of speech squeezing at his head, Lloyd decided that it would be best to portray the intently single-minded driver. But the expectant turns of her face raked at him, called to him, and only later on, when Anna seemed resigned to simply watching the landscape pass by, did Lloyd begin to loosen his hands on the steering wheel, to curve his spine slightly.

Outside, the trees and plants were being transformed from multi-leaved, evergreen, to small-leaved, naked; from soft-edged to spiny; from tall to dwarf; from crowded together to widely scattered, solitary. South of Albuquerque the land turned arid and there were only mesquite bushes and an occasional yucca, like a tousle-haired beggar child. To the east were mesas rising from the desert, their plateaus as flat as the horizon at the end of the highway.

Lloyd stopped at Roys but he still felt unprepared to talk. He took out his slide rule at the table and wrote a page of meaningless figures while Anna ate and watched intently. After a time he thought that this had worked out for the best—he felt an admiration in Anna's gaze. And he felt her joy at being free, on the road.

But south of Socorro, she spoke to him in the car. "I'm very hot, Dr. Coulter. Very thirsty."

Lloyd opened his mouth to reply but he didn't know what to say. He gave her a brief glance and squeezed the wheel. The car was very hot; he was aware of the steel top and sides and hood of the car and the windows seemed ridiculously small, the rush of air through them only moved the heat more quickly over their bodies; there was no cooling effect. The dust smelled of alkali and Anna said, "Please can't we stop? We won't give away any secrets, surely."

Lloyd knew he could not say no to Anna on this. She needed to stop, to drink, and he felt he had to provide these things. They turned east on a two-lane blacktop—their approved route—and in the little junction town of San Antonio they approached a low wooden building with a clock-face gas pump outside and a hand-painted sign: Jaime Lopez, Gas, Beer, Food.

Lloyd braked sharply and turned in and Anna yelped in pleasure. He pulled the car through the gas pump lane and around to the side of the building. He stopped, but before he turned off the engine he had a further thought. He put the car back in gear and drove around to the rear of the building, shielding the car from view of the highway.

They got out of the car and Lloyd's feet and legs and arms still throbbed faintly in vivid recollection of the motion that had just ceased. Chickens clucked nearby in a wire mesh pen and a car rippled past on the highway, its engine cycling lower in a Doppler curve as it withdrew.

Inside, there was one large room. The air was thick with suspended dust visible in long columns of sunlight buttressed down from the two windows in the western wall. The tables were empty and the room—beyond the columns of light—was dim. Before Lloyd, the southern wall was filled with bottles—whiskey and wine and beer; the bottles covered the wall on shelves like books. A smiling, nearly bald Mexican man in a white bib apron nodded from behind a counter and waved them to a table. They sat down, Lloyd facing the wall of bottles.

The Mexican approached and Anna smiled up eagerly at him and ordered a beer. Lloyd stammered a bit and ended up ordering the same. "Si, señor," the Mexican said, and before he moved off he paused and smiled broadly at the two of them, nodding at the private's stripe on Anna's uniform, nodding at Lloyd's tie. "You are from Los Alamos, yes?" he said.

Lloyd almost leaped up from the table, but the Mexican's hand came out, his voice oozed. "No, señor, it's all right. Many of your people stop at Jaime Lopez's. I am very discreet. My chickens will guard your automobile. No problem."

The Mexican moved off and Lloyd was sweating. He wiped

at his face and decided they should pay at once and leave. But when he turned to Anna her eyes were bright and she was stifling a laugh. She leaned closer, across the table, and she began to talk to him. For a long while he didn't hear her words. He knew she was talking about the sights along the highway—letting out all the things she'd wanted to say on the way—but he didn't hear anything specific that she said. He let her ardor, her joy buffet him like a wind off the ocean, he tilted his face to it, breathed it in, smiled into it, but it shook him like a wind, it frightened him too, threatened to throw him down.

Eventually though, as he held his ground, he grew less fearful, more comfortable with the movement of her words and he began to hear her. "I knew some bad girls before I enlisted. I mean, I was getting a little old to hang around with some of these girls but I didn't know better then."

"Where was this?" He said.

Anna looked briefly puzzled and Lloyd realized she'd already explained where and he'd missed it. But he felt the urge now to talk with her, to understand what she was saying.

"In Chicago," Anna said. "Remember? I was living in Chicago with my mother."

"Yes. Ah yes. Of course."

"The war was just getting started and these girls were—I don't know—going crazy over all these uniforms, I guess. Men in uniforms. So we all wore the same sort of things—we had our own uniforms. Sloppy Joe sweaters, bobby sox and saddle shoes, hair ribbons. Even I wore that stuff for a little while. Then we'd hang around the Navy Pier downtown, from there to State Street. But listen, my career as a V-girl was very short, I assure you, Dr. Coulter. As soon as I realized what those girls were *doing,* you know. Momma raised me right. And of course those poor guys came to *expect* what it was the girls were doing and it wasn't those guys' fault, really. It wasn't even the fault of the guy I had to punch." Anna paused to laugh.

Lloyd felt himself staring stupidly at Anna; he knew he appeared uncomprehending—and in some ways he knew he was—but only in the superficial ways. He appreciated her. He appreciated her dynamics, he liked her eyes and even the slightly too-long curve of her nose. He wanted to put his hands out to her but he just stared stupidly and now he saw in her face the effect of his stare.

"Oh but I'm just jabbering, aren't I, Dr. Coulter. I'm not usually like this. I went to college for two years. Loyola. I'm not this talkative usually. It's just . . . I'm glad to be out doing something. I was excited about . . ." She lowered voice. "You know, the project and all, being assigned to it. But I got stuck in that supply room and I was going crazy in there and I really appreciate your seeing that." She stopped abruptly. Then she said, very quietly, "I'm doing it again."

Lloyd looked past Anna to the wall of bottles. The wall stood on the side of the building facing the desert. The place Oppie had chosen for ground-zero was perhaps forty miles away. Lloyd thought the chances were very good that the bottles would fall. There was even a chance that this whole room would be disintegrated. At this thought, Lloyd wanted even more to reach out his hands and touch Anna. He realized she was silent. Without any premeditation at all, he said, "I've never been married. I guess I've been too preoccupied. Or too inward. A scientist can be very . . . self-absorbed." He heard now what he was saying. He realized he should be distressed— a foolish non-sequitur—but he didn't care. He was glad he said it; he was glad she knew it.

But he didn't like the flicker of confusion—did he even see fear?—in her face. She stammered a bit about how that was all right, his being preoccupied, and she fell silent. They sipped their beer and a car droned by outside. Lloyd could hear the chickens rutting beyond the wall of bottles. He suggested to Anna that they leave.

In the car he wanted to turn to her, to apologize for alarming her. But she said, "Thanks for stopping. I enjoyed our talk." And even though her voice sounded a little flat, he felt things had been restored.

They drove the remaining leg of their trip in silence. It was a rough, circuitous route into the desert and finally, near sundown, they passed the ranch house where Lloyd and Oppie had conferred in their earlier visit. A small Army truck sat outside. On the porch two soldiers turned their faces blankly to the passing car. Lloyd felt something odd about the faces. He passed the old cattle cistern near the ranch house and picked up a new blacktop into the camp area. The low-slung lab building still had its south-end unsided, roofless, only the clean, yellow timber frame standing. That would be part of his task, to oversee the completion of the lab, the installation of the equipment.

Again Lloyd felt something in the slow looks of the men he passed—men near the lab, men gathered on the steps of three wooden barracks, and then near the command center he saw the flag flying at half-staff. He parked and he and Anna got out of the car and she said, "Oh my God, no," even before they crossed the square and Oppie greeted them in the command center, his eyes bright with grief.

"Lloyd," Oppenheimer said.

"This is Anna Brown," Lloyd said and he felt her quaking beside him, as if she knew something already.

"Lloyd," Oppie said, "President Roosevelt's dead."

Anna began to sob. Oppie's eyes grew brighter still. Lloyd felt nothing; but this in itself made him feel a vague regret at his own distance.

THE NEXT MORNING DARRELL awoke with the thought of the rancher in his head. He'd slept on the captain's warning for two nights now and he could not put it aside. He rose and dressed and he hesitated to leave Betty and Thomas alone but it was daylight and he had to find out what was being done to protect them. He got into his car and drove south.

Soon he was on an adobe road and then it changed to blacktop—a smooth blacktop still smelling of tar and Darrell felt a disquiet run through him that was as smooth as this road. The feeling quickened as he saw up ahead what seemed to be a town, a neat little town full of trucks and new cars and strung with wire—thickets of wire high on solid, unweathered posts. Darrell did not know what prompted his uneasiness, except perhaps for the incongruity of this community out here in the desert, the further lie given, in retrospect, to Dr. Oppenheimer's claim that their explosives work was routine.

An Army man with a white helmet and a rifle held across his chest stepped out into the road and made Darrell stop. He came around to Darrell's window. "May I ask your business, sir?" he said.

"My name is Dr. Darrell Reeves. Dr. Oppenheimer . . ."

"I know your name," the soldier said. "Follow this road to the flagpole. Dr. Oppenheimer is still here, I think. In the command center."

"Thank you." Darrell drove on and ahead he saw the flagpole. The flag was flying at half-staff. At once he remembered Dean Felker's words about Roosevelt's health. Darrell pulled into a parking row and got out. He went up four wood-plank steps into the biggest of the buildings on the square. Inside he found a large space in frozen chaos: a wall was half constructed that would close off a small outer room; beyond the exposed beams and scantlings, the inner room had a stacking of crates marked "fragile," electronic gear half-assembled, tables and chairs scattered around. But no one attended to any of this. Half a dozen men sat idle in the inner room. Darrell did not see Dr. Oppenheimer. Nearby, a woman sat beside a desk. Her position at the desk was ambiguous—she was not clearly a worker here but she wore an Army uniform and he said to her, "Is Dr. Oppenheimer around?"

She lifted her face and Darrell felt his breath catch. She had very large, dark eyes—the eyes of one of the King's women, the dark eyes of a Pre-Columbian Indian. That was his instant impression and it did not fade even as she spoke in a flat, Midwestern voice.

"He's just out for a little while. He'll be back," she said.

Darrell nodded at her, and he saw that she'd been crying. The eyes that caught him were a little bit puffy, a little red. He'd had his first impression in spite of this. He wished she'd not been crying—how like the King's wife she would seem then. And her nose, too, was long and sharp. Only her skin was too pale.

"Why have you been crying?" he asked.

The woman cocked her head. "You haven't heard?" she said.

"No," he said and he thought of the flag outside—that matter had vanished from his mind when he'd stepped inside this building.

"The President's dead," the woman said and her voice quavered.

Although he'd suspected this was so as soon as he'd seen the flag, the words sucked a hole in the center of his chest and he leaned against the desk. The woman leaped from her chair.

"Sit here," she said. "I'm sorry. I couldn't imagine you didn't know."

Darrell was surprised himself at his reaction. He thought he'd long ago come to take Roosevelt for granted, had come to know that the world would be the same even if the man were gone. But he felt anxious. That more than grief. He felt anxious, as if something important—like his mason's trowel—had been lost.

He waved the woman back into her chair and he lifted a leg up to perch on the desk, to rest for a moment. He thought of Roosevelt, the man's eyes made very round by his glasses, as round as the optic foramens behind them. He thought of Roosevelt's skeleton being unearthed—a long age from now—Roosevelt's bones being brushed clean, the pelvis measured, the signs of his paralysis visible in the joining of his bones.

"Are you all right?" the woman said.

"Yes," Darrell said.

"It's a terrible thing. He was like a father," she said.

"Or a King."

"You a Republican?" the woman said.

Darrell almost laughed, in spite of Roosevelt's passing. "No," he said. "I'm an archaeologist."

He could see the same struggle to repress a smile in the young woman. "I'll give the archaeologist candidate a careful look next time," she said.

Now Darrell let himself smile. "I didn't mean to call him 'King' out of political scorn. Kings for archaeologists are seen a little differently."

"You find lots of treasure mixed in with their bones."

"Now, is that what you think of us? Treasure hunters?"

"Are you really an archaeologist?" Her voice had quickened. Darrell felt his breath beginning to catch again, just as when he'd first seen her face.

"Yes, I am," he said. "I'm conducting an excavation about ten miles north of here."

"No fooling?"

Darrell was having trouble figuring out the woman—her mind seemed very quick, she seemed aware, even educated, but there was a coarseness to her as well, a vigor. He liked both parts of her and he chided himself for trying to classify her.

"No fooling," he said, gently. "It's a King, too. An ancient burial."

"Can I come see it sometime?"

The prospect of this was so pleasurable, Darrell could not speak for a moment. Then he said, "Of course. Yes."

"I'm Anna Brown . . . *Private* Anna Brown, as you see."

"I'm Darrell Reeves. *Doctor* Darrell Reeves, as I sincerely hope you *cannot* see."

"Why's that?" Anna asked. "You're not ashamed of it."

"No."

"You're not *that* humble, are you? You don't go around worrying about people finding out you've got a PhD and thinking you're really hot stuff, do you?"

"No. No . . . It was false humility, I guess, Miss Brown." Darrell watched the tilt of her head, and he knew she was ready to ask, What was that for, to impress me? Darrell knew she was thinking this; he knew she was capable of speaking it; he was prepared to confess. But she let it pass. She smiled, as if to say, You know what was next.

Darrell noticed that she had bad teeth, crooked and faintly discolored, and he could see them in a skull, he could see himself touching her jawbone, the teeth, trying to deduce her life, missing entirely this sharp edge to her mind, seeing only weakness in her mouth.

"I really am interested . . ." Anna said and there was a clomping on the wooden steps outside and the door to the center opened. Darrell rose from the desk and faced a tall, bony man—Oppenheimer—and the short, powerful man who'd come with Oppenheimer to the excavation site. Coulter was his name, Darrell recalled. He watched Coulter's eyes slide over to Anna and there was nothing but the movement of the eyes to her and a brief fixing, but the look chilled Darrell.

"Dr. Reeves," Oppenheimer said in muted greeting.

Darrell turned to Oppenheimer and he was still very conscious of Anna Brown. An idea began to shape in him and he said, "I'm sorry to come on a day like this. I only just now learned about the President . . ."

"Of course," Oppenheimer said. "You were cut off down there . . . We all have to press on. What is it that brings you here?"

Now Darrell knew what he wanted to do. He put his concern about the rancher in momentary abeyance and he said, "Two things. First, I want to remind you of my need for help at the excavation. So I can get out of your way expeditiously. If you can spare anyone at all . . . I could use even part-time help with the dig." Darrell could not bring himself to turn to Anna and suggest her. He silently cursed his own timidity.

THE KING WAS FREE. He lay on his pedestal and his feet were tight together and angled like a diver's. The earth around him was smoothed and leveled and Darrell could not cast off the impression that the King had not been reached by digging but, rather, had himself risen on the narrow platform through a corridor in the earth. The cape of shells seemed only recently shrugged from the King's shoulders. He'd come now when he was needed. One King to succeed another.

The light was growing dim and Darrell turned and crossed to his tent and he thought of a time he had seen Roosevelt in Santa Fe. As a faculty member Darrell had been on the dais and he'd seen two strong men straining to lift the President from his wheel chair and up the steps. He'd known, of course, that Roosevelt was unable to walk. But the voice was so firm on the radio, the face was so commanding in the photos, the body itself always seemed at ease in the newsreels. This moment had shocked Darrell. He'd felt suddenly uneasy in his own sense of command.

Darrell sat on his rattan chair in the center of his tent and he did not light the lamp. For a moment his mind fretted about, testing Oppenheimer's assurances that the rancher would be apprehended, that the Army that was sweeping through Europe could roust a maverick rancher. He grew concerned, though, about the King and, as if in answer, he heard Thomas's voice, and Betty's, and then the snap of the tarpaulin as they covered up the dig for the night.

Darrell closed his eyes against the fading light and he felt the sweat still draining down his neck, his chest, and his mind began to follow its own, unexpected course: Roosevelt again, his broad smile frozen in the center of a newspaper front page; the stack of papers in Darrell's apartment; his brother in Washington—did Frank take the death coolly, pursing his lips and saying nothing, feeling as little as if it had been the death of his only brother? Darrell's thoughts snagged on Frank for a moment, but his mind was too weary to be controlled and he had an image of cherry blossoms; Frank's letter had seemed oblivious to the irony of this detail, for the trees had been a gift of the Japanese from before the first war, a little bit of Japan reflected in the Tidal Basin. There would be great

57

mourning in Washington. The newspapers nagged at Darrell—
there was some other association for him there—but he couldn't
place it; he saw instead the woman's face, Anna Brown's, the
eyes of the King's wife and Darrell wondered if she'd heard
his hint, wondered if she'd ask to come. Her dark eyes rose
to him and they touched him in a different way now, reminding
him of a woman he'd known before his wife, briefly, a week
or two, sitting in a restaurant, sitting in the parlor of her parents'
house, unable to touch; she was a Jew. He thought of the Jews.
That was what he'd tried to think of from the newspapers.
What was happening to the Jews? Or was it simply the madness
of the one-legged man? But the Jews faded now quickly again.
Roosevelt's death was stronger in him. He saw the President
lying in a coffin, his glasses pinched onto his nose. And the
next connection was so obvious, so easily anticipated, that it
came with the illusion of having come by an act of Darrell's
own will: he thought of his father, lying dead, too, in a wick-
er casket, less than a month after Darrell's twenty-first birth-
day. The timing had impressed Darrell. The distance esta-
blished between them by his father's reasonableness suddenly
seemed filled with unspoken understandings; the man had
timed his own death to correspond with Darrell's coming of
age. Surely there'd been more between them than had ever
been spoken.

Darrell rose now from his rattan chair. He circled it and sat
back down. No. Darrell's second thought as his father had lain
in the parlor, natty and silent, was that this was the whipping
the man had never given him.

"JACK BENNY IS DEAD," Anna said. "That's what they say at
the mess hall."

"Jack Benny?" Lloyd said. He hesitated by the car. Anna
did not pause but got into the front seat. He had been thinking
about the lab. They'd drive over there now and Anna would
begin to work near him. She would see how orderly his mind

could be. But Jack Benny? The President and now Jack Benny? He didn't understand the randomness of these things. He got into the car.

Anna said, "Do you think it's true?"

"What?"

"That Jack Benny is dead?"

Lloyd started the car. "I have no idea."

"No one seemed to know where the news came from . . . Somebody else said it was Al Jolson who died. He'd heard it from someone who'd been talking on the telephone to New York."

Lloyd pondered the reaction—and he thought how it might be like the splitting of the atom. Roosevelt's was not a normal death; he was a critical mass. When the President died he split apart and he killed Jack Benny who split apart and killed Al Jolson, escalating, the famous had all died within seconds, a chain reaction, Frank Sinatra, Charlie Chaplin, Errol Flynn, Joe DiMaggio, Jack Dempsey, all of them exploding, their pieces flying off, killing others.

"I don't believe it myself," Anna said. "People are just shook up."

They drove the half mile to the laboratory in silence. After they parked, though, before they could get out of the car, Anna said, "Are you going back up to Los Alamos soon?"

"Probably day after tomorrow," Lloyd said. "For just a couple of days."

Lloyd was struck by her interest in his plans. He smiled but kept his face forward. The smile was for her but he could not yet turn it clearly on her.

Then she said, "Whenever you're back at Los Alamos I'm going over to help at that excavation that's going on."

"No," Lloyd said. It was faint but immediate and beneath the faint sound his arms had grown suddenly very strong, very tight, though they did not move; his chest had compacted. On the periphery of his vision he saw her face jerk toward him, but he still did not turn to her.

"I've already asked Dr. Oppenheimer," she said. "I volunteered. He said it was all right with him."

"I thought you'd go back with me to Los Alamos."

"My orders transferred me down here. That's what they say. That's the letter of the rules . . . I guess you could change that, but please, Dr. Coulter, I so appreciate your rescuing me . . ."

She paused briefly and the sweet flutter of her voice, her calling him her rescuer, made Lloyd's arms turn slack, weak. But he thought of that pale-eyed archaeologist and he wanted to grab Anna and shake her.

"I can't go back up there," she said. "Not for awhile. Please."

He said nothing; he could not imagine what to say or do but he felt her hand touch his. "Thanks," she said. "I knew you'd understand."

He heard her open the door and get out of the car and he sat motionless for a time and he concentrated hard on the spot on the back of his hand that her fingers had touched.

THE FIVE-FOOT SQUARE TO the King's left was more than half excavated and so far it was empty. By mid-morning Darrell climbed from the hole, vaguely discontented. He looked at the King to reassure himself. The fleshless grin suggested a sense of humor now. The King teased Darrell: what did you expect? a store-house full of pendants and pottery? I'm a simple man, really, for a King.

Darrell heard a car and he turned to see an Army sedan approaching across the desert, seeming to have an enormous fire inside, from the great cloud of dust trailing behind it. Darrell was suspended between a hope and a fear—either the rancher had been captured or the right to continue the excavation had been taken away. But as the car slowed and curved to a stop, Darrell saw that the driver was not the captain and there was a passenger in the car. Before he actually saw who the passenger was, he took a step forward as a different hope formed.

The door opened and Darrell saw Anna Brown, dressed in fatigues, climbing out of the car. He crossed to her at once, her smile fixing him briefly and then shifting behind him to the camp, the excavation. She squeezed twice at the smile, no doubt to acknowledge Betty and Thomas in the hole, and then she turned her face back to Darrell as he reached her. Only now, in retrospect, did Darrell sense a brief disappointment—even alarm—in her face at the look of the place.

"Perhaps it's not quite what you'd expected, Miss Brown?" Darrell said.

Anna didn't reply at once but stuck out her hand and Darrell wiped off the dust across the front of his shirt and he shook her hand. "Don't you worry about that, Dr. Reeves," Anna said. "I've adjusted already."

A man's face became visible in the passenger's window as he leaned across the seat. "I'll be back—when?"

"Not till nightfall," Darrell said.

He walked Anna very slowly toward the excavation as the car sped off. He said, "You're going to meet three people here. My two assistants and an ancient King. Try not to look too closely at the King—who's lying in the center of the excavation—until we've gotten the other two introductions accomplished."

Anna's eyes were very bright and she said nothing but only nodded at this and Darrell realized that not a word of explanation had passed between them about why she was here.

"It seems you've come ready to work," he said, looking at her hair pulled back in a ponytail. From his first sight of her he remembered her hair in a longer line, sleek, down one side of her face. He liked her hair pulled back, although it made her seem very young and that was unsettling, hinting at a barrier between them.

Darrell introduced her to Betty and Thomas and he watched Anna's gaze holding carefully on the faces of the two assistants, not moving farther on, just as Darrell had told her. He smiled at this. When the greetings had died and Darrell had explained that Anna would be helping with the dig, she turned to him expectantly.

"Now this," he said, taking her arm, "is the man we're working for."

He moved her around the edge of the hole and watched her face as she turned it to the King. Her eyes widened and then she ducked her head slightly and said, "It's like seeing him naked."

She said this without looking away from the King and Darrell felt naked himself beside her, felt a prickling down the front of his body and he sucked in a deep breath to stop the rush of his feelings. He wanted to touch Anna's shoulder, just put his fingertips on the point of her shoulder. But instead he forced himself into his teacher-voice and he explained how the King was found and what the excavation plan was and then he turned her over to Betty and Thomas and retreated to his tent. He sat and sweated in the heat and he listened to the grainy whisk of the wind and he waited until the trembling inside stopped. When he returned to the dig, Anna was at work at the rocking screen. She smiled at him but returned at once to her work with a vigor that touched him and threatened to stir his desire once more.

Darrell worked separately from the others all afternoon and they stopped at their accustomed hour with a foot-wide strip of earth left to excavate on the edge of the second square. There was still no trace of artifacts in this part of the grid. Normally that would have been the object of Darrell's intense speculation, but an hour of sunlight was left, an hour before the car would return for Anna, and Darrell was faced with the opportunity that he'd instinctively arranged for himself.

While Betty and Thomas were occupied with putting away the digging tools, Darrell came near to Anna, where she sat by the rocking screen. "Tired?" he said.

"Yes," she said, drawing her wrist across her forehead, leaving a dark streak of dirt in the perspiration there. "But I'm happy I came out."

"I'm sorry we didn't find anything today. Tomorrow perhaps . . . Are you interested in coming back?"

Anna angled her face higher and smiled at him. The smile was twisted slightly to one side, suggesting a wry perception that she was withholding from him.

"What is it?" he said, surprised at his own directness.

"I didn't see much of you today," she said at once, and her directness surprised him even more than his own. She said, "It was like you were driving a car a long distance and you were afraid of running off the road."

Darrell glanced toward Betty and Thomas. They were unrolling the tarp. He looked back to Anna and her eyes did not waver in their hold on him as she drew her wrist across her cheek and left another streak. The streaks on her face made him smile. "You've got a little while. Would you like a cup of coffee?"

"How about something cold," she said.

"Tepid is the best I can do," Darrell said.

"Tepid is okay."

Darrell helped Anna to her feet and led her to his tent. As they entered, he looked back and saw Betty and Thomas jerking their faces away, holding back smiles. He didn't give this a thought; already he was turning to follow Anna into the tent, watching her ponytail, still pert and in place.

He wished he could make her talk again about her regret at his working apart from her during the day. He realized now that he'd done it deliberately—he'd been unprepared to face the strong feelings in being near her. But he wanted Anna to talk about it again. She was facing him in the center of the tent, smiling, and he wondered once more at her directness, her boldness. I didn't see much of you today, she'd said with undisguised regret.

He wanted to say now, You're a very modern woman. But he thought about it for a moment too long and instead he said, "I'm afraid I only have bottled water."

"That's all right," she said.

He poured the water for them and they sat in two chairs, she in the rattan, and they sipped in silence for a time. Then she said, "I'm tireder than I thought."

"It's not easy work."

"Are you very disappointed we didn't find anything today?"

"No. There's more. That old fellow isn't alone in his grave, not a man who rated a cape like that. We'll find more."

"You mean there are other . . . bodies?"

"Perhaps. But I was referring to artifacts, really. Pottery, ceremonial . . ." He felt himself growing professorial and he stopped. He didn't want to retreat from her now, not alone with her in this tent, not with less than an hour left of her company.

" 'Ceremonial' what?" she said.

"Whatever. Things."

"You don't have to be simple for me," Anna said with vigor, but without any hint of offense.

"It's not that," Darrell said.

"I've been to college. I'm a very bright girl," she said.

"I'm sorry," Darrell said. "That's not why I was being so . . . vague. I'm sorry to make you say those things."

Anna tilted her head at this. Then she smiled gently. "It's all right. It's not painful for me to tell people I'm bright."

Darrell leaned slightly nearer to Anna. "I just don't want to sound dry to you. Sound like a teacher. I think what I do is exciting, but sometimes when I try to tell people . . . it's difficult."

"Tell me the most exciting thing you've ever done in your work," she said.

Darrell paused only briefly—to appreciate the incline of Anna's body toward his, the eagerness of her voice—and then he told her about Cahokia, about his work in the ancient city that flourished seven centuries ago in the Mississippi River bottoms, a city that could have been the largest in the world in the twelfth century and the center of a great empire of trade. He told her of the vastness of Sun Mound and he told her about a King there, buried like this one on a cape of shells—twenty thousand mother-of-pearl discs—and with half a dozen copper tubes and fifteen ground discoidal game stones and a bushel of mica and a thousand arrowheads from all over the Midwest. And with four men killed and buried to serve him in the afterlife. Darrell told her about the early autumn twilight with a mist rising in the fields of soybeans and horseradish out across the highway beyond the empty plaza clearing—Indian summer when the souls of the Indians rose to hunt in vain for the long-vanished deer. He told her of the steel mill five miles off, in Wabash, the sky streaked with red smoke from the hot-strip, like a distant Indian pyre. He spoke to Anna with great passion, a passion he genuinely felt for that time in his life, for that ancient city, but also, he realized, a passion for Anna that he was deflecting into his memory of Cahokia.

When he stopped she whistled. He grinned at this, this thin little whistle from this alert mind.

She said, "I understand your love of all this."

"Yes."

Darrell glanced away, out the tent flap. He realized it must seem to Anna that he was thinking further about Cahokia, but in fact he was thinking of her, trying to slow himself down, trying to detach. The light was fading outside; the sky was not yet dark but the sunlight had slid past them, would only be on the mountains to the east now. He turned back to Anna and she too was staring out of the tent. After a moment she grew conscious of Darrell's gaze and she looked at him and smiled.

"I learned a little about archaeology in school," she said. "We studied Pompeii and Herculaneum."

"Yes," he said. "Of course."

"Can I ask you a question, since you're an archaeologist?" She smiled suddenly, but her eyes narrowed, giving her a mischievous look.

"Yes."

"Have you ever felt *thankful* for the eruption of Vesuvius that buried those two cities? I don't mean to put you on the spot, but I bet it's easy for a scientist not to even think about all those private disasters when you compare it to all the things that have been saved for you."

Darrell sat back in his chair and put his hands on his knees. Yes of course he'd been thankful. Even when the notion was put this way now, his mind quickly sorted out its priorities and he found that the people of Pompeii—all the shopkeepers and actors and bureaucrats and teachers lying where the sulphur had choked them and the ash had covered them over in the midst of their busy early morning—all these people were part of him, part of the world, and he felt tenderly about them in their state of preservation and yes he was glad they were there for him, just like that, in spite of the agony they went through on that August morning in the year 79. But realizing this did not suggest an answer for Anna. She'd made him consider a feeling he'd never been conscious of and he was delighted by her for that. But at the same time he was a little ashamed at the feeling, particularly since she'd put it the way she had.

The silence stretched out and she didn't seem inclined to let the question go unanswered. Her smile persisted, her eyes had relaxed but they wouldn't let him go. He said, "I've never felt thankful because I never got that far. I just accepted the existence of the people of Pompeii and Herculaneum. They exist for me, even now. Not dead, really, though I know that's a mental trick . . ." He paused and he felt that her smile had changed from mischievous to tender, though he had no idea what gave him this impression. "Your point is well taken," he said. "Any archaeologist is prone to that kind of . . . crust."

"I didn't have a point, really," she said. "I just like to hear you talk about all this."

A car horn honked outside. Darrell and Anna turned their faces to the twilight beyond the tent. "He's early," Anna said. "There's still some light."

"Come back again," Darrell said.

"I will," she said.

DARRELL LET BETTY AND Thomas begin without him the next morning. He lay on his cot for a time after his coffee, his hands still clean, his body still dry, and he thought of Anna. He wondered if she would come today. But soon he began to pose questions to himself, as she had done yesterday with Pompeii, sharp questions. Was he not *thankful* when his marriage broke up and he was left alone? Was he not incapable of giving another person—a *living* person—any reasonable measure of devotion, any understanding? He thought of his wife. While he was working at the Cahokia site they'd lived in a house in Wabash, a fragment of a house, a basement that had a flat, tarpaper roof and a front doorway that stood up like the remnant of the house left after a tornado. There were other basement-houses like this one in Wabash in 1935, compromises of homes begun and cut short during the Depression. He blamed himself for his wife's anger, for her gradual withdrawal, for the divorce that broke her heart and her parents' hearts and shamed her. He wondered if she'd overcome the stigma at last somewhere. He blamed himself. His preoccupation with his work. That seemed a simple fault, a common fault, but he knew it must have been very bad to have driven her away. Toward the end she complained often about the dirt that never seemed to come out from under his fingernails. He knew it wasn't that. It was his preoccupation. And he blamed himself for even more. He failed to understand her, understand what she wanted, what delighted her, what made her sad. When they'd met in college he had talked to her at great length about this feeling for the past that had seized him. They were the

67

same age, fellow students, but perhaps she'd fallen in love with him as she would with an interesting course. He talked to her and never really moved beyond her response to his words. The thing he knew best about her was that she liked to hear him talk. When that wasn't enough, when his love for pre-history turned inward, she became a stranger. Once, he had come home and found her gone to the store. He went into the subterranean stillness of their bedroom and he looked around, trying to read their life together. He went to the dresser to see her artifacts. One at a time he picked up the objects there; he turned them over in his hands, trying to read the clues. Her hairbrush, the bristles worn and bent, black hair tangled there: how thrilling this would be in an excavation, how much he could deduce. From the hair of the woman he could learn about the chemical balances of her body, her age, her health, perhaps her diet. From the brush itself he could learn about the artisans of her society, her economic status, whether she was right-handed or left-handed. But he could not say from this brush why his wife had married him or why she would soon leave him. Perhaps if I could see her bones, he thought. If I could touch her bones. But he knew nothing and he put the brush down.

Now he feared: was he doing it again to Anna Brown? He had told her of Cahokia and she said she loved to hear him talk about these things. But what did he know of her?

"Dr. Reeves." It was Betty's voice. Fitting into his thoughts, her words seemed to be announcing Anna's arrival.

"Yes?" He rose up quickly. He thought, I'll ask her about herself today; the hour before dark we'll sit and talk about her.

"Dr. Reeves, we've found something," Betty said, her face peeking into the tent.

Anna vanished at once from his mind, although he was conscious of her vanishing and so he felt it was all right. He moved past Betty and out to the excavation and Thomas was still working with his trowel. Darrell jumped into the hole and drew near.

68

In the margin of the second square, at the same depth as the King, Thomas's hands were rapidly uncovering a stone. It was a smooth, flat stone barely fashioned beyond its natural shape and surface. But Darrell knew at once what it was. It marked a sacred enclosure. The man on the cape of beads was indeed a King and this stone—and others Darrell knew they would find—had held the sacred ritual of the King's burial, of his return to the gods for whom he was a special son.

Darrell stepped back and looked first to the King and then to the stone, gauging the distance. He stretched out his arm and pointed to a spot, also in the marginal strip of the square, a little less than a yard from the stone. "Another will be there," he said. "And there. And there," he said, and he proceeded on, placing the stones, tracing a large circle around the site with the King at its center and the mystery there, too, deeper now. Why was the King here?

They uncovered two more stones of the sacred enclosure that day—just where Darrell had said they'd be—but Anna did not arrive.

Late in the afternoon there was shooting in the mountains to the east, the sound thin and faint from where Darrell stood by the pit, his knees aching, his hands and forearms covered in the alkaline dust. He saw a sand devil swirl up out on the desert and he expected the rancher to suddenly step from the vortex of dust, rifle in hand; but then Darrell's concern shifted to the south, where for some reason Anna had been prevented from coming back to him. The gunfire was in the mountains and surely she was ten miles to the south, in the camp, but as irrational as it was, he feared for her safety.

LLOYD HAD SEEN THAT his return to Trinity-site after only one day at Los Alamos had clearly surprised Anna; she had even seemed disappointed that morning, as he came in to the mess hall and he found her in a fatigue uniform, her hair pulled back. Her quickly suppressed disappointment had clashed in him with the beauty of her ears, their pale convolutions. He had never seen her ears before and they had finally prevailed.

But by late afternoon, as he went over the list of needed lab supplies that she'd been making with him through the day, Anna's enthusiasm had begun to wane. She'd smiled at him all day, her eyes had widened often at the equipment he explained to her as they'd gone over the lab-site, but now she seemed tired and it reminded Lloyd of that moment in the mess hall when she'd been disappointed to see him.

He grew angry at this but the anger was pulled back by his desire for her—as if by the mass of a great planet—and the anger bent and began to trail words through his mind. As she slid into the passenger seat beside him for the drive back to the barracks area, Lloyd wanted to speak to her of his feelings; but he felt the words slowing, fading.

"Are you still happy you're down here?" he said.

She turned to him and her enthusiasm returned. "Yes," she said, "I am. Yes."

"I knew you wanted to get out of that supply room. I felt it."

"You were right. I'm very grateful to you."

Lloyd turned on the engine and drove off and he felt strong, he could speak to her now, he was learning how to reach her. "Scientists sometimes have intuitions," he said. "We're not as rigorously rational as we sometimes seem." He glanced at her and found her face on him, smiling. He said, "Like when I knew you were unhappy." This sounded repetitive to him; he grew afraid again of seeming foolish. But instead of silencing him the fear made him bolder. "I also needed your help," he said. "Not only here but back at Los Alamos, whenever I needed to go back there."

"Oh Dr. Coulter, are you going to make me go back and forth?"

"I wanted you to help me," he said. The car approached a large crack in the blacktop but Lloyd's arms were too rigid to curve around the spot and they jolted twice as they ran over the crack.

70

"I'm helping you down *here,* aren't I?" she said.

"It's not enough," he said and he was conscious of the hardness in his voice.

She didn't respond at once. He glanced toward her and her face was lowered. He felt sorry for her, sorry for his harshness but he said it again, "It's not enough," wanting to put his hands on her, shake her, pull her against him.

"I'm sorry," she said. "I'm not being grateful enough . . . You were very nice to me . . . I want to help." Her voice was quavering.

The steering wheel wobbled and Lloyd looked to the front. He'd forgotten his driving and the car was going very slowly now, running half off the road. He put on the brakes and stopped entirely.

"I'm sorry," he said and the tears that were beginning to make Anna's eyes shine made his own eyes grow warm. He knew he would soon cry too and he could not accept that. "It's all right," he said. "Please don't . . I'm at fault to press you back. I'm sorry. It's just . . . my work is so important. This is all so important, what I'm doing."

"I know it is," she said, and her face lifted, she seemed in control of herself now. Lloyd took a deep breath; his own tears had never pushed out; they both kept control and he was glad. But he'd let her stay at Trinity again. "It's very important and I've been trying to share the work with you," he said.

Anna smiled the firm, admiring smile that she'd given him several times before. "I'm grateful. I know how important your work is, how important *you* are."

He made a little sound in his throat that he heard clearly as his own desire for her. But still he could not bring his arms forward, could not even open his hands.

"I *mean* it," she said, and he knew that the sound had struck her as modesty. "Listen," she said, "when it's *very* important I come back with you, I'll do it. Okay?"

"Yes. Okay."

"But please make sure it's *really* important for your work. Promise?"

Lloyd hesitated. He was happy to have this much from her, but he wanted to take her with him because of himself, not because of his work. But he was trapped now. "I promise," he said.

I'M A MAN OF my word, Lloyd said to himself, over and over, when he'd gone back to Los Alamos alone. It was a pitiful compensation for his terrible mistake, he thought, for ietting Anna stay down in the desert while he came up here, for not lying to her and insisting that she was vital to his work on this trip—on all the trips. Now he stared at the thin silver tracks on the black photos. He laid them all out on the tabletop, the corners of the prints curling, two days' worth of explosions recorded here and the particles' thrust across the chamber was still not enough. They could never begin the work of the bomb. More than that, the cloud chamber itself wasn't operating properly. Half the prints had false tracks, the ghosts of previous particles. I'm a man of my word, he said to himself, swiping at the prints, scattering them onto the floor. This phrase, too, crossing his mind, had a ghost of itself tracking behind it. The phrase had gone through Lloyd before, long ago, and its image had not been cleared away.

He burst from the lab and crossed to the two Army engineer assistants who crouched near the explosive caddy between the blockhouses. Their faces turned at his quick stride and Lloyd wanted to grab each of them by the throat, he had one hand for each; but he stopped short and put his anger into his voice. "Dammit to hell," he shouted. "Don't you idiots check the chamber before you shoot your goddam charge off? I've got garbage ions all through those photos. I don't care if it takes all afternoon for one shot, you've got to run those electrodes long enough to clear the vapor." After this outburst, Lloyd abruptly took a step toward the two men and they both reared back in fear, one of them losing his balance and falling backwards. The man sprawled and his arms flailed and he lifted up, his face rigid in fear, and Lloyd felt his anger tail off. The man's falling back was enough; Lloyd felt as if he'd hit him.

Turning away now, the tension suddenly gone from his arms, he heard the phrase again in his head—I'm a man of my word— and the voice was not his own. Then Lloyd saw Oppenheimer coming up the rutted path toward the lab, and the voice spoke again in his head, more loudly, and Lloyd knew it was his father who spoke, a memory of his father.

"Where the hell did you come from?" Lloyd said, low, to the memory. At once Lloyd feared that Oppie had heard the words and thought they were for him. But Oppie's face was on the path as he climbed; he trailed the smoke of his pipe; his eyes were hidden by the brim of his hat. Lloyd saw his father sitting in the kitchen, his felt hat on the tabletop beside him, and one at a time he took from his pocket six cigars wrapped in lead foil. He laid them in a row before him.

"Lloyd," Oppie said, approaching.

Lloyd nodded but he watched his father lay the last cigar before him. It was payday. Each payday his father bought six cigars in lead foil and as soon as he got home he laid them on the table and then he took one up and unwrapped it, the lead foil crackling and making Lloyd's hands twitch in desire. He wanted to take the foil and role it up tight and add another foil around it and another. But he never asked for the foil and his father never offered it, folding it instead and putting it in the side pocket of his suitcoat.

"Lloyd," Oppie said, standing before him, "everything's going into implosion now. I'm sorry you were down at Trinity when the final decision was made."

Lloyd wondered what ultimately happened to the lead foil that disappeared into his father's pockets. Did the man have his own gigantic ball of foil hidden somewhere?

"Lloyd," Oppie said.

"Yes?"

"Did you hear me?"

"I'm sorry," Lloyd said. "There are troubles clearing the

tracks in the cloud chamber. And the particle energy is still not nearly what we need.''

Oppie puffed hard at his pipe. Lloyd saw his father lift the cigar—his first cigar on payday, the first thing he did when he came home—he saw his father lift the cigar and begin to lick it, lick its two ends, lick all along its length, lick every part of the cigar to moisten it, to make it burn smoothly. He saw his father licking at the cigar and Oppie said, ''We've got to solve these problems soon, Lloyd . . . We've got no choice now but implosion.''

Lloyd's hands jumped up, his mind cracked in two—on each side of his mind he had a clear image. Oppie said that implosion had won. It was the only approach now. Neddermeyer had been right. Lloyd's little operation here was suddenly at the center of the bomb, their only bomb, the only bomb they could possibly make. On the other side of his mind his father said very clearly, ''I'm a man of my word,'' and then his powerful arm went back and pistoned forward, his fist catching Lloyd's mother squarely in the face and the cracking sound cut through Lloyd's head and his mother flew backward across the kitchen and fell with another crack against the floor, her head bouncing, her apron settling delicately down upon her.

''We have to get the lens mold settled soon,'' Oppie said.

''I understand,'' Lloyd said. His father had apparently warned his mother about this. He'd promised her a beating for something. There'd been other promises, but Lloyd had never known what issues were behind them. Those secrets were locked far tighter than the heart of an atom.

''I don't know where you're needed most at the moment, Lloyd,'' Oppie said. ''I want to set up the test blast at Trinity site. A hundred tons or so of TNT to test our instruments.''

''Out where the real bomb will go?''

''The same spot.''

''I can help at both,'' Lloyd said.

''I don't want to stretch you too thin. These experiments here are crucial now . . .''

"I can handle them both," he said firmly, afraid he'd be delayed in Los Alamos without Anna.

"All right, Lloyd. Keep splitting your time, if need be."

"I promise you it'll be all right," Lloyd said. He almost added, I'm a man of my word, but his mother lay very still and he crept back from the kitchen door, out of his father's sight. But he heard the man breathing; he smelled the smoke of his cigar.

THERE WAS A PARTY that night at the Ranch School lodge building. There was always a party somewhere; Los Alamos was stuffed with five thousand workers and their families and Oppie encouraged a casual spirit here, a testimony, Lloyd always thought, to Oppie's uncertainty about when or whether this job could be done. Lloyd wanted simply to lie in his room and wait for the night to end. But he felt Anna's distance so keenly that he went out and wandered toward the lodge, the windows top and bottom lit up, shadows moving there, the front doors open wide, the gabble of many people filling the night, obscuring even the chirring of the crickets. Lloyd approached. He would edge around the room, watching, letting the narcotic sound and motion dull his senses, make the night tolerable.

But once inside he was troubled. The main hall was full of people trampling in the space where the top scientists met weekly to exchange ideas. All the canvas chairs, the blackboards, had disappeared and instead people stomped and jiggled and drifted in the open space. A small dance band played somewhere, hidden by the crowds, and the band segued into a rhumba; hips began to jut as Lloyd eased along the wall, watching these people make fools of themselves. He stopped and crossed his arms on his chest and he saw a ripple in the crowd on the other side, a chain shaping, and the line rhumbaed around the room, curling and growing. The head of the line emerged from the crowd and Lloyd was surprised to see a slight young man there, leading all the others, a man with a wide, bulging forehead and round glasses, a man who had always struck Lloyd as being sensible, as being a scientist with the same strengths and limitations as himself—intense, open, watchful, but slow to make the graceful leaps of intuition. The man was here with the British team. His name was Klaus Fuchs and he was making a damn fool of himself and because of Lloyd's previous sense of kinship with him, Lloyd himself felt foolish.

Lloyd moved on along the wall and a view opened up to the far side where a corner of the hall had a rug, reading lamps, a couch and overstuffed chairs. Oppie stood in the center of the rug and there was a small crowd around him, as there always was. At the inner ring of the crowd were four young women straining for each word, each gesture. The women always fawned on Oppenheimer and Lloyd couldn't understand it. Oppenheimer stood there in his tweed suit, puffing at his pipe, his spindly arms folded awkwardly in front of him, a fist supporting the elbow of the other arm that rose to his face where the hand clutched the pipe—the whole thing was a patchwork scaffold and Lloyd couldn't understand why all the women loved him. Lloyd could take Oppie up in his hands and snap the man in two. Why should the women desire this brittle stick-man, he wondered. Coming here was a mistake.

He turned abruptly and began to move toward the door. The end of the rhumba snake whipped near him and he pressed against the wall.

"It's dangerous out there," a man's voice said.

Lloyd turned and a young man and woman were standing against the wall. The woman's right hand was hooked in the man's arm and her left hand lay on top of it. Lloyd looked at her wedding band and then up to the two faces, near each other, smiling at him.

"I'm Peters," the man said. "Ted Peters. I work with Kistiakowsky at the X Division. I've seen you there a couple of times. This is my wife, Kay."

Lloyd had difficulty making his mouth shape into a smile

76

even though he had a strong feeling for this couple; he appreciated their being here to distract him from Oppie and the others; he liked their being married. "I'm Dr. Lloyd Coulter," he said.

"Right," Peters said. "Dr. Coulter. I did know your name."

"Nice to meet you," Kay Peters said.

"Nice to meet *you*," Lloyd said firmly. "Nice to meet you both." This was what it was like, he thought. This was a vision of what it was like. He felt suddenly close to Anna. He felt her hand on his arm.

"Do you come to many of these parties?" Peters asked.

"No," Lloyd said. "Do you?"

"No."

"It's crazy," Kay said. "Los Alamos has all the dance bands you want but we can't even find enough pairs of diapers at the PX to keep our baby dry."

"I don't think they got this band at the PX either, dear," Peters said and the couple laughed together, turning their faces to each other in a sudden, exclusive intimacy that Lloyd wanted to reach out and touch; he wanted to reach out and spread his hand and touch these two faces that had come so near to each other.

"There's a shortage of diapers?" Lloyd said.

"Yes," Kay said. "And milk. I don't know why they let all the wives and kids in here."

That sentiment reverberated in Lloyd; he'd asked that once himself, for a different reason. But right now—with men and women snaking around the floor, the saxaphones blaring, Oppie puffing away for his own little group of V-girls—Lloyd was glad this couple was here, self-contained, detached, to show him what it was like.

MORE THAN ANYTHING ELSE, Darrell wanted to walk with Anna out on the desert; the mountains to the west would be crested with a thin-air sunset and he might try to take her hand. But he could not bear the scrutiny of Betty and Thomas. Or worse, he could not bear being out on the desert with the two of them mooning around out there themselves; that would force Anna to be conscious of a relationship that Darrell hoped would grow between them but which was still not ready for her conscious examination. So they sat in his tent for a third night and they talked. He had encouraged her to talk about herself; he had determined to listen, to understand her; and he'd heard about her youth in Chicago living alone with her mother, about her mistaken time with a group of V-girls hanging around State Street, about her life in the Army, her initial feeling of liberty, escape, and then her boredom, entrapment.

"Now I know how much I miss the big city," she said. "I never knew there were no Army jobs in the city."

Darrell did not answer and Anna seemed absorbed in a thought. He tried to see how he could use this knowledge of Anna to make her closer to him. Anna's mother was abandoned by her husband when Anna was three; Anna had no memory of her father, though she seemed to recall other things from about that time; in her early twenties Anna fell in with some bad girls for a while but she never did the worst things herself; she went to college for two years, where she liked every course equally; she felt very happy in Army basic training, far from the streets and housefronts of her childhood. These were the things that had stuck in Darrell from the talk of the past few evenings, these and a few other details like them. He had no need to deduce the physical woman or her culture; these were givens. He could abstract and systematize her likes and dislikes but he did not see how he could use that, moment to moment, to love Anna better than he had his wife. Darrell compacted his fists together, squeezing at himself, frightened.

"I want to go to New York City," Anna said.

"Yes?" Darrell's voice was faint.

· "New York," she said. "I've never been there. I'd really like to go to New York City."

Darrell had been in New York City for about six weeks of

work at Columbia University, a professional seminar, but he did not speak now. He could mention the city, she could ask him what it was like, he could tell her about the Columbia campus, the Hudson River, Harlem, the skyscrapers, and would that bring them together? These desires and appreciations were things he'd understood about his wife, as well. Over the ten years since the divorce he'd forgotten them; but yes, he'd known. His wife liked to row. They would go on the trolley to Forest Park in St. Louis and they would rent a boat on the lagoon and his wife would row. They had done that together on a Sunday, more than once, and it had done no good.

He watched Anna's face as it held patiently on his, waiting for him to speak. He nearly said, I was in New York once, but he had a rush of impatience. He was impatient with himself for dwelling on his wife and for his own failings; he was impatient with the pace this culture expected him to maintain in his approach to a woman; he was impatient to draw nearer to her.

"What else do you want?" he said.

"What else?" She tilted her head.

"You want to go to New York . . . What else do you want in your life?"

"What any girl wants, I guess."

"What's that?"

"The usual things."

Darrell felt her resistance. She was smiling, her face was calm, but he felt her discomfort. She must have meant that she wanted to get married, but she was resisting the declaration. Was that because she didn't want to encourage him? he wondered. Or was it just shyness?

"I've been digging in the ground for maybe fifteen years now," Darrell said. "I'm not sure what the usual things are anymore. Can't you tell me what you want?"

She stretched her smile just a little wider and she said, "A family."

Darrell thought: she would not say "husband" to me, not

even "marriage." He felt a heaviness in his legs, his arms. He feared now that she had no interest in him.

"An interesting life," she said.

"That's a little vague."

"I've got an open mind about it, is why I'm vague."

" 'A family' doesn't necessarily mean an interesting life?"

"Not necessarily. No . . ." Her smile faded a bit; but it did not disappear altogether and she leaned nearer to him. "My . . . husband would have to be interesting. His life would have to be interesting."

Darrell did not know if this meant he should proceed with her or withdraw. He felt as if his chest were being slowly squeezed in a clamp. "Big-city interesting?"

"I like cities," she said. "I'd like at least to go to them once in awhile. But I wouldn't necessarily have to live in one."

"His work would have to be interesting?"

"Yes . . . But lots of things interest me. I'm not really as limited as I'm sounding."

Darrell could speak no more. He tried to weigh the nuances of what she was saying, tried to read the implications for his own hopes with Anna, but he couldn't even decide if implications were there to be read at all or if she was speaking with utter insouciance.

"Am I confusing you?" she said.

Darrell cleared his face, concentrated hard to take away whatever outward signs of his distress had led her to ask this. "No," he said. "You're perfectly lucid to me."

Anna laughed at this and riding over her laugh came the honk of the car that had arrived to take her back to the base.

She turned her face to the honking and she frowned. "We never seem to have enough time to talk," she said.

Darrell wouldn't even let this statement into his mind; he had been tantalized enough and he wanted no more phrases to pick at on his cot through the night.

Anna began slowly to rise and Darrell rose with her, though more quickly. After she'd said good-bye and disappeared into the twilight Darrell remained standing in the center of the tent for a long while. He moved only after deciding that no matter what were the risks, he would soon have to become clearer about the fullness of his interest in her.

INSTEAD OF ANNA GETTING out of the Army sedan that pulled up the next day, it was Oppenheimer and his assistant, Coulter, and the captain. Darrell climbed out of the hole at once, pushing through the stiffness and twinges in his joints so he would meet these men on their own level. He squeezed hard at the trowel to siphon off the surge of energy he felt and the anger, building already even without knowing the reason for their visit.

"Good morning," Oppenheimer said, not offering his hand. Darrell didn't feel any withdrawal of courtesy from the man but, rather, a matter-of-fact acceptance, as if Darrell were working for him.

"How are you, Dr. Oppenheimer?" Darrell said.

"I'm interested in seeing how you're coming along," the man said. The morning air was already very warm, the desert was shaking off evening more quickly now and with greater vigor. But Oppenheimer was wearing a tweed suit and a tie knotted tightly at the throat. Darrell itched at the sight of him, although the scientist did not show a drop of sweat on his face.

"You can see for yourself," Darrell said, turning, leading whoever wished to follow over to the excavation. When he turned back, Oppenheimer was at his elbow and Coulter was drawing near more slowly, his eyes restlessly darting around the whole camp. The captain stood by the car.

"He's a fine specimen," Oppenheimer said.

"He was a King," Darrell said, not liking the man's choice of words. "The cape of shell-beads tells us that. Also the stones." Darrell pointed to the three stones uncovered in the square to the left of the King and to three stones an equal distance to the right of the King. They had begun excavating this third five-foot square at its farthest edge, with Darrell having put three stakes in the surface dirt at the beginning, predicting the placement of the three stones precisely. The excavation of this square was now approaching the place where the King lay, with only a two-foot column of dirt remaining immediately next to the skeleton.

"What do the stones signify?" Oppenheimer asked.

"A sacred enclosure. The burial rites would be quite elaborate for a man of great stature, like a King. And these rites always took place within an enclosure, a great circle that described the universe for the Indians."

Oppenheimer looked at the two gentle curves of stones, two arcs each of forty-five degrees, like a set of parentheses. Darrell watched his eyes and knew he was extending the arcs around the far side and then back down until he looked over his shoulder, recognizing that the circle closed behind them.

"We're in the circle now," Oppenheimer said.

"That's right."

Oppenheimer looked at the King and then down at his own feet.

"The great mystery," Darrell said, "is why he's out here in the desert. There was a mound here when we began. This man's cape, the stones, the mound, are quite foreign to the cultures of this desert."

Oppenheimer traced the circle again with his eyes. "Is it just a matter, do you think, of uncovering the other stones of the circle now?"

"I certainly hope not. No. There should be some burial artifacts. With luck we'll find some clue as to where he came from."

"So there's a lot left to do?" Oppenheimer said, turning his body half-away from the King and pulling a pipe out of his coat pocket.

Darrell glanced to Coulter who was looking off to the eastern mountains. The indirectness of the two suddenly seemed ominous to Darrell, seemed like a tactful approach to an unpleasant subject. "There's a lot. Yes."

"Can you remove what you've got so far?" Oppenheimer said, tamping the half-bowl remnant in his pipe with his fingertip.

"No," Darrell said and the angry energy rushed back into him. "Not until it's done. The physical relationships of things are important and they're sometimes subtle. I have to keep the contents in situ until it's done."

Oppenheimer pulled his pipe away from his face unlit and his thin, sad face did not show any change. But Darrell sensed turmoil in him. Darrell had trouble focusing his anger on this man, this fragile-looking man with the earnest, rational alertness that Darrell valued in himself.

"Very soon," Oppenheimer said, "we're going to have an explosion out here. A test. We're going to stack a hundred tons of TNT off to the southwest and detonate it."

"What would the effect be on this site?"

"We can give you something to cover this over. And the tents will have to come down temporarily . . . But Dr. Reeves, I must tell you I'm concerned. Your work is not resolving itself quickly enough. There are other experiments scheduled out here that will make it impossible to protect your King and his grave."

"How much time do I have?"

"The first test will be within two weeks. The other test— I can't really say. But believe me. Time is running out."

The threat to his work, the threat to his King, lifted Darrell's hands before him, tightened his hands into fists, the mason's trowel was still in his right hand and Darrell saw it rising there in the narrow space between him and Oppenheimer and he felt something like pity for the trowel because it wouldn't be able to do its work properly, a bizarre flicker of feeling before the anger came; crude, protective anger. "Listen to me," Darrell said. "This is an extraordinary find. There are secrets here that are . . ." He felt a trembling in his chest and he paused to steady his voice.

Oppenheimer said, "I'm sorry we . . ."

"Secrets that need care to solve. You can't force this . . ."

"Dr. Reeves," Oppenheimer said.

"My brother in Washington is very highly placed in . . ."

"We know who your brother is," Dr. Oppenheimer interrupted. "But our authority here is the highest. And our work is just as fragile as yours. Just as time-sensitive."

Darrell saw the other man's face, Coulter's face, emerging from behind Oppenheimer's, slowly but severely, the two faces like alien moons with Coulter's just coming out of eclipse. The face hung now over Oppenheimer's shoulder, frankly threatening and Darrell imagined Coulter pushing Oppenheimer aside and with his thick hands trying to grab him and he thought of thrusting the trowel up to the man's throat, touching the larynx lightly but insistently, the thick hands retreating, beginning to tremble.

"This is a very difficult position . . ." Darrell began, but he stopped. Having faced down Coulter in his fantasy, the anger faded enough for him to get snagged on Oppenheimer's reasonableness. This man's work, too, was time-sensitive; and there was a war on, after all; Darrell himself had had inklings that the explosives work was very important, much more important than these men had pretended in their first visit. All that was reasonable, and Darrell couldn't make his own reasonable position confront this other reasonable position, no matter how deep was his fear.

"I know it's difficult," Oppenheimer said.

"Listen," Darrell said, "you're a scientist. If you were on the verge of an important discovery and time was running out . . ."

"I am and it is. Time's running out for me, too."

"All right," Darrell said. "I'll do the best I can. Please, though, if you can give me some help here. The resources through my own university are very limited . . . The woman you've been sending. If you can let her come more often. She's a big help."

"Yes. All right," Oppenheimer said and the face that still hung over the man's shoulder suddenly contorted, its features wrenched and Darrell first thought of the rancher, thought that Coulter had just been hit in the back by a bullet fired beyond hearing from far off in the mountains.

But Coulter's face jerked, the eyes raged at Oppenheimer as the man said, with a quiet rationality, "That's a fair request. We'll see if we can work something out."

Coulter's face had jerked back again to challenge Darrell and Darrell raised the trowel and wiped the blade across the front of his shirt, high up, near his clavicle, where Coulter could see.

"Good-bye, Dr. Reeves," Oppenheimer said, and he moved off toward the car, leaving Darrell Reeves and Lloyd Coulter standing before each other, their faces neutral now but hard, their bodies motionless but oscillating within, waiting for something drastic.

After a long moment, Darrell said, "We're men of science, you and I. Men of the mind."

Lloyd wanted to answer this. These words were as surprising as if the man had lunged at him with that blade in his hand, and he wanted to deflect the words, knock them aside but his hands were useless, the strength that had been clotting in his arms since Oppie walked away was useless and he could not speak. He wanted to say yes, yes, I'm a man of the mind, of course I'm a man of the mind, I kept my promises to myself, I've become the man I wanted to be, a man of the mind just as you say, just like you. But Lloyd also wanted cause now to vent off this power in his arms, to twist the stalk that held the pale-eyed face erect. And perhaps that would help hack away all the tangled feelings that wrapped Anna within him. But this man hadn't lunged, he hadn't spoken the expected words, and Lloyd couldn't challenge what he had said. Of course I'm a man of the mind, in spite of what's happening in the world, in spite of all that I've seen. I just want to be near this woman. Then he realized he had to stop Oppie from giving Anna away full time. This let Lloyd keep silent, let him hold back his hands, let him turn and follow Oppie to the car. And then this very restraint let him think clearly. He knew Oppie had been patronizing the archaeologist. Lloyd had heard the tone often before. There was no real danger from Oppie. Only from Anna herself. And Lloyd still was unclear how to handle that.

THERE WAS NO TIME for Darrell to dwell on the visit of the physicists. He moved off toward his tent after the car had turned its tail to him and vanished behind a swirl of dust it began to trail across the desert. He thought briefly of Coulter, his visible agitation when Anna was mentioned and he remembered the vague fear he'd felt at the way Coulter had looked at Anna in the outer office of the operations center the day Darrell had first met her.

Darrell noticed Betty and Thomas beginning to work and he paused at the mouth of his tent, thinking, From what Oppenheimer said, I have no time to go in and speculate. Then Darrell heard Thomas cry out in surprise and he knew there was something in the excavation. He ran to the hole and leaped in and the two assistants turned their heads to him and pulled back. This final strip of dirt in the third square had gathered a fruitful promise even as the rest of the square proved to be empty. And now it yielded what they'd expected—an artifact. But when Darrell leaned down to look, he gasped aloud. He straightened back up and turned to Thomas but he did not see his assistant's face; his head spun from the vision before him in the earth: a round stone, its surface filled with the carving of a spider, its legs spread flat, its mandibles open, two large eyes in the top of its head. A stone gorget made to be worn around the neck and clearly a design that spoke of a cult Darrell had found before. He took out his brush and cleaned the face of the spider, its eyes round and open very wide, as if in great fear.

Then on a hunch he began to dig to the right of the gorget, nearer the King, only a reach of the King's arm away. He quickly crumbled the soil and scooped it off and his knife caught on a stone; he cleared it with the knife and then his fingers and then the brush and a second gorget emerged. This stone was sharply tapered at the bottom so that it formed a sunken-cheeked face. The forehead was shallow, the eyes were two holes set wide apart, and from the eyes fell jagged lines down the face. Weeping eyes. Darrell saw anguish in this face, anguish and fear, fear like the fear in the face even of this spider.

"My God," Darrell said now, with both of these gorgets before him.

"What are they?" Betty said in a low voice, almost a whisper.

"It's the Southern Death Cult," Darrell said. "It was first found in the Southeast, but there have been traces of it among the mound builders of the Midwest. There was even one artifact that *could* be traced to the cult at Cahokia. That piece was not so clearly connected, but these . . . My God, these are unquestionably from the Death Cult."

"This spider?" Thomas said.

"Yes."

"And the other . . . These look like . . ." Thomas's hand timidly approached the stone face.

"Tears," Darrell said. "This face is weeping. These are the signs of a religious cult that flourished from the middle of the fifteenth century to the middle of the seventeenth. It's thought that the cult gained its intensity from the wild rumors that spread throughout the continent of the Spanish conquest of the Aztec empire. The Aztecs had been ravaged by these men who came as if from another planet. The Indians had never seen horses or armor or crossbows or muskets. The death was new and unimaginable and after that the Indians were never the same. They were seized by a feeling of impending doom. They had a vision of a new violence. Their society had violence in it, but it was in their own forms, traditionalized, passed on and assimilated like the way to plant corn, the way to set the stones for the burials of their kings. The rumors they heard were altogether different, a new age, and they were forced to confront death in a different way from before. It was no longer sufficient to let death be the rejoining of the spirit to its natural element. It became necessary to make death part of a higher ritual, to reconcile its finality and its terror. And this cult began and spread and the spiders and weeping eyes externalized their terror, objectified it.''

Darrell paused and the two faces that looked up at him were wide-eyed now, a pair of gorgets, as if filled with the terror the Indians felt. Darrell's brief lecture had drawn his own feelings away, distanced him. But the wonder and fear and pity he read in the faces of Betty and Thomas clutched at him, dragged him back and he turned once more to the two stones. The very spiders that crawled in the King's grave felt the terror, the bravest men of stone wept. And this King? He'd felt the terror, too. He and his followers fled from the rich, wet mound-building soils to this alkaline desert to die.

THAT NIGHT DARRELL SENSED the King's fear rising in the dark. The moon was full and he stood for a long while before his tent and he felt the King still shuddering where he lay, plagued by bad dreams of this new death. And the King may have been fleeing into the Spaniards' very arms by coming to the Southwest. But at least he did not die at their hands, for he had been buried by his own people.

Darrell went into his tent and closed the flap and intended to sleep. But on his cot the anger of the morning began to stir again. The King had died his Indian death and been buried in his Indian grave. Now the physicists were pressing Darrell to rip these bones from the earth in careless haste. Darrell knew how to reverence the King, give these earthly remnants the care that the King would require. And the first requirement was that the whole site be kept *in situ*, just as it was arranged four centuries ago, until the entire excavation was complete. Then he could photograph it all and remove each bone, each artifact, with the precise relationships recorded. The King would reach his next burial site, in Darrell's own photos and notes and hermetic cases. He would take the King into his care. And not Oppenheimer, not Coulter, not the captain, not the entire Department of War would prevent this. Darrell found himself standing in the center of his tent, quaking in anger, his fists clenched.

To clear his mind he stepped outside. The moon was very high and the stars were so profuse they struck him like thoughts, countless conflicting thoughts, and that was exactly what he wanted to escape. He looked toward the excavation, where the tarp glowed in the moonlight like the flank of a great deep-sea fish. Then he heard a man's voice, a single syllable, without meaning but clearly a voice beyond the tents on the far side of the excavation.

Darrell's first thought was of the rancher. Darrell moved past the hole and quietly approached the equipment tent. He strained to hear another word and he heard a brief scuffling sound; he realized he had no weapon. He held back briefly and then crept along the side of the tent and looked around.

This was the edge of the camp; the desert stretched away from here, visible but colorless beneath the moon; and a hundred feet away, out in the mesquite, were Betty and Thomas, naked. Betty was turning her back to Thomas and beginning to run farther out into the desert and Thomas began to run after her, their bodies the same now as they receded, silver and thick and their bottoms churning, the moon's image rippling in a pond. They ran naked and silent and Darrell drew back. He turned away and crossed to his tent. The paternal outrage he expected did not come. Instead, he thought of Anna; he undressed her in his mind and sent her running across the desert before him.

ANNA HAD COME WITH Lloyd on this trip to Los Alamos; he'd had to press her only slightly to make her comply; and this took the sting out of Oppenheimer's words. Anna was waiting for Lloyd in the lab as Oppie stood in the center of the main room at the lodge—the dancers had gone, even their scuffs on the floor were gone, the canvas chairs and blackboards and the project chairmen had all returned—and Oppie summarized the plight of their project.

"We're having trouble," Oppie said, "diagnosing how the implosion assembly will work. We still don't have a fix on the energy of the bombarding particles."

Lloyd ducked his head at this. He was glad he was sitting toward the rear, with his face invisible to most of the other faces in the room.

Oppie went on, "And our old nemesis predetonation is rearing its ugly head again. We just can't seem to get a detonator to work right. We need, at worst, a one in ten thousand failure rate and I'm not sure we can get even one in a hundred. The firing circuits have to be produced on the outside and they need improvements we don't have control over. The lens molds are still in short supply and we can't improve the design without more of them to test. We still don't have enough plutonium from the Hanford plant and all this just pushes the bomb back, pushes it back. I'm not sure we can try our gadget before the end of July now."

A groan rippled through the men and there was a great scuffling of feet and a squeaking of chairs.

"And then we've got the fizzle problem," Oppie said. "We still haven't made enough progress on the problem of recovering the nuclear core in case the gadget fizzles."

"And what if it works too well?" one of the younger scientists said, a man Lloyd didn't know. "What if we erase the whole state of New Mexico." The young man laughed and the rest of the scientists laughed and Lloyd laughed, too. They all laughed in release, they laughed because that was a problem with a consolation to it—the bomb at least would have worked very well if that were the hitch. And Lloyd felt this problem of the other extreme swing the mood of the men back to a rationally moderate level of concern.

"For the recovery of the core," another voice said, "how about putting the whole bomb into a big brown jug."

The men laughed again but Oppenheimer held up a hand, his coat and shirt sleeve falling back from his bony wrist. "Perhaps it's not a joke," he said. "Large enough, thick enough . . ."

And the scientists began to discuss in earnest a plan to build an enormous steel shell to try to contain the nuclear core if the bomb fizzled. Lloyd let his mind creep away from this subject; a foolish subject, in his judgment—the bomb would not fail. He thought of Anna waiting for him in the implosion lab. He had a plan to work out, too, though his mind felt it shaping without pushing it. He had seen a poster earlier in the day at the mess hall—tonight a play was being given by an amateur group at Los Alamos. There had been a time when Lloyd scorned all this recreation, all these social activities, but now he saw them as opportunities. A vague plan had begun to form the night of the dance at the lodge and now this poster advanced it rapidly. The play was called *Arsenic and Old Lace* and the poster promised a surprise appearance.

Lloyd turned the elements over in his mind—the play, Anna waiting, the threat of the archaeologist and the need for Lloyd to act, the coming evening, cool and full of stars on this mesa—but he did not yet put them together into a specific course of action. Then the meeting ended and he went out of the lodge and an aide gave him a lift in a jeep to the implosion site. At last he opened the door to the lab.

Anna was there, although Lloyd found that he had prepared himself for her absence. She rose up from a chair at a desk on the far wall and she said, "Are you sure I was necessary on this trip?"

She did not sound angry, but Lloyd's plan for the evening stalled just as it was about to find words.

"Yes," Lloyd said. "I didn't lie to you."

Anna crossed the room to him. "I didn't mean to say that."

"It's all right," Lloyd said, her sudden approach making him ready again to give her whatever she wanted. "I know you don't like to come back here."

"Not to sit," she said.

"I'm sorry today's meeting lasted so long. You have to understand. This is a difficult task we have and things aren't going well right now. My need for you isn't always easy to anticipate."

"It's all right," Anna said, her hand rising to flick away his apologies, her voice betraying her restlessness.

"I'm sure tomorrow I'll need your help," Lloyd said. "We have to plan out the next sequence of implosion tests . . . I'll need you then."

She did not speak but she nodded. Her shoulders slumped slightly.

"You need to relax," Lloyd said. "Why are you driving yourself?"

"Why are you?"

"My work . . . It's important."

"I want to have that reason too."

"You *are* important," Lloyd said and the words startled him, made him stop without adding, "to me."

"Does your work scare you?" Anna said, as if she hadn't heard him.

"Scare me?"

"I mean, this enormous bomb. Doesn't it scare you?"

"The only one who really has to be scared is Louis Slotin. He has to tickle the dragon's tail."

"What's that?"

"He's been doing the critical-assemblies testing. When we were working with hydrides he'd have to drop a slug of uranium hydride into an almost critical assembly of the same material. The whole thing then became supercritical, but he'd keep the slug in just long enough to measure the prompt neutrons. It gave us evidence that an explosive chain reaction would occur.

92

But it was delicate work to keep a reaction from happening there and then.''

"That was the dragon's tail?''

"That's what Slotin calls it. He always says, 'Tickle it, but don't make him turn on you.' ''

Anna nodded and grew thoughtfully quiet. In this silence, with her near, with the ease he felt in talking about his work to her and seeing her sincere interest, Lloyd's plan began to shape again.

She said, "I guess I meant some sort of more general fear. The fear of the final thing itself.''

"The test?''

"Not just that . . . I don't know.''

"Anna,'' Lloyd began and he paused to relish saying her first name. Her eyes focused on him when he spoke her name; this odd distraction over the bomb seemed to vanish. "Anna,'' he said again, "why don't you . . .'' An appropriate word would not come and Lloyd almost panicked, but then he said, ". . . relax tonight.'' Relax, he repeated in his mind. It would do. "There's a play being given. *Arsenic and Old Lace*. The posters promise a surprise appearance . . .'' He now confronted the crucial moment and he hesitated. Anna said nothing. Her eyes were on him—her wonderful eyes—and they seemed comprehending, but she said nothing to help him. Perhaps she had no idea what was coming. Lloyd had to proceed. He'd come this far and he had to proceed. "I'm going to the play . . . Would you like to come along?''

She smiled at once. Not in mockery. Not in mockery, he told himself and he believed it; her eyes were soft. "How nice,'' she said. "How nice, Dr. Coulter.''

He didn't know what to feel at this. She sounded flattered, happy, but why "Dr. Coulter''? Wouldn't she use his first name too? He waited for more information. She was still smiling gently at him—was it affection or condescension?—his hands began to stir.

"Thank you so much for asking me," Anna said. "Normally I'd say, Yes of course."

"But you can't now?"

"I'm very tired. The trip."

Lloyd wanted to believe her and he concentrated on her warmth, her animation; signs of sincerity. But she wasn't going to go with him and so he still had no clear indication that she might be able to feel for him the way he felt for her. "I thought you'd like to go to a play," he said. "It would help you feel better about coming back to Los Alamos."

"Perhaps," she said. "Yes."

He saw her thinking, saw her mind opening to his insistence. He felt a restlessness in himself again, as he hung between hope and despair—was she thinking of another excuse, another way to put him off? or was she trying to overcome her weariness so she could go with him?

"Listen," she said. "Let me go to my room and rest awhile and see how I feel . . . You're going to the play anyway, aren't you?"

"What?" He tried to figure out quickly what the best answer would be to this, but he didn't know how clear to make his own motives. He had no interest in the play except as a way of being near her, of letting her know he wanted to court her; but trying to decide how to put this was too complex and he gave it up.

He did not reply and Anna said, "You go on. See the play. I'll try to meet you there."

"You might come?" he said, trying to keep the eagerness out of his voice. He could not appear to plunge, he knew. It could frighten her, or it could raise his own hopes dangerously.

"I might," she said. "Yes. You go on and enjoy yourself. Don't *depend* on my being there. I *am* tired. But I'll try."

Lloyd felt a sudden anxiety. He wanted to speak to her firmly, to take her by the shoulders and square her around before

94

him and say, Will you or won't you? I have to know. But he didn't speak. He let her vagueness stand.

THE PLAY BEGAN AND Lloyd stood at the back of the hall and he did not watch the platform where the two women and two men— one a character who looked like Teddy Roosevelt—sat talking and generating flutters of laughter in the audience. He looked at the two empty chairs halfway down the center aisle where he'd laid his coat, and then he looked behind him at the door into the hall, and then he looked at each head in the audience, making sure he hadn't missed her. She was not there. Not yet.

He saw the married couple he'd met in the lodge. They laughed at a line of dialogue and their heads bent near each other. Lloyd moved a few steps down the side aisle so he could see more of their faces. They had identical smiles focused on the stage. Against the woman's chest, an infant slept. The infant who had trouble staying dry because of the diaper shortage at Los Alamos, Lloyd recalled. The woman stretched her smile and laid her head against the point of her husband's shoulder and Lloyd grew conscious of the same spot on his own shoulder. He looked away from the couple but their influence on him remained. They held him here, gave him the patience to wait for Anna; and he watched the stage for a long while, barely hearing the voices as he stood there, his body rigid in its suspension.

Not until a man climbed through the window on stage did Lloyd stir. He recognized the body slung over the man's shoulder and he heard the gasps and then laughter as the audience recognized the body, too. The body was Oppie. The man came through the window with Oppenheimer limply folded over his shoulder, portraying a dead body. The man looked about and opened a window seat and dumped Oppie inside. Lloyd had a glimpse of Oppie's face as he played his part; his sharp-edged features were blank, his eyes were closed, he was dead. The window seat lid thumped shut and the audience burst into applause and Lloyd knew Anna wasn't coming. He went to the center aisle and strode down to the two empty seats and picked up his coat and rushed out into the night.

Outside, he stood in the rut of the road and he slowly put his jacket on and he had trouble breathing. He blamed the thin air of the plateau but he knew he was disappointed. She was very tired. Very tired, he said again in his mind in order to keep out the alternate thought. But it came in anyway: she was not tired but repelled by his interest in her. She was not tired but lying, staying away from him, hoping he'd never try to get this close to her again.

He stood in the center of the road for a time and then he moved off toward the quonset where she was staying in a visitor room. He wanted simply to remove the doubt; he wanted simply to determine her feelings for him; and his mind and body moved mechanically toward the quonset village with no preconception, no speculation, with the open-mindedness of scientific inquiry.

But as he saw the low, stretched, half-moon of her building, he felt a quaking begin inside him. He thrust his hands into the pockets of his coat and moved more quickly.

The door of the quonset opened into a narrow, central hallway. Her room was the second on the left. He approached it. There was no window and he put his ear to the door, but he could only hear his own pulse in his head. His hands were still in his pockets but had clenched tightly into fists now. He wanted her to be inside there, sleeping. She had to be inside and asleep. That was the only option. It was all he could let himself believe. His hands came out of his pockets and he reached and touched the doorknob. He turned it and it yielded and he pushed the door open very gently and there was darkness and silence. He felt his breath rush out quickly, as if in relief, but the proof was not yet sufficient. She could be away from the room.

He stepped inside and closed the door behind him. He waited for his eyes to grow accustomed to the dark and he listened for her breathing but he could only hear his own, coming in shallow gasps. He thrust his hands back into his pockets and he tried to keep his thoughts from rushing ahead into options.

There was a sound outside. The outer door to the quonset. He turned and faced the room door as he heard the scuff of feet. But they passed by. They passed on and he found his hands free in the air and he turned. His eyes could see shapes now and he took a step toward the bed. A form was there.

He bent near. He could see Anna's face. She was lying on her back and he could make out her features in the dimness, her closed eyes, her still mouth. He eased down onto his knees and drew his face very close to hers. He listened and he could hear her breath, the faint slip of air. She slept. She had been very tired. His face grew warm and he felt tears coming to his eyes. He rose and retreated into the night and wept in pity for her weariness and in relief that his anger had not begun.

NOT EVEN THE SIGNIFICANCE of the death cult symbols, not even the consequent heightened anguish over the need to rush the excavation, could keep Darrell's mind from picking through the words at the last meeting with Anna. She had not returned to the dig for over a week and Darrell vacillated between a fear that he'd scared her off by pressing for her attitudes about marriage and a hope that she was simply busy with the work of the physicists and that his questions had made her begin to think of him in a more intimate way. He could find no clear indication in her words to decide the matter and both hope and fear finally blurred together into a dull, unshakeable depression.

All three central squares were done now and the find so far consisted of the King, his cape, the two gorgets to his right, and six stones of the enclosure, three on each side. The slices of the projected sacred circle above and below the excavated strip had grown so full of promise that when he stood in those spaces, the soles of Darrell's feet were as touchy as the pit of his arm.

It was time to go back to Santa Fe to report to Dean Felker.

Darrell didn't like to leave the excavation with the scientists to the south pressing him, but Felker had to be informed of the discovery and perhaps the gorgets would motivate him to find some more workers for the excavation.

Darrell decided to do a test hole in the square just below the King and then go up to Santa Fe tomorrow. The trip back was still on his mind when a swirl of dust to the south turned out to be the Army sedan and Anna emerged, dressed in her fatigues, her hair pulled back. She crossed quickly to the dig, as Darrell rose up, trowel in hand, and the car sped off behind her. Darrell tried not to smile too broadly, fearful that in the pleasure at seeing her he'd end up pressing her again. But he knew at once that he would ask her to go with him.

"Hello," she said.

"Hello."

"Were you afraid I wasn't coming back?"

"No . . . I didn't know . . ."

"I was up in Los Alamos for a few days. Then the last two days I've been busy down there." She angled her head slightly to the rear, over her shoulder, back down south toward the scientists' camp.

"It seemed odd," Darrell said. "I had just asked Dr. Oppenheimer if he could let you come out more often. He seemed amenable to that idea."

"Really? That's funny . . . But the man I usually work for is doing very important research. I have to be on call for him."

"Is his name Coulter?"

"Yes," Anna said. "How did you know?"

"I met him."

"He's a very bright man," she said.

"Is he?"

"Yes."

Darrell measured the warmth with which Anna had declared Coulter's brilliance and it gave him a queasiness in his limbs that he recognized as jealousy. "And today?" he said.

"He went back to Los Alamos this morning. I asked him . . . that is, his work on this trip didn't require my help."

"So you can help me?"

"Yes."

"Are you permitted off this desert?"

"As I said, I go to Los Alamos . . ."

"I mean could you go somewhere with *me*."

"I don't know. Yes. I guess I could get permission," she said.

Darrell listened closely to her voice. He wanted to hear an eagerness, but he heard only a thoughtfulness in her tone, as she apparently tried to figure out how to go about it. But he was instantly critical of himself. He'd asked her only generally, theoretically; he could not expect her to get excited over that. "You seem to like cities, new places," he said.

"Yes."

"Santa Fe isn't so big, but I have to go up there to see a colleague about the excavation. We've made a discovery you'll be interested in."

"Wonderful," she said and her voice began to soar now in him, began to take on the eagerness he liked so much about her.

"I thought you'd like to go up to Santa Fe with me. We'd leave tomorrow morning and come back . . . Let's see, tomorrow's Friday. We'd come back Saturday night. I'd find a place for you to stay up there."

"Is Santa Fe nice?"

"I like it. It's not big. But I think this weekend there's a fiesta of some sort. The first weekend in May there's always a Spring Fiesta. It'd be interesting for you, I think."

"All right," Anna said. "I'd love to go."

Darrell held back the leaping of his hands, his feet, his voice. "Fine," he said, his voice flat, passionless. "Fine. You see if you can get permission."

THE NEXT MORNING LLOYD missed Anna by less than an hour. He had gotten a ride with a night convoy of supplies down from Los Alamos and he was willing to suffer a night of sleeping in his clothes, his head angled against a car-door, for the sake of bringing Anna back to his side, grabbing her from the presence of the pale-eyed man. But the security captain told him she'd gone. No one expected Lloyd back today and Oppenheimer happened to have been around to clear her request to go with the archaeologist up to Santa Fe until tomorrow night.

Lloyd did not make a sound at this, kept his face blank; he turned and went out of the operations center and he stood for a long while in the road near the flagpole. A shrike cried out as it fell on an animal somewhere in the desert; Lloyd looked down the road toward the sound and he saw a sand devil swirling there, reminding him that his neck hurt, his feet felt clammy and hot, his clothes itched; an Army deuce-and-a-half whined by full of crates. Lloyd wasn't expected at the lab. He tried briefly to readjust his schedule in his mind but he had no patience for this now and he quickly gave it up. He had to follow them. It was as simple as that.

He went back into the operations center and got the keys to one of the sedans. He drove slowly out of the compound, waving at the guard who knew him well, drove at a moderate speed along the new blacktop and then began to go faster as the camp receded, he drove faster and turned hard onto the county highway, the car fishtailing, scaring him, making him see the car in his mind, rolling there, but he kept his foot on the accelerator. The car straightened and raced on toward Santa Fe.

ON THAT AFTERNOON, DARRELL talked with Dean Felker in the man's office, explaining the new discoveries.

"Splendid," Felker said, a word he had repeated several times—but without strong feeling—as the tale of the Death Cult had unfolded.

"Is there some way to get more workers?" Darrell said.

Felker hesitated; his thick body appeared less apt to move than the bare white wall behind him. "I don't see how," he

finally said. "Even if we could persuade the women and crip-
ples left in our classes to go down there in the desert and work
for you, we don't have the money to support them." He had
described the current students with no harshness in his voice
but with a weary resignation.

For a moment Darrell snagged on Felker's gathering sadness
and he said nothing; but then he thought of the scientists pushing him, the time running out. "Listen," he said. "They're
going to ruin all this. These physicists are trying to make me
rush the excavation. I need help to preserve this find . . ."

Felker spread his hands. "There's nothing we can do. Go
on back and preserve as much as you can."

Darrell rose and muttered a good-bye and hurried out into
the square. He found Anna sitting on a bench under an apricot
tree, an oval of sunlight quivering on her chest as if she were
suckling it. She saw him approach and began to rise but he
moved his hand to keep her there. He sat down beside her.

"Can he give you more help?" she said.

"No."

Anna puffed in exasperation and Darrell looked at her. Her
bottom lip had pushed up and her eyes had grown sad. She
seemed to care deeply about his work. Darrell wanted to put
his arm around her but this was not quite the time and certainly
not the place. He looked around the plaza. Even Felker's office
had a window with a view of this bench.

Anna said, "Is your discovery going to be ruined?"

"We still have some time."

"And it's not as though you won't be able to recover the
things themselves."

"That's true . . . It's just so much better to keep it all in
place—especially for this kind of discovery, where the physical
relationship of things was carefully thought out. The real
meaning of it all could be utterly lost without detailed study
of . . ." Darrell felt the words growing small and hard in his
mouth, as if his teeth had all broken loose and were rattling
around. He cared about his excavation. But sitting here on the

campus of his school, his words turning abstract, his thoughts ratcheting into the clockwork of his learning, he felt himself drawing away from Anna; and even from the King in some fundamental way. He stopped speaking, turned his face from Anna and his anger lurched back, the tiny words were gone and he was very angry at Oppenheimer. He wouldn't let them out of their car next time. He'd thump Oppenheimer in the chest, force him back inside his car, tell them to get the hell away. And Coulter, too, the bulging eyes, the square face. The man had some connection to Anna. As if Coulter had punched him in the face, this realization stunned Darrell, made him turn back to her.

"What is it?" she said.

Darrell knew his distress was showing but he didn't know what to say.

She studied his face, trying to read him, and she said, "I hate to see you so upset. Is it really *impossible* to finish the excavation before the big test?"

He was glad she had jumped to a conclusion that let him avoid talking about the actual concern of that moment. But at the same time he wished he could resolve the matter of Anna and Lloyd Coulter directly. He thought of the man's face twisted wildly in anger at Darrell's mention of Anna to Oppenheimer.

"I'll come to help you whenever I can," she said, reaching out to touch the back of his hand. Before Darrell could turn his hand over and take hers, it retreated again.

"Let's get our minds off all this for a little while," he said. "The fiesta has started. There'll be good food . . ."

"Yes," she said, rising. "I'm ready for that."

They walked across the plaza side by side but just far enough away from each other so that they did not bump arms in the little variations of their movement. Darrell thought about bearing in a bit more so that they might occasionally brush into each other. He decided against it and then he surprised himself by considering something even more radical—he thought of taking her hand. Yes, he decided at once, sometime before tomorrow afternoon he would take her hand. But not now. He wanted more time to pass between them, more words, a meal first.

They walked through the archway and into the view of Lloyd Coulter who sat fifty yards up the street in his car. He slumped down in the seat and watched them pause before the arch. He held his breath now. The two of them together. It was only a college campus, the archaeologist's college. But they were to-gether—heading where? They stood speaking to each other and Lloyd heard himself letting out breath, hissing in the car like a desert snake. He waited like a snake, too, waiting for movement, waiting for a lizard to betray its camouflage with a tiny movement: he watched for this man's hand to come out and touch her, touch her hand or her arm or even the small of her back, a movement that would betray the camouflage of this college, the archaeological excavation, her fascination with subjects of the mind. Where were they going now? Lloyd came up to the next question—where would she sleep tonight?—but he didn't let that question shape itself. He would have to leap from the car at that question and he wanted to watch. He was a man of the mind. He just wanted to understand all this. He was a man of the mind. He felt gentle. His hands were very soft. Would a woman admire that? Surely she would. His hands were soft and loved to move slowly, gently, thoughtfully. Thoughtful hands.

Anna and the pale-eyed man began to walk up the road. Lloyd turned on the engine and crept after them in his car, letting them move farther ahead so they wouldn't suddenly turn around and catch him. He expected them to walk on—still there was no touching—but they crossed to a car and the man let Anna in at the passenger side and went around to drive. Lloyd stopped and waited, fretting at their leaving the street, at their sitting together in an enclosed space, their hands out of his sight.

The car drove off and Lloyd followed as they went down

Canyon Road, past the adobe houses and quiet yards—Lloyd was conscious of the houses, conscious of the lives inside them, coupled, touching—and the traffic thickened, some cars, many carts, horses, Indians in shawls and mantillas and sombreros, carts full of food, rolling on wooden wheels, raising dust on the road until the pavement began and then the wheels grinding on the hard surface. Lloyd concentrated on the car ahead and it approached the central plaza and he was conscious of crowds on the periphery of his vision; he heard guitars and shouting. The archaeologist turned onto a sidestreet and parked. Lloyd followed and drove on past their car and down the street and also parked.

He watched in his rearview mirror as Anna and the man got out. The two were formal-seeming, but Lloyd was growing very suspicious of that; it struck him as contrived, a pose. At this thought Lloyd opened the door of his car.

The sudden movement of a car door down the street nearly drew Darrell's glance, though purely by reflex, without conscious interest. But at the same moment Anna said, "Hear the music?" and Darrell did not look.

"Yes," he said. "In the square."

"I'm very glad I came," she said.

"Good."

Again he was faced with the possibility of taking her hand or offering his arm. But he felt constrained still. He was conscious of his age, ten years older than she; he was uncertain of her interest in him; he was indelibly impressed by his own past failure at all this. So he still withheld his hand, still withheld his arm.

They walked up the street and crossed into the square behind an Indian driving a cart full of children. Anna broke away through the crowd; following the sound of guitars, Darrell knew, and he lunged after her to keep up. He found her standing in a ring around the music, her back to him, and he came up and stood directly behind her. He could smell her hair—cutting through the smell of dust and corn and horses was the smell of her hair, she was so close. And for now this was as good as touching her. Before her, Indian women swirled in their long skirts, their bare feet stamping and skipping and pointing in the dust and Darrell filled himself with the smell of Anna's hair. His shoulders lifted slightly, a gesture Lloyd saw.

But Lloyd couldn't see Anna. She was blocked off by this man and he wondered if there was a space between the two or if the man was pressing against her. Lloyd took a stride forward, a body brushed past and stopped him, he moved now to the side and he saw Anna. Lloyd moved further and the archaeologist's shoulders were still raised, his head was inclined backwards just a bit but his hands were at his side, there was a space between the man and Anna, a clear space, though even a half step back by Anna would make them touch.

Lloyd knew he couldn't go on like this. He could not watch them without somehow acting. But they were in a public place. At worst the pale-eyed man would take her hand or she would take his arm. Would Lloyd act then? And how would he act? He wanted only to learn. But the evening would tell more. He reasoned: if they touch in this plaza, they would also touch as they ended the day somewhere; he could take himself away now and wait for them to return to their car; he did not have to watch them in this public place. He wheeled around and disappeared into the crowd and soon after, Darrell lifted a hand and touched Anna's shoulder.

But when Anna turned to him, Darrell took the hand away, as if the touch had been merely to get her attention. The guitars suddenly thumped, went silent, and then thrummed on, prompting shouts of mimetic passion from the dancers. Anna looked back briefly into the circle and then returned to Darrell and said, "Have you ever danced like that?"

Darrell laughed in surprise. "Impossible," he said.

"Since you live here and all . . ."

"Wrong blood."

She said, "Do you think your King in the desert ever danced like this?"

"I've never considered that, really. It's a wonderful question. Perhaps he did. More likely his wives and children did."

"Would the dancing have looked like that?"

"The guitars have something to do with this dance, I suspect. My King had pipes and drums. The drums could probably find this pace."

"Can we watch some more?"

"Of course."

Anna faced the dancers again and when Darrell raised his eyes, he saw, on the far side of the circle, the one-legged veteran, Hendricks, just lurching away.

For a moment Darrell focused on the dancers, wishing the man would leave his mind in the way he had left the circle. But Darrell remembered the Jews and he remembered his forgetfulness. The veteran's rumors had plagued him for a day or two and then had disappeared. He challenged himself: Down what hole in my mind have the Jews gone? There was a dark center of gravity even in himself, he knew, that could suck in such a thought as that and let him live with it; live as he always had, digging in the dirt and even being stirred by a woman, even beginning to love a woman. And as this idea suddenly bloomed in him—that he was falling in love with Anna Brown—the veteran disappeared again in his mind. But Darrell sensed him go and he bent near to Anna and even as he spoke into her ear and felt her hair against his cheek and he knew he was beginning to love her, he said, "I see someone I have to talk to. I'll be back here in a few minutes."

"Fine," she said without taking her eyes from a man and woman dancing furiously beside each other, not touching but staring at each other intensely, their feet racing in place in the dust.

Darrell moved away, around the circle, and when he got to the far side he couldn't locate Hendricks. He was surprised to find himself panicky at this. He began to push his way through the crowd, lifting up on his toes, straining his neck, frantically searching in all directions for the one-legged man. Then he glanced out beyond the plaza area and saw Hendricks passing the old governor's palace, moving rapidly in a smooth, swinging lope on his crutches. Darrell broke from the crowd and ran after him, dodging through the carts and revelers, finally in the clear, leaving the plaza just as Hendricks disappeared down a side street. Darrell pumped hard, sprinting to the corner and stumbling as he turned. He regained his footing and stood and saw Hendricks at the end of the street, about to turn again. Darrell tried to shout but his panting snipped off the sound. His chest ached and his temples throbbed but just as the veteran pivoted on one crutch and swung into another turn, Darrell cried out his name. "Hendricks."

The man at the end of the street paused. He looked back over his shoulder.

"Wait," Darrell cried and he began to walk toward him. But Hendricks paused only briefly and then disappeared.

This action so startled Darrell that he stopped altogether. A low-grade panic fluttered back into him and he began to run. His legs were stiff now and his chest hurt but he ran as hard as he could to the end of the street. He lurched to a stop and made the turn, his hand groping for support on an adobe wall and there, sitting on the running board of a parked car, was Hendricks, his crutches leaning stiffly beside him, his leg stretched out straight, his face turned calmly on Darrell.

Darrell could not speak. He struggled to catch his breath and Hendricks looked at him closely. "I thought it was you," the veteran said.

Darrell nodded at this and he approached the car. "I wanted to talk with you," he said.

"I'm not very good company these days," Hendricks said.

Darrell sat down beside him on the running board. "I never have been."

"That sounds faintly patronizing."

Darrell looked at him. "I'm only patronizing myself."

The veteran shook his head at this, a contemptuous, private gesture as if he were suffering a fool. Darrell felt no anger. He said, "Have you heard any more about the Jews?"

Without pause, without urgency, with only a flat weariness in his voice, Hendricks said, "It was true, of course."

"What do you mean?"

"It was true." The man sounded patient in his flatness.

"How do you know?" Darrell felt a clutching in him that he couldn't clearly identify.

"It was even in the newspapers. A couple of weeks ago. Didn't you see it?"

"In the papers? No. No, I've been out in the desert."

Hendricks laughed a quick, sharp, near-silent laugh. Then he spoke in a flat tone. "You might have missed it even if you'd been keeping up on things. Belsen. That was the site of one of the camps. It was liberated on April 15. Allied soldiers walked right in and looked it right in the face, looked at the ovens, looked at the stick-creatures that were left there in the vague shape of men. They walked right in and put out a news story that got stuck somewhere among a bunch of other events, like it was just the same kind of thing."

Darrell leaned his head back against the car door. He could hear the guitar music faintly thrumming in the distance; he could hear laughter up the street, behind an adobe wall. But he felt passionless. And that frightened him. He tried to picture a Jew, a specific person—the woman he'd not quite courted for two weeks—being stripped and stuffed into . . . what? An oven? The vision turned bizarre, like a Grimm's fairy tale. An oven. He waited for the next turn of his feelings. The first encounter with Hendricks had at least haunted him for two days, had made him feel something directly. This time there was an immediate distance. Hendricks sounded the same way.

"You don't seem to be feeling as much about all this now," Darrell said.

"I decided the newspapers were right," Hendricks said. "It's an event like others. I could go back to the clerk at the veterans office—the little woman with her hair in a bun who shouted at me this afternoon—and I could kill her with my hands. I could crush her throat in my two hands, and the papers would put that right there on the page with the next camp they walk into and they'd be right, see. The fucker who threw the fucking grenade that blew my fucking right leg off would go there too. And if I could have stayed conscious and could have seen that fucker coming over to search my body and I had a knife in my hand I could have stuck it into his groin and heard it go in and twisted it and my leg would be paid for and they could put that right there in the paper too. I could even kill your buddy back there at the university. That fat man Felker. I could walk into his office and blow his fucking head off and that could go right there alongside the third camp they liberate."

Hendricks was quaking now, his fists were clenched before him and his body was shaking and Darrell expected to be repelled and fearful—his mind offered those reactions as his logical response even as, in fact, he responded in an utterly different way, so different that he was not conscious of it for a long moment, not till he found himself leaning nearer to Hendricks as if to a fire on a cold desert morning; he found his own hands raised in kinesthetic empathy; he found his own throat open, as if these curses were passing through him. And as for fear, Darrell briefly imagined Hendricks turning on him, grabbing at his throat and he saw himself picking Hendricks up and throwing him against the wall, slamming the threats out of him, making him stop.

"Stop it," Darrell said. "For God's sake, stop it, man."

Hendricks half-turned his face but he did not look at Darrell. "Just leave me alone. You don't want to hear any of this. Quit following me."

Darrell rose and he felt suddenly distant from Hendricks, he wanted to say something supportive, wanted to offer him some sort of assistance. But he had nothing to say to him, nothing to do for him, and he moved away.

"Fucker," Hendricks said low and Darrell saw himself

picking up Oppenheimer and throwing him against the wall, the physicist crumpling into the dust beside Hendricks, and then Darrell grabbed Coulter, lifted him off the ground, held him there long enough for the dark face to widen in fear.

Darrell stopped. An awareness of what he was doing slipped into him as quick as the flash of his trowel blade. Even still, the image of Coulter lifted up needed completion and Darrell threw him against the wall and the man cracked there and fell. Darrell sucked hard at the dusty air to clear this all away. He struggled with the rage that made his body feel strong. Ahead was distant music, furious music; behind was silence, Hendricks might have fallen into a crack in the earth, his curses had stopped so completely; and Darrell stood in the empty street afraid at last. He'd found the hole in his mind where the Jews had disappeared.

IT WAS NEARLY DARK and Lloyd sat slumped in the seat, the rearview mirror angled sharply down so that he could see the archaeologist's car. He had watched the car without ceasing, without letting his gaze wander for more than a few seconds, all afternoon and now into the early evening. The hours of daylight were stretching out and he was glad for that, he was worried that when dark came he would not be able to see well enough to learn what he had to know. He'd kept his mind fixed on the car—a physicist's discipline, like poring over data in an experiment—but he felt weary from his night of awkward sleep in the convoy from Los Alamos, and after a time his nerves wouldn't sustain him any longer and the thin rectangle of street, the car grill, the dusk in the mirror began to blur. His father had a tattoo. A spider clutching a globe in its eight legs. The tattoo was high up on his left forearm and he never referred to it and Lloyd never asked about it. Even as it hung in this half-dream Lloyd didn't wonder why it was there. His father's corded veins ran through it when his arm flexed and Lloyd looked closely to see if the spider had a face but he could not see it clearly enough and then two bright eyes opened, two eyes in the center of the spider's head and Lloyd sat upright, awake. He looked into the mirror and the two eyes were the headlights of the archaeologist's car.

The car was moving; it passed Lloyd and he started his own car and followed. He was conscious of nothing around him but the movement of the tail-lights up ahead. They surged and slowed and turned and surged again for what seemed to Lloyd a very long time. He would not let himself consider where they were going and he gripped hard at the wheel and tried to depersonalize this whole process; he had a laboratory procedure to complete—trace the movements of these two red lights. When the lights eased over and brightened briefly and stopped moving, Lloyd went on past and parked up the street. He had no idea where he was. The street was dark. He could sense trees around. The headlights in his rearview mirror went off and he could see nothing there. He eased out of his car as quietly as he could. He saw a tree a few feet away and moved to it and hid there and peeked around to observe.

There were no walls on this street, but little frame houses with tiny yards. Lloyd had a clear line of sight as he watched the archaeologist moving to open the passenger door for Anna. But the night sky was overcast and the lamppost was distant and he could not see the details he wanted. While the archaeologist was on the far side of the car, Lloyd crouched and dashed to a closer tree. From here he heard their voices. Anna's eager. The man's plying. Lloyd peeked and watched the two moving up the yard of a house. They entered into porchlight and Lloyd crept closer, keeping low but scorning the trees now, his mind straining hard to keep out the conclusions. This man's house. His house. The phrases tumbled in Lloyd but he would not act yet. Not yet. He could see them in the light and they were not touching and they stopped at the door. Lloyd stopped too. He coiled down near the grass and he was at the edge of the yard, exposed but coiled low in the darkness and he expected this all to be resolved, but the archaeologist raised his hand and knocked at the door.

The door opened and an elderly woman appeared. There were words and the screen door swung out and Anna and the man went inside. Lloyd rose up. He felt an odd regret. An inconclusive experiment. He saw figures in the front window, pausing there, sitting down. Lloyd considered going onto the front porch, but he didn't want to be exposed. He crept to the side of the house where a window looked through a dark sewing room and into the living room. He could see the archaeologist in a wing chair and Anna opposite him on a couch. Beside her was the elderly woman.

The three spoke, their voices muddling together, no words clearly emerging, and Lloyd waited, his fingertips on the windowsill. After a time, the elderly woman stood up and, after a murmuring nod to Anna and the man, she left the room. Lloyd's fingers curled, but the tips stayed on the sill. The archaeologist bent slightly in Anna's direction and he began to speak. Lloyd strained to hear the words but he could not.

In his mind Darrell was cursing himself for his cowardice on this day. Never did he take Anna's hand. Never did he try. Now he was caught in Mrs. Galen's parlor. "Mrs. Galen will take good care of you," he said to Anna.

Anna smiled. "I'm sure she will."

"She's been the registrar for thirty years," he said, feeling compelled to carry his cowardice to its logical end now. He would wallow in triviality with Anna.

But then she said, "It's been a lovely day," and her voice was rich and cast very low, low enough that Mrs. Galen could not possibly hear.

Darrell's mind lagged back at this; he found himself thinking in a detached way about Anna's warmth even as his feeling rushed forward and made him say, "I want to kiss you good night." He was as surprised at these words as Anna seemed to be.

112

Lloyd watched both Anna and the archaeologist abruptly lean back in their seats and look at each other without speaking for a long moment. Lloyd's hands spread against the window screen, he pressed his face there, frantic over this mystery. When the voices resumed, there was almost no sound at all that reached his ears. The two bodies leaned far forward again, first the man's, then Anna's soon after, and the lips moved but Lloyd nearly cried out in anger at the silence.

Darrell wanted even more strongly to kiss Anna now that he'd spoken it. "I don't know why I said that."

Anna said, "I'm . . . I was surprised."

"It just rushed out . . . I've hurt you."

"No. Of course not."

Darrell wanted to say more but he didn't know what and though he opened his mouth he only spread his hands before him in a gesture of vague apology.

"I was surprised," Anna said.

Darrell nodded. "I was too."

"I never realized . . ." She left the sentence unfinished.

"You didn't?"

"No."

"I'm sorry," Darrell said. "Listen, if it hadn't even occurred to you . . ."

"It hadn't," she said. "I was very interested in you . . . In your work. In the things you were saying. But I really hadn't gotten around to thinking of you like that."

"Ah." Darrell felt suddenly weak. He'd mistimed all of this; he feared he'd ruined the possibilities between them, like displacing the objects in a dig. But something about her gave him a hope—her persistent warmth, the hint of possibility in her words—was that actually there?—she said she hadn't *gotten around* to thinking of him like that; she didn't say she *couldn't* think of him like that. He became aware that the swirl of this analysis was making him gape at her in foolish silence. "I'm sorry," he said. "I didn't mean to . . . force anything on you."

Anna laughed gently. "That's the last thing I'd think of you."

Darrell laughed too. "I'm a fool."

"No," she said. "Don't say that."

Darrell expected her to say more, but she didn't. She sat back and her face became thoughtful but she said no more. Suddenly he realized how unresolved this all was. The time they'd talked about her goals of marriage, he'd been raked for a week by the ambiguities. "I'm sorry I was so heavy-handed," Darrell said. "But it's true that I . . . like you, Anna. We have a rapport . . ." Darrell felt that word thump onto the floor between them and then he stopped. How could he say this in the way that he felt it? Anna waited. She was giving no help and Darrell felt a trickle of anger at her, a thin trickle but very hot, running in his chest, along his arms.

Finally she spoke. "I like you too. But I just haven't begun to . . ."

She was repeating the same tantalizing words and Darrell tried to moderate his voice, keep it calm, friendly. "Please don't repeat that," he said. "I did this all wrong, but I need to know . . ."

"If you'd done it a little more gradually, maybe I could tell you," she said and the trace of anger in her instantly changed his own anger to despair.

"I'm sorry," he said.

"Please," she said, leaning forward again, her hand rising as if to cross the space between them and pat him. "I wish I could give you an answer. But I'm telling you the truth. It's just too new. Sometimes my interests in things are misunderstood. I'm not throwing myself at men."

"I never thought so," Darrell said.

"I know you didn't. But I'm not really sure *what* I want. Much less *who* I want . . . I'm much more . . . cautious than my enthusiasm for things makes me seem."

"I understand." Darrell rose to go. He could not bear to listen to more of this.

Anna rose too. "'Please understand. I don't want to hurt you. I just don't *know* yet."

"I understand," he said, thinking: I understand nothing.

Anna smiled at him very sweetly. Darrell knew it was a sweet smile preparatory to a kiss on the cheek and he wondered if he could endure this ultimate ambiguity, and out in the night Lloyd sensed that things would resolve themselves now. But the elderly woman suddenly bustled into the room with a tray of teacups and Lloyd watched Anna and the pale-eyed man turn woodenly to her. The man made apologetic shrugs at the old woman and bowed slightly to Anna— a grotesque ruse, that bow, an infuriating sham that made Lloyd yank his hands from the screen and double them into fists.

The archaeologist turned and disappeared out the front door; Anna sat down with the elderly woman and Lloyd pulled back from the window. He took a step toward the front of the house, to follow the archaeologist, to stop him in the street, before he got into the car. But what was next? This was still unresolved. He pressed back against the window and the voices of the two women pattered against him and he had no clear data, no answers. His intuition told him the truth, but he was a man of science, a man of the mind. He needed more. This was no good, he knew, this thrashing in him. He couldn't pass a night like this. Then he heard the archaeologist's car drive off. Lloyd focused on Anna, the sleek straight line of her hair, her thin, gently curved nose in profile, her moving lips. She sat on a couch, in a living room in a house. He liked her there. He blotted out the elderly woman and concentrated on Anna in a house, contained, safe, he felt himself just out of view, in a chair with a reading lamp.

Lloyd turned and moved away. He cut across the next yard, heading back to his car, and he saw, behind the house next door, a row of clothes dangling dimly in the yard. He stopped. A tricycle sat near the house and he moved toward the clothesline with only a half-conscious intent. Hanging on the line were dresses, childrens' shirts and pants, and, on the far end, diapers. Lloyd looked about him. He was alone in the night and he moved to the clothesline. He reached up and he paused briefly; then he took down six diapers, his hands working quickly but gently. He folded the diapers together and put them under his arm; then he moved away to his car.

ON THE TRIP BACK to the desert the next day, not a word was spoken between Darrell and Anna about the night before. Anna chattered for a time about Mrs. Galen's kindness and about the fiesta and about her concern over the excavation and for awhile Darrell was grateful for the total disregard of the incident. But then his feeling veered sharply and he despaired. The incident was so absurd to her that it was as if it had never happened; he had no chance at all, he feared. He grew less and less responsive and Anna eventually fell silent and watched the landscape.

At the base camp, Anna looked as if she might say something serious. Her face grew solemn, as she began to get out of the car; her eyes fixed on Darrell with great intensity; then she said only "Good-bye." But before she disappeared, Anna reached out and squeezed Darrell's hand.

He grew angry at that gesture as he drove back to the excavation. What the hell does it mean? he finally shouted at her in his mind. And he immediately regretted the outburst—just as if he'd actually confronted her—and his anger returned to himself, for his foolish, impetuous words. I want to kiss you goodnight. "Damn," he said out loud.

He cursed at intervals until he pulled into the excavation area and he saw Thomas and Betty rise up and come running.

"What is it?" he said, even while he was opening the door, before they could hear him.

As he emerged, Betty said, "Dr. Reeves," and she and Thomas turned and dashed back to the excavation. Darrell followed and he did not let himself look at anything until he fixed on the King in brief obeisance, appreciating his constancy, and then he followed the length of the King's body, his feet stretching into the five-foot square beneath him and there, a meter below the King and half a meter to the right, was another skeleton.

The body was twisted to the left, its eyes averted from Darrell. He drew near and stepped into the trench beside the body; he moved slowly, his limbs stiff-hinged, as if he moved to a bridal bed. He sensed it was a woman and he peeked at the pelvis and found that he was correct—the sciatic notch was wide and shallow. He let his eyes glide along the smooth line of bone into her pubis where the symphysis also was shallow.

He felt as if he were rushing things, he felt vaguely embarrassed even as his heart raced, as he wanted to touch her, wanted to cry out in joy that she was here. And he looked at her face. The curve of the skull was long and unbroken, the jaw was open only slightly, the teeth were even and not one was visibly worn. She was young, hardly out of her teens. Her arm was pulled up, crossing the curve of her ribs. That arm would have covered her breasts, as if the gesture had been one of modesty before the man who had placed her here. But she was dead by that time. She was dead.

A row of shell beads—once a strand—lay about her neck. Their color, their form, made them look like tiny vertabrae, as if she'd been strangled by the spine of a child. He shook away the thought. They were shells, taken from the shore of the gulf two thousand miles and four centuries distant. He bent nearer. There was a thin line of fracture in her neck. The weight of the earth, Darrell's mind insisted. He did not ask further how she'd come to this burial. He let the Indians persuade him. She was the servant of the King; perhaps a daughter of the King. She'd simply gone with him on his journey to the sun.

THE MEDICS SWABBED THE inside of Lloyd's nose. They had a station set up outside the mess hall at Los Alamos for a routine radiation check. The sudden smell of cotton made him think of the morning, the airy smell of the diapers, the look on Kay

Peters's face when she came to the door of her trailer apartment, the baby clinging to her chest, and he gave her the diapers, opening the screen door for her and thrusting them into her hand and moving off before she could speak. He had heard her sputtering thank-you behind him and he had felt pleased, he felt even now that the couple and their child were taken care of.

"Okay," the medic said and Lloyd went into the mess hall. Oppie appeared as soon as Lloyd sat down with his tray at a table.

"Lloyd, I want you to do me a favor," Oppie said.

"What is it?" Lloyd noticed a wisp of cotton caught in Oppie's nostril.

"We've set day after tomorrow for the test of our instruments."

"The hundred tons of TNT."

"Yes. We need to have a team go out there and take down Dr. Reeves's tents."

Lloyd bowed his face toward his tray.

Oppie went on, "I want you to go with the team and make sure our archaeologist friend is kept calm."

Lloyd lifted his face. "Meaning what?"

Oppie hesitated a moment, and Lloyd clarified his question. "What am I supposed to do with him?"

"Be sympathetic. Take him with you."

"Take him . . .?"

"Take him out to one of the instrument sites. Get him involved. He's a scientist, after all. Of sorts. Get him interested. I don't want any trouble from him, Lloyd. Don't let him out of your sight."

Lloyd wanted desperately to explain how all this was impossible for him to do. But he couldn't think of a lie that would let him say no to Oppie for the first time ever. And the truth was beyond explanation. Lloyd could only squeeze at the silverware in his hands and wait for Oppie to leave.

"Stay with him every moment till it's over," Oppie said.

"Yessir."

118

Oppie disappeared and Lloyd left soon after, without touching his food. He went to his room and opened the window wide. The night was warm, even up here on the plateau, and he lay on his bed expecting to find his mind full of the archaeologist, expecting to worry about the coming ordeal of being with the man alone in the desert. But he found that his initial distress was fading. The pale-eyed man would be under Lloyd's authority. Lloyd could speak or not speak, act or not act, as he wished.

A warm wisp of breeze blew in Lloyd's window and he thought of being down in the desert and then he let himself go to the breeze and he remembered a time without his father, a hot summer in Kansas City and his mother and he and his infant brother slept on the back porch of their flat at night because of the heat. And he'd heard the neighbors talk about the second summer. It was the crucial time in a baby's life when the children who were to die usually died. The neighbors warned that the children should never be fed new potatoes or peaches. They whispered about diptheria and scarlet fever and typhoid and tuberculosis in the second summer but often the baby would just get diarrhea and get weaker and weaker in the terrible summer heat and die. Lloyd remembered grabbing the bedclothes as the sky lightened and they scrambled back into the house at his mother's urging so that they wouldn't be seen. And his little brother died in his second summer and Lloyd tried to remember the tiny face but the features were vague and yet he knew the child. Clyde Coulter. For a time Lloyd was a brother and then the child died in his sleep. "Clyde," Lloyd said aloud. Sleep on, Lloyd thought. Sleep on, young Clyde. You would have hated your name. Sleep on.

BEFORE DAWN DARRELL WENT out of his tent into the dark and he folded back an edge of the tarp and he entered the excavation, his stealth quickening his heart. The moon was nearly down but the residue of its light and the light from the stars were enough for him to see the young woman. He knelt beside her and drew his face very near hers. How did you die? he whispered in his mind. Were you his lover? Did you insist on going with him? Or did his dying words tell his eldest son: I want her with me. Darrell could see her eyes widening only briefly as she stood beside her King's body, the body she had so recently covered with hers.

Darrell's hand rose and he touched her head, he touched the forearm that she'd laid over her breast. The bone was smooth, nearly as warm as the air. He closed his eyes, angled his head, waited for her to whisper in return. How did you die? he prompted in his mind. But he felt her shyness. He felt gentle over her. She did not turn from him, did not turn away, he had exposed her and she waited for his touch. His hand rose and it quaked and he moved it down and he touched her hip. And his fingers moved gently into her wide sciatic notch. He breathed deeply and waited to understand her. A rush of intuition to understand this woman, her life and death in this desert. He moved his hand around the ridge of bone and down into the shallow, fibrous trough of her pubis. He thought how little a man can know of a woman this way, how the mystery only deepens and he heard a distant rumbling.

At first he thought it was the bombers beyond the mountains. But the engines were drawing nearer and he rose up and in the south, coming at him along the desert flats, were lights. Pairs—two pair, three—lights and a grinding, rumbling sound before dawn. The lights advanced, roaring at him, and Betty and Thomas appeared in the mouths of their tents as the lights came and transformed themselves finally into trucks—two trucks and one car—and the trucks broke away from each other to surround the camp, stopping one on each side. The car kept coming, it raced toward the excavation and Darrell braced himself but the car slammed to a stop at the last moment. The headlights stayed on, glaring in his face, after the engine was off. The driver-side door opened and Darrell could only see a shape moving, a man coming around, his torso and legs a dark block

120

and stumps outlined with a penumbra from the lights. The man's head was invisible to Darrell's throbbing eyes. The figure stopped and its arms rose and angled akimbo and it waited.

Darrell shaded his eyes, squinted, and he could see the face dimly and he recognized it at once—Coulter. Darrell lowered his hand and straightened up but he had no time to outwait the physicist because figures were moving around him now, men in Army uniforms carrying wooden planks and stacking them by the excavation.

Darrell scrambled out of the pit. "What is this, Coulter?" he said.

Lloyd felt a surge of anger—something he'd been trying hard to hold back—at the archaeologist's flat, harsh use of his last name. But Lloyd still felt restrained. He was in this man's camp. There were all these other people moving around, all the confusion. Things would be different soon. "Tell your workers to get dressed," Lloyd said. "You all have to be out of here in half an hour."

"Is this your damn TNT blast?"

"The tents have to come down. The planking goes over the hole. You can oversee all that, if you want, but when it's done I have orders to take you with me."

The two men stood without any further words, without any movement, and then in his periphery Darrell saw an Army man bending to the tarp. Darrell moved quickly off and Lloyd returned to his car to wait.

After the tents were down, the hole boarded over, the trucks loaded, and the two assistants ushered into the truck with their gear, Lloyd turned on his engine and his lights. He saw the archaeologist cross in front of him and Lloyd revved the motor.

Darrell opened the passenger door and climbed into the car with Coulter. "When am I going to be brought back here?"

"In about four and a half hours."

"Good," Darrell said, immediately uncomfortable at showing his relief to this man.

Lloyd put the car in gear and backed out and drove south only far enough to pick up one of the paths the Army engineers had graded heading east.

Darrell was instantly conscious of their direction and he felt an oily fear begin to seep into his chest. "Your camp is south, isn't it?"

"Yes," Lloyd said and he said no more. That was the best way to proceed in this whole ordeal, he thought, say as little as possible. Just wait. If more reaction were inevitable—driven by laws like those he worked with every day—then it would happen and he'd know his part when it came.

"So why aren't we going that way?" Darrell insisted.

"I was told to take you out to one of our instrument sites."

"Those mountains are supposed to be dangerous now, aren't they?" Darrell realized that his thought of the maverick rancher came only after the first impulse to fear. That first fear had been of Coulter himself.

Lloyd turned his face to Darrell and thought, Is he referring to me? Lloyd felt confused. He hadn't considered himself dangerous. Not quite. Not clearly. Not yet. "We're men of the mind," Lloyd said, quoting Reeves from their last confrontation, but with sincerity.

Darrell didn't understand the answer at first, even though it fit his true fear. "Have they caught the rancher?"

"Rancher?" Lloyd looked back to the road.

"The rancher who was put off his land . . ." It struck Darrell now that the physicist had understood his fear of him. "The rancher who . . ." Darrell's voice clenched and he cleared his throat. "The rancher who was shooting at people out there."

"I don't know."

The two men did not speak again as they drove. Panicky little fantasies spanked across Darrell's mind, fantasies of leaping from the moving car, of running into the sheltering dark of the desert; and in Lloyd's mind there was only a sense of its own walls, of the concrete bunker of his mind, holding instruments like the bunker they were heading for, the instru-

ments in his mind measuring the energy impulses of this creature near him, measuring and waiting, measuring and waiting.

Three miles east, Lloyd found a marker and he braked hard,
the beams of the headlights swung around and stopped on a
cinderblock bunker with a dirt mound mounting its western
wall. Lloyd switched off the engine and shut off the lights and
the archaeologist opened the door at once and disappeared.
Lloyd sat for a moment in the car and Reeves's quick exit
reminded Lloyd of the man's fear of him. Lloyd felt angry at
this but before that feeling could grow he realized that Reeves
was out there somewhere on his own and Oppenheimer had
warned Lloyd not to let the archaeologist out of his sight. Lloyd
felt a rush of panic. Oppie wanted the man watched and Lloyd
had let him get away.

Lloyd flung open the door and jumped out. "Reeves," he
shouted. "Reeves."

Darrell was standing only a few yards from the car, letting
the kinesthetic stretch of the desert fill him, calm him, when
Lloyd began shouting his name. He drew back further into the
dark. Was Coulter going to push this now? Darrell's hand
moved to his belt. An instinctive gesture. But his trowel was
not there. It was in his tool pack in the back of an Army truck
and Darrell gasped audibly in fear, cursed in silence for not
keeping his trowel with him.

Lloyd heard the gasp out in the dark and he turned to it. He
could not see. The sky had clouded over and he could not see
but the gasp was clear. "Reeves," he said, almost in a whisper.

Darrell drew back further.

"Reeves."

"What do you want?"

The faint hum of the desert silence filled the next moment.

"Reeves."

"What is it?"

Lloyd still could not see the man. The voice had receded.
He said, "What are you doing with Anna Brown?"

Darrell nearly laughed at the irony of this. Nothing, he

thought. Not a damn thing. But before the laugh could shape, the question struck him as ominous. Was Coulter mad? Would the rage Darrell had once glimpsed in the man's face assert itself out here in the desert? Darrell could see Lloyd only because he knew where he must be standing, near the car door. The physicist and even the car were only vague shapes, the color of the night. Darrell looked around. No light at all came from the sky. Darrell backed further away.

"Reeves," Lloyd said.

There was no answer.

"Reeves," Lloyd shouted. "Did you hear me?"

Darrell stumbled on a stone. He bent and picked it up, gripped it tight.

Lloyd heard Oppie's warning again, as if the man had just bent down and whispered to him. Lloyd's anger tumbled and turned into fear and he shouted again, "Come back. There's danger."

Darrell stopped. "I think the danger is you," he shouted in return.

Focused as Lloyd was on his own fear, this charge hurt him. "We're men of the mind," he cried.

"Why do you ask about Anna Brown?" Darrell answered, moving as soon as the words were spoken, circling in the dark so that Coulter could not get a fix on his position. He stumbled against a creosote bush and stopped.

Anna, Lloyd thought. Her name in this man's mouth swung his feeling around again. He closed his hands on the top of the open car door and he squeezed hard. He didn't want this. But then he let the door go and he moved away from the car. He moved a few steps in the direction of the voice—it was distant and his fear of disobeying Oppie rushed back—and then he stopped. There was too much inside him. Too much. "Reeves," he shouted.

Darrell said nothing. He felt a scrambling in his chest, his face grew hot. The man's voice had drawn nearer. Without thinking, Darrell threw the rock he was holding into the desert, off to the right. It landed with a thump and skitter and then he moved in the opposite direction as quickly as he could without making any noise.

Lloyd heard the thump and looked toward it. His thoughts began to clutter together and this was his greatest fear. He was a scientist. He knew the danger when a man couldn't control his mind. He slowed himself down. Out here, the archaeologist could do no harm. Not to the test blast. Not to Anna. Lloyd couldn't let himself be confused by this man. And he couldn't allow him to speak her name again. Not at all. Not even for Lloyd to get answers. And they'd be lies anyway. This all was logical. Lloyd felt better and his mind went on. He would work all this out with Anna herself. She'd been sleeping, the night of the play. She'd been tired. "Reeves," he shouted. "Listen to me. Sit down. Find a place and sit down. Face the east and after the TNT goes, we'll return. We don't have anything more to say to each other, you and I. Just sit down wherever you are and wait."

Darrell did not reply. He thought it might be a ruse and he stood very still for a long time, listening; but there were no sounds at all and finally he felt around and found an empty patch—no stones, no bushes—and he sat on the desert floor and waited.

The night stretched on but finally the mountains before him began to show as a thickening of the darkness. That was his first perception, though in fact it was the eastern sky above them that was losing its intensity. He looked hard to see the rim—the black still blended there—and suddenly the mountains leaped at him, their flanks were spotted with scrub and the ridge fissured across the sky. There was a great light and he turned around to look.

A bright orange ball crouched on the desert and a stiff breeze bumped Darrell and then a crack of sound as the ball rose up shimmering, cohesive, it rose higher, tendrils extending to the ground and it rose and then even the tendrils broke. Darrell felt oddly unmoved by this display. They'd stacked some explosives and made a bright light. The desert held its illumination for a moment and Darrell looked toward the car and he saw Coulter standing only a dozen yards away. Darrell's breath caught at the man's nearness and at his face—Coulter's face was wide in wonder— and Darrell looked back at the fireball as the ambient light faded quickly. For the first time on this day Lloyd had no thought of the archaeologist. Lloyd knew how small this cloud of fire was. From three miles off it was only as large as two suns. There would be much more. And at this, he thought of Anna. Lloyd lifted his arms, his hands clenched, he lifted his arms high at the expectations of his life.

AT THE END OF their wordless return to the excavation site, Darrell and Lloyd found the surrounding scrub bushes and cacti singed and angled to the east and there was a long, curving scorch mark on the wood planks covering the hole. The two men stood by the car and Darrell's detachment from the explosion vaporized, he saw how far that fire had reached—even into his own camp, even licking over the body of the King— and he was afraid. Lloyd's eyes followed the scythe of black on the wood planking and he felt a lift at the puniness of a hundred tons of TNT and then he saw the astonishment in the archaeologist's face as it gazed at that same scorch mark and turned to look far off toward the blast site. Lloyd felt he'd made his point. He opened the car door and he heard faint gunfire—as distant as a memory—and then he got into the car and drove off, leaving the pale-eyed man with the message of this blast.

Lloyd drove across the desert with a palpable vision of fire around him, the great fire to come. And since Dr. Darrell Reeves had been defined this morning, had been grabbed by the throat and shaken, he no longer had power over Lloyd. None. There was only one thing left to do. He knew it with the suddenness of the morning's detonation: he would ask Anna to marry him.

Back in the camp there was a briskness to the workers Lloyd passed. The test had given them all strength. Lloyd turned onto the blacktop leading to the operations center and two deuce-and-a-half trucks immediately passed him, heading out toward the desert. The archaeologist's gear and assistants, Lloyd assumed. Only after he'd stopped near the flagpole did it occur to him that Anna might be on one of the trucks, going out to work at the excavation again. But this was too troubling to consider. He put it out of his mind. She'd be waiting for him, to see if she were needed. He smiled at this thought; he needed her permanently. That was the next step. He went up the porch of the operations center in two strides and Anna was not in the outer office, where she often waited for him. He entered the inner area and there were people moving quickly through the rows of desks, there was a din of voices, telephone wires stretched to faces, papers fluttered and before Lloyd could focus on the faces to find Anna, Oppie appeared.

"How did it go with Dr. Reeves?" Oppie asked.

"Just fine."

"You haven't heard the news." Oppie said this with no inflection of inquiry. He stated a premise.

"No."

"The Germans have surrendered."

There was only a brief blip of silence between them and then they spoke together, their words garbling into each other: Oppenheimer began, "The field recording conditions . . ." and Lloyd said, "Where is Anna Brown?"

"Sorry," Oppenheimer said, but then without pause he repeated his own thought. "The field recording conditions were very hard on the laboratory instruments. That's the main problem that came with the test blast."

Lloyd nodded at this and said, "Where's Anna Brown?"

"I haven't seen her," Oppenheimer said.

Lloyd turned at once and went out of the operations center. But before his worst fear could begin to swell in him, he saw Anna coming up the road, past the flagpole. She was moving quickly and when she saw him she smiled brilliantly and Lloyd descended the steps of the operations center with the slow precision of self-confidence.

"Isn't it wonderful?" she said.

"What?" Lloyd said, thinking—though he realized it was foolish—that somehow she already knew what he was going to ask.

"The German surrender," she said.

"Yes," he said, hardly hearing the statement, that matter having been taken care of in the interval of silence between Oppie and himself; there was still the need to press on, there was still Japan to lead them on.

"It's so wonderful," she said.

"Anna." Lloyd felt strong. He realized that his nerves would hold fast, the words would come. "I'd like to marry you."

Anna's eyes widened, but all that was in Lloyd's head was the unexpected phrasing. He'd meant to pose it as a question, the way it was supposed to be done. He corrected himself, "Will you marry me?"

"Oh, Dr. Coulter," Anna said and she seemed to Lloyd to be overcome with feeling, ravished. Her face dipped modestly—he squinted to see the blush he felt certain was there—and he wondered if he should take her hand now.

Anna raised her face. It was still dilated—with what strong feeling? Then Lloyd recognized it. It was the face of a woman seeing a great explosion. This is the face she'll have when the atomic bomb fills the sky, he decided.

"I don't know what to say," she said.

Lloyd hung now between his immediate desire for Anna and his pleasure at stunning her, making her stand in awe. He knew he could try to press her instantly into the answer he wanted, but that would take away this look. Her face was open to him; but it had not been her choice, it had been his choice, he had controlled it; and her openness held a trace of fear, as if the bomb blast she watched threatened to rush over her. Lloyd found that he wanted to keep her face just like this for a time.

She said, "This is . . . so sudden."

"Yes," he said, looking closely at her wide eyes, her drawn mouth, the stretch in her forehead, her cheeks. He memorized her face like this. He was in control now. The face was braced, as if she were about to be struck. "I understand," he said. "We can talk again." And Lloyd moved off. He went to his room and closed the door and sat in the dim room with Anna's face before him.

LATER THAT MORNING LLOYD began to debrief each field-instrument group leader. He sat in the operations center and Anna was at his side making a list of operational suggestions that emerged from the series of dialogues. Oppie was right, Lloyd thought. The instruments that worked well in the laboratory became unstable and unreliable out in the desert. But as his mind struggled with the task of making suggestions for improvement, a list that he began to realize would please Oppie, he was conscious of the woman near him. Anna was still stricken with the force of Lloyd's question. He sensed it. He was holding her fast with his question.

After one of the group leaders left and the next one still had not appeared and the focus of the open operations room was clearly on the other side—no one was near—Lloyd allowed himself the luxury of leaning back in the wooden swivel chair and thumbing his suspenders. Anna leaned near him at once.

"Dr. Coulter," she said.

"Yes?"

"About this morning—what you suggested."

Her voice was steady, her face was calm, and Lloyd felt suddenly frantic. He lowered his hands and leaned closer to Anna. "Really," he said. "I just want to let you think about that awhile."

"Yes," she said. "I appreciate that . . . It's just . . ." Her eyes began to search his face, began to leap about, and Lloyd wanted to put his hands on her to stop her.

"I just want to let you . . ." he began and he realized he was about to repeat himself. He was losing control of all this.

"It's so sudden," she said.

"I understand," he said firmly, trying to stop her.

"I'm not the kind of girl I sometimes seem . . ." She hesitated a moment and then wagged her head with a little smile, a smile Lloyd could not bear. But before his anger could form, she said, "I guess I just don't understand how I come across, sometimes."

Lloyd realized the little smile had been in self-deprecation. He didn't understand what she was referring to, but he suddenly felt gentle about her. He said, "It's all right." He wanted her look of awe to return, he wanted control, but he didn't know what to do.

"I like you," she said.

Good, he thought. He'd take that for now, even without her face being right.

"I just haven't gotten around to thinking like that about you," she said.

Lloyd didn't let all of this into his mind. He was aware, in what she said, of the implication of possibility for them and he'd take that too. Things were going well. The first blast had gone off, the archaeologist had been answered, the final bloom of atoms was drawing near; all this was growing easier for Lloyd.

Anna continued to talk and Lloyd felt like an indulgent parent. He let her prattle on; the words came clearly into his head, but he perceived only the flutter of her confusion, her need for him.

"You know," she was saying, "I thought for a time that men were all alike in the way they responded to women. But the image I had was of those Navy men along State Street, as similar as their uniforms, clucking and whistling and posing . . . *obvious* about their interests. Now I've been around scientists and you're all the same, too. But in an altogether different way. For a while I thought that a desire for women was just . . . left out of your whole equation. On the surface you're so preoccupied. Shy even. And then all of a sudden something comes up from somewhere inside you and you make demands and in a way the demands seem as oblivious to who I am as if they were from those guys on State Street . . . They make me feel . . . I don't know . . . *abstract*, I guess . . . I'm not making this very clear . . ."

Lloyd grew tired of these sounds. "Be still," he said firmly. "It won't be long before you'll see what I've been doing."

The feelings he desired in her face flickered briefly there. He felt now he could have her whenever he chose. As if he'd made a breakthrough with the implosion work, he found the right shape of his mind, the right explosive charge, to get what he wanted.

"What do you mean?" she asked.

He didn't understand her question. Though he felt only a darkening in himself, his face must have shown puzzlement, for Anna said, "What is it you've been doing?"

She was a child. A slow-witted child. "The atomic bomb," he said, very low. "That will make everything clear."

There was suddenly a commotion across the room, near the front door. Anna looked sharply over her shoulder and half rose up. Lloyd followed her gaze and with the irritation of having been interrupted at a delicate moment, he, too, stood. Lloyd crossed the room and the trail of distracted, agitated people led out of the operations center and onto the front steps. Oppenheimer was standing out in the road with the security captain and a group of soldiers. They all strained to see into the rear of a jeep. The latecomers, the operations center personnel, were peeking and turning away at once. Oppie was angled toward the jeep and wagging his head slowly while the captain bent near, talking.

Lloyd went down the steps and pushed through to Oppie's side. Oppie gave him a glance as he arrived and Lloyd looked into the jeep. An Army sergeant lay in the back seat, a small, dark red vortex in the center of his chest, his shirt front swirled outward from this point with blood, his head cocked to the side; a dead man, dead without doubt; Lloyd leaned near, struck by how primitive this death was, the body still here, limp, slick with blood. The bomb would carry each molecule away in its bloom, a natural process, evaporation into the hot rays of the sun.

"The rancher out there has finally killed someone," Oppie said.

"Move ground zero to the foot of the mountains," Lloyd said. He expected Oppie to at least smile at the elegance of this joke, but the man sucked at his pipe and his eyes grew very sad and before the man could begin quoting some Hindu text, Lloyd moved away, unwilling to waste his anger.

THE NEXT WEEKS PASSED for Darrell with his desire for Anna restrained, from shame and fear. He found a second woman laid out beside the first. She was the same age, perhaps eighteen; she had a shell bead necklace; she was laid out in the same pose, turned slightly away, an arm over her chest. Anna arrived at the site soon after the discovery and Darrell took her into the pit and talked to her about the devotion of these women to the King. She listened to him quietly. She seemed quieter now than when he first met her and this worried Darrell, but he didn't mention it. Still, he saw her now and then watching him. Beginning, he thought in his better moments, to consider him in the way he wished; falling away from him, he thought in his worse moments, even her interest in the Indians unable to sustain her enthusiasm, now that he'd blundered with her.

"Are you all right?" he finally asked at the end of one day.

"Yes," she said. "I'm sorry. Have I been very quiet?"

"No."

"Yes I have. That's why you asked."

"I have no right . . ."

"Yes you do," Anna said softly. "I'm not ignoring your feelings. Really I'm not."

"I wish you'd forget . . ."

"No. It's just my life overall is beginning to confuse me. I'm sorry if I'm moody. I've got things on my mind."

"I'm sorry I've complicated all that."

"Stop now." Her voice was firm almost to the point of anger and Darrell cursed himself for beginning to push again. He knew he had reopened his torment. He'd pay for this in a week of dissection on his cot.

For now, he was silent; but he did nothing to preclude further conversation. They leaned against a balk in the pit, the day's work done but with their hands still gloved in dust. The Indians nearby seemed patient to Darrell. Very patient, and he tried to emulate them; he stretched his mind out beside them, made it be still.

After a time, Anna said, "Not confused, exactly."

"What?"

"I said my life is confusing me, but that's not quite true. Not the way it sounds."

Darrell waited, kept himself as still as his King.

"I've always appreciated things," Anna said.

"Yes?"

"You know, I met a guy in Chicago who was assigned to a battleship. That really interested me. I made him tell me every detail. You look at a picture of a battleship and all the structures there on deck seem so complex. It seems you'd never know how to move from one spot to another. I made him draw me a plan. He showed me the gangways and how they all fit together."

Anna paused and Darrell let himself peek at her face. She was staring out into the pit, and then with a tiny start she seemed to focus on something. "I'm really very fortunate. Look at what I'm doing now. I've got two whole worlds that are the most interesting things I've ever known. Dr. Coulter and . . ."

There was a hesitation in her. A sympathetic response? Darrell wondered. He himself had felt a shuddering pause at the mention of the physician's name. But Darrell did not truly believe Anna sensed his own feeling, and if she didn't, then what caused her to pause? He veered away from any consideration of that and Anna was speaking again.

"That battleship I learned about," she said. "It seemed pretty simple, finally. Logical. Once you got the connections figured out, that was all there was. Down at Trinity-site, you'd think it would be the same. The way science is supposed to be, you'd think it was just a matter of a few more hidden connections waiting to be found. Then all those physicists would get what they want. But I see them sweating and arguing and pouting and—I don't know—I wonder if it's so simple. If it's ever really as logical as they want to think."

Anna paused. Darrell was watching her frankly and she seemed unaware of it. Her voice; the movement of her mind; her eyes, as they fixed now on the bodies in the pit: this sense of Anna prickled along the surface of Darrell's skin, ran beneath the layer of dust and chilled him with desire. But he did not move.

"And here," she said. "Sometimes you forget where you are, what you're actually doing. You get caught up into the physical task—digging and sifting, digging and sifting. You forget. But oh my, then I stop and look around and there are these people here. Especially those two young women. I can see them, how they were. They're like friends of mine. Slender girls with figures I envy and they're always primping. They braid their long black hair and they put feathers in the braids and they wear soft animal skins. That's how I see them both. Then the King comes to them and they're awed by him but they feel giggly. And he makes a very serious request. He wants them to be with him as he goes after something very big. The gods themselves. He's going to travel to the gods and he wants them to be with him. But those are *his* gods, really. And I feel afraid for my two friends. I'm afraid, but the King is very impressive . . . Did he love them?" Anna suddenly turned to Darrell. The question was for him.

"Yes," he said without hesitating, even without thinking. "Yes."

She paused only briefly, then said, "Did *they* love *him?*"

"What do you think?"

Anna looked back into the pit. Darrell followed her eyes to the two slim girls curled up at the feet of the King. "I don't know," she said.

FOR LLOYD, WEEKS PASSED with his further plans for Anna in abeyance. He still relished his control of the situation. And he felt his work moving now in the way he knew it must go. Then at last he could seek her out with news: he burst into his office at K-site to find her waiting. He said, "The time has come," and she must have misunderstood because she said, "I'll be able to tell you my feelings as soon as I understand them myself."

Lloyd drew back at this, puzzled. His puzzlement made her blush. "I'm sorry," she said. "I jumped to a conclusion."

"Yes?"

"What's come?"

"This," he said and he sat her at his desk and laid the photo out before her, holding the curling corners down with the spread of his hands. He waited for her to become thoroughly baffled and then he said, "Do you see the thin white line running across the photo?"

"Yes."

"That's the track of a neutron. It has just passed through an explosion focused by a molded lens. What it shows—by the distance it travels here—is that the implosion method is going to work."

"The bomb's going to work?" she said, raising her face

with the features stretching, as in a great wind, as in his proposal of marriage.

Lloyd smiled. "You never doubted it, did you?"

"I guess not. No . . . But this shows . . .?"

"This shows we're almost there. This is fundamental. There are going to be a lot of nervous scientists around here straining at problems until the final shot, but in my own mind this is all I need to know." He thumped the photo with his knuckles. "The rest will yield."

And at this Anna smiled with such wanness that Lloyd knew how frightened she was and he straightened up before her. He wanted to comfort her, this woman who would soon be in his protection forever, he wanted to cup her in his hands as if he held a delicate slug of plutonium that would fly apart without gentleness. But he did not touch her and the distress in her face persisted and then he'd waited too long to comfort her, for she was making him angry, the power of the bomb was his own power and so it was he that she was afraid of and he knew that fear taunts power, fear challenges power to show itself, to complete the equation, fear sucks at power, like the suck of sex. He took up the photo and left, unsettled now, the patience he'd had beginning to wither.

THAT NIGHT, JUST BEFORE sleep, Lloyd had a brief glimpse of his mother's face. Lloyd's father was coming up the back steps of their flat. He had been gone for weeks to wherever it was he went and Lloyd was sitting with his mother at the kitchen table and they could not see Lloyd's father but they knew who it was from the sound of his steps. Lloyd's mother smiled a wan, frightened smile. Lloyd touched her hand and in his bed at Los Alamos he fell asleep. Two hundred miles to the south, Darrell lay on his cot and he thought of his own father. The man was angry at Darrell and he prided himself on never hitting his son. But the man's forefinger rose and waved in emphasis, his face grew red and his words grew so logical they fortified that finger with steel and it came jutting out. His father never hit him but that finger came forward and tapped in emphasis on Darrell's chest, tapped with the force of his impeccable logic, and the tight little spot on his chest began to hurt and the pain gathered quickly and the finger prodded again and again against him and he felt as if his chest would split in two. And Darrell also slept.

THE FOLLOWING WEEK DARRELL uncovered a third young woman. He knew where to dig—she completed the symmetry—three young women lay side by side at the feet of the King. Darrell exposed her head first, the teeth as smooth as the others', the face turned to the side. Thomas and Betty were sitting in the shade of a tent flap eating lunch and Darrell did not call for them. The sun squeezed at him, the smell of alkali was making him faintly dizzy, his knees ached as he shifted his position slightly, but he had no physical hunger in him—not for food or drink or shade now. He was meeting another of his King's women and he was content. The four figures had a sense of confraternity about them—they shared the burial space, they shared the rites that brought them there, their bones were a striking uniform. Darrell's hands rapidly pulled the dirt away. Her jaw was long.

And he found the tiny crack in her neck. The second one had had it too. He'd seen it and let it pass but now all three had it in the same place and he knew he'd closed his mind before to this detail, he knew he'd chosen instinctively to be discreet about his King's rites. Darrell's hands worked and worked and then he found a pair of stones at the back of the young woman's neck. The stones were elongated and each had a hole in one end. Handles.

He sat back and a gritty wind blew past his raised face. She'd been the third to die. The stones were handles—what was left of the cord that strangled her, strangled all three of them. It wasn't unusual. He had no reason to hesitate over this discovery. This was natural to the Indians, after all. But he felt a prickling along the backs of his arms and he decided it was the irony. The irony, he thought. These Indians of the Death Cult had fled the rumors of violence and they brought their own violence with them. But these three women knew what was expected of them. They were merely stepping out of the vessel of their flesh to be with their King. And Darrell thought of Anna. He turned his face to the south and wished she were with him. This leap of his mind felt perfectly natural to him and went unquestioned. But he rasped a wrist hard across his forehead at the thought that she was somewhere at that moment in the presence of Lloyd Coulter.

LLOYD GREW STILL AND hard when he arrived from Los Alamos and could not find Anna at the desert base. He felt he'd done this too many times. Too many times he expected to find her and he had to go through this same cycle of fear and anger and even when it ended in relief he was reminded that in fact he had no control. He went to her room and down at the end of the quonset hall was an open door and beyond was the desert, and in the distance—as if this hall were the tube of a telescope looking at a distant world—were the San Andres Mountains. Before Lloyd knocked, he remembered the dead Army man. He thought: Put the bomb right there and wipe the rancher's mountains away. He knocked loudly. There was no answer. He turned the handle and it yielded and he opened the door.

Lloyd's distress reached its apogee now—a new force made it curve and begin to fall. Anna wasn't here but he was alone in her room. He felt an intimacy with her that the savor of her awe in the past few weeks had denied him. Since she had two rooms—one in Los Alamos as well as this one—there were few personal objects. But the bed was vaguely rumpled—hardly military, he thought with a smile—and there were some objects on the top of her dresser. He noted their existence without seeing what they were—he'd save those for last. The room was small, but there was a large wardrobe at one end and a rod, holding a drape, beside it. He went to the drape and pulled it open to reveal the wash basin. On the basin was a bar of soap worn smooth and small by her hands. He touched it lightly with his fingertips, but it felt sticky and he didn't like it. He drew his hand back and wiped his fingers hard against his shirt with the fleeting, inchoate fear that sex was like that.

He backed away and then turned and stepped to the dresser. He opened the top drawer and the soft lumps of cloth there made him tremble and he closed the drawer hard. Again he felt an anger beginning to shape, but the objects on the dresser-top distracted him. They were hard, they could fit his hands in some sensible way. A gold compact, a comb, an enameled tube of lipstick, a hairbrush. The hairbrush made him stop. Anna's dark hair was tangled in the bristles. The individual hairs began to snake into him, the long curves of these hairs, but they did not trouble him because they were held tight by the bristles and the bristles in turn were held by the hard plastic stem and handle. He picked up the brush and gripped it in his palm. He was conscious of the touch of the ends of some of the hairs. He grasped the brush by its handle and he slowly raised it to his head. He would run the brush through his hair, her hair entwining with his. He trembled now, but he lifted the brush.

Then he heard a sound outside. He put the brush down, turned, considered a confrontation, and rejected it, he strode over to the wash basin and closed the drape behind him.

He heard the door open and close. Only for a moment did he fear she would discover him. He heard her sigh and the cot creaked and he held back his breath, he measured it in and out in silent little bursts. He was all right, unseen, and he eased to the edge of the drape and peeked into the room.

Anna was sitting with her profile to him. Her face was bowed and still. She was thinking of him, he knew. He watched her face shaping in her thoughts and he could read her clearly: he's in control of me; he's too powerful; I'll lose track of myself; but that's going to be all right; I'm just a little afraid. Lloyd wondered at his own intuition. Neddermeyer was an imbecile by comparison. Lloyd felt his powers growing, just as the bomb was growing in all the labs at Los Alamos, growing but not yet ready.

Lloyd waited, watching. At last Anna looked at her watch and jumped up. Lloyd read her: he's looking for me; he needs me; I have to go. And she crossed to the door, and paused there. She began to turn toward Lloyd and he moved back from the edge of the drape. He waited. There was no more sound in the room for a long moment and he waited. Then he heard the scuffle of her feet and he didn't know if she had come back into the room or left it, but he suddenly felt like a damn fool, hiding here, and he grabbed the drape and yanked it open. The room was empty. He heard her clearly in his mind: I have to find him.

DARRELL THOUGHT HE WAS going to be very calm when he saw the captain's car pull up to the site. The tarp had only just been removed and Betty and Thomas were still folding it. Darrell was sweating already in the morning heat but he felt reasonably fresh. And his senses were distracted by too much useless fretting over Anna—rethinking his fumbling, re-examining her ambiguity, wondering what she was doing when she was away from the camp. He had not spoken again about any of this to her. She came out to the dig now and then and sifted the desert soil quietly and earnestly and she asked only about the Indians and he talked only about the Indians, though he actually thought about them less than he had ever done on a dig. So he felt detached from the captain as the man approached. Darrell was ready to be aloof.

"Dr. Reeves," the captain said.

"Captain."

"You still digging out here?"

"Yes we are."

The captain's eyes shifted to the excavation and Darrell followed his gaze and he saw the recent work afresh, as this man might be seeing it. And that made Darrell feel even more calm.

The site was smooth-edged and prim. The King lay stretched on his cape of beads which was beginning to shine in the early morning sun as if in a faintly kindled recollection of the King's worship, his rising up and opening his arms to the sky and turning so that his cape caught the sun and blazed. The King lay on a smooth, scraped dirt pedestal and beside him, on a separate pedestal, were the gorgets, the weeping face, the spider. Below him were the three young women, each on her own pedestal, each flexed slightly, each turned slightly away, each with an arm drawn up to her breast. And the sacred enclosure curved, unbroken, for over two hundred degrees. The stones marked the ancient compass of the world, swooping from one side of the King to the other, suggesting their still uncovered completion in the three five-foot squares remaining to be excavated.

Betty and Thomas moved to the upper right square with their tools and shaking screens. They looked at Darrell and then, with a trace of fear, at the captain. He turned to the man who was still gazing at the excavation. Darrell studied the captain's eyes; they were fixed on the three skeletons below the King.

"They're young women," Darrell said.

The captain jerked his face to Darrell as if he'd been startled. "Who?"

"Those three there. You were looking . . ."

"Not at all," the captain said, "I was just thinking . . ."

"You were staring at them."

The captain's eyes narrowed.

Darrell felt angry. "Don't try to sneer now. You were looking at them for a long while without speaking. You were interested."

The captain's face crumpled in wry condescension.

"Don't look at me like that," Darrell said. "I don't like you, captain. And I don't really care what you think. But I saw you caught by these Indians and you can't deny it. I saw it."

"You're making this very easy for me," the captain said.

"You and those damn physicists down there think you're more powerful than history . . . This is all just rubble to you."

"Very easy," the captain interjected.

But Darrell wouldn't stop. He wanted to grab this smug, hard man by the throat. "Well, those four people lying there have more humanity to them right now than your whole camp full of hobbyists and tin soldiers."

"You've got less than two weeks, Reeves . . . You've really made this very pleasant . . . I'm gonna run your ass out of here in maybe ten days no matter what you've got done in your rubble heap."

"This can't be rushed," Darrell said, an expression of fear that he immediately regretted showing to the man.

"Then you're in a bind, Reeves." The captain spun around and marched back to his car and Darrell's mind thrashed around for a few words of defiance, anything to make up for his display of weakness.

Just as the captain opened the car door—the last chance for him to be answered—Darrell shouted, "Crow to . . ." He'd begun to call him crazy and then shifted to go-to-hell and the blend made him sound like a fool. The car door slammed and Darrell expelled a sharp, wordless sound. A gritty spiral swirled through his head like a sand devil. He squeezed at his mind but the sand devil spun on and he knew that when it stopped all the fragments of fears and failures held aloft would settle on him like a burial mound. He turned and Betty and Thomas were looking at him with wide eyes.

"Get to work," Darrell said sharply.

The two faces contracted with pain and Darrell said, "I'm sorry."

Betty and Thomas looked about them at the earth as if they didn't know how to proceed. Darrell felt a pulse in his hands and feet, a sudden quickening. "Wait," he said. "I'll show you where."

He moved around the exposed curve of the sacred circle and he knew when he crossed it in the unexcavated square. He felt contained here. "Back away," he said to his assistants. He stood inside the circle and closed his eyes briefly. The sensitivity had intensified in his hands and feet. He opened his eyes and looked at the King. He looked down at the yellow-gray soil, pocked with stones. He moved around slowly in the invisible boundary of this five-foot square, feeling along with the soles of his feet as if in a strange, dark room. He stopped on impulse and looked off to the King, and he could imagine a body laid out in this place, perhaps an attendant. He said, "Start here."

Darrell backed away and Thomas and Betty set up on the spot and began to dig. They worked quickly with spades until they neared the horizontal level of the King and the three women. Darrell kneeled with them and soon he saw Thomas switch from trowel to grapefruit knife and then, as the young man took up a brush, Darrell said, "Something?"

"Yes," Thomas said.

Darrell looked into the hole and watched Thomas uncover a knob of bone—a calcaneus, the heel bone—and then Darrell joined him, their four hands working quickly, understanding that all their work must be done as quickly as possible now. The ankles and feet appeared—crossed, as if they'd been bound together. The bones were large. And as the tibia and fibula were gradually exposed, this impression of largeness grew stronger. Darrell had internalized a sense of size and proportion for the Indians from all his work with them and these bones stretched beyond his expectations. Not grossly, but enough that he was certain of it.

The three of them worked hard, without stopping even for water, though the day had grown very hot. The legs were free and after that the pelvis, and the man's sex was confirmed. Then they found the wrist bone, lying across the back of the hip. An unexpected positioning until Darrell remembered his first impression of the ankles. They'd been bound. Darrell's trowel followed the wrist bone to the hand and the other hand was there and they were crossed behind the man's back. They too had been bound together.

Now Darrell paused, though he did not speak. Betty and Thomas retreated into shade to drink and rest and Darrell was aware of how remote he'd been. His assistants asked him no questions; they seemed to sense that he had grown unapproachable. The claim that this realization had on him surprised Darrell, for the discovery they'd just made in the pit was in some ways unusual. It should have been dominating his thoughts now. But even as his mind began to shape hypotheses about the Indians, some part of him contemplated his own mood, his effect on the people around him. He sat back on the ground and took off his hat and wiped his brow with a handkerchief and he thought perhaps this train of thought was a good thing. He'd uncovered a trace of consideration in himself that might serve him well with Anna.

He looked at the half-exposed skeleton, the hands crossed and bound, the cord long ago rotted away but the hands unable to seize the advantage of their freedom. This man didn't want to die, Darrell thought. Then it struck him that he'd been a tribal rival of the King. That would make sense. On his deathbed, the King took precautions with his succession. He had his rival killed and then took the man with him into his own burial to serve as captive slave.

Darrell opened his canteen and lifted his head to drink and he saw a cloud of dust—the trail of a vehicle—approaching from the south. His mouth felt brittle and he drank first and then rose. He felt shaky on his feet, his legs hurt and he didn't feel like another confrontation. But he could not let this all be destroyed. Not a bone could be moved till it was all done and he would do what he needed to do.

But when the Army sedan stopped, it was Anna who got out. As the car roared off, she stood for a moment watching Darrell and he stood watching her. She'd slowed down over the past seven weeks. Just as Darrell had an internal sense of the proportion of his Indians' bones, he had a sense of Anna, her warmth, her animation, her pleasure. And these impulses in her had diminished over the weeks. Darrell knew this with certainty. The diminishment was not always obvious but he was certain it was so.

Anna was walking toward him now and he moved out to meet her. She smiled a slow, wide smile—its final state was similar to all the impulsive smiles of enthusiasm that had enchanted Darrell two months ago, but there seemed to be an act of will behind it.

"I'm glad you're here," Darrell said. He kept his voice flat, vowing to himself not to get caught up and push her again.

"I'm a little late."

"It's all right."

"Dr. Coulter needed me this morning."

Darrell felt a ripple of unease.

She said, "But he's gone out on the desert for the rest of the day, so I'm yours."

So I'm yours: her tantalizing words were unconscious; Darrell was convinced of that. But they still scraped along his skin as if they were her fingernails on his chest, not quite causing pain, not quite causing pleasure. He felt suddenly weary and hot and he could not do the smart thing—get immediately back to the isolated concentration of work—so he said, "We're on a break. Shall we sit in my tent?"

"Yes. I'd like that."

He put her liking it immediately out his mind and led her away, pointing out the King's rival as they passed, diverting their minds into the safety of the sacred enclosure and hypotheses about the past. He was still discoursing when they entered the tent—he was talking about the problems of royal succession, how they've been the same since the most ancient of times, how all societies had only a small range of workable solutions.

Then, as he moved to the lesser chair, Anna stopped him and insisted he sit in the rattan. He protested but she said, "Please. I want you there."

"Thank you," he said and his mind filled with varied explanations of her gesture and he knew it was a terrible mistake to bring her into his tent. He'd maintained the working distance between them so effectively for these weeks that he feared this nearness now.

"Are you going to make it?" she said.

He knew what she meant but his response shaped very slowly, as if he were being etherized.

She said, "The excavation. Will . . . we finish in time?"

He was slowed down further by her conscious choice of "we." Finally he said, "I will not move these bones until the excavation's done."

"That doesn't quite answer . . ." She sounded fearful.

Darrell felt the fear too, for a beat, and then his anger prevailed. "The 'time' will have to wait. I won't move from here till it's done."

"You should realize," she said, "that these men are very determined."

"So am I," Darrell said.

Anna puffed in concern. Darrell felt buoyed by his defiance, by its display before Anna. "So am I," he repeated.

"They can force you."

Darrell shrank inside but he just hardened his face, turned it away from her logic. There had to be some way to stall them, or maybe work around them. He thought of the crouching ball of flame he'd seen, just one clean lick of flame over the site.

"How many tons of TNT can they be possibly planning to stick out there?" he said rhetorically, thinking that somehow the King could be shielded for the brief bellow of the blast.

Anna said, "There are things coming together out there that you're not aware of . . . *I'm* not even sure what exactly may happen and I can't really talk about what I do know. But you've got to take these people very seriously."

"I do."

"I'm worried about you," Anna said, almost in a whisper.

146

Now it was Darrell who puffed out air in a moment of concern. He had to work as quickly as he could at the site and not paralyze himself planning for a final confrontation. He would react when the time came.

"When this is over," Anna said. "And it will be soon, I think . . ."

"That's what I'm told."

"What will you do then?"

"Do?"

"Say you get the excavation finished all right and you clear out of the desert . . . What then?"

Darrell looked closely at Anna, afraid of her careless language, but afraid, too, of not remaining prepared for the moment when she might open to him. "I'll go back to Santa Fe, I suppose," he said.

"Do you expect to make your whole career in Santa Fe?"

Darrell smiled. It had been some years since he thought in those terms. Maybe not since his first year or two of marriage. "I don't know," he said. "I'm absorbed by my work—the exploration, the reconstruction, the theorizing, the teaching. As long as I'm doing those things, I seem to be satisfied."

"I see."

"Do you admire ambition?" Darrell grew fearful of making a mistake with her again, but he also felt a sensitivity in his hands and feet, as if he were standing on an excavation site.

"I guess I do," she said.

"My university isn't a big name in archaeology."

"I feel embarrassed," she said, lowering her eyes but not her face.

"Why?"

"For pressing like this."

"It's all right." Darrell hesitated and knew he'd have a very bad time trying to figure out if he'd passed or failed some sort of test. So he asked, "Are you trying to decide about me . . . about whether I could presume to . . ."

"I'm sorry to get like this," she said.

"Don't say that," he said firmly. "For heaven's sake, don't get ambiguous again or circumspect or apologetically vague . . ." Darrell heard his sharp tone and he stopped. He felt himself panting, his face burned and he wiped the sweat away with his hand.

He looked at her startled face and he felt ravaged with regret at his harshness and even as the impulse formed to apologize, Anna said, "Now don't *you* do it either."

"I didn't want to speak that way to you."

"Yes you did."

He paused only long enough to note that there was no irritation or hurt in her voice. "Yes I did," he said. "And you wanted to pry."

"Ambition *is* important to me," she said. "I wish I could figure out a way to have it for myself. But at least a man who wants me to . . ."

"If I'm going to have a chance with you, I've got to get ambitious, is that it?"

"I'm . . ."

"Don't apologize, dammit."

"Yes then. All right. Yes."

"Ambitious in a way you can identify."

"Look," she said, her voice pitching high. "I didn't *ask* to start thinking about you like that. It's not like it was *my* idea to make demands on you."

"Can I be ambitious? Sure. Do I want more as an archaeologist? Sure. I could use this discovery here and write a hell of a paper and play the journals against each other and make them feature it and get myself a presentation at one of the conventions. Then I could play the colleges against each other and dump Santa Fe and get into Wisconsin or Columbia and start politicking for money, a big expedition somewhere in Mexico or Peru and go after the shiny stuff, the golden artifacts instead of the clay, the stuff for the Metropolitan Museum. Then I could play that into a post abroad and an even bigger expedition, a score of PhD's and five hundred natives at my command out in the jungles of Central America.'' Darrell found himself standing, his chest and arms taut and trembling, as if in anger, as if he were in the middle of a fist fight. He looked down at Anna. She smiled at him with a smile that was part wryness and part pride. The pride split Darrell's feelings like a birthing amoeba.

"That sounds sensible to me,'' she said.

Darrell looked at the two feelings swimming in him: he was lifted by her pride, he'd reached her with this improvised plan for his life in a way that no kiss in a parlor could have ever done; but this feeling of tautness in him, the vigor of aggressiveness, scared him, for it had come unbidden, as if it had leaped from beneath the earth, had pierced through his sensitive feet and spread through him.

"Doesn't that life interest you?'' she said.

"My ambition right now is to preserve my King out there and his grave.''

Anna rose. "All right,'' she said. "That was first in the big plan anyway.''

"Anna,'' Darrell said.

"Yes?''

"Would you definitely expect that other life from me?''

Anna's face—eager at her rising—relaxed into a moment of thoughtfulness. She smiled gently. "Don't you know how much trouble it is for me to focus on what I want? I mean *one* thing I want in a lasting way?''

"Is it hard?''

"Yes . . . You've got something stable in your life. I don't.''

Darrell wondered if what she said about him was true. "You mean my work?''

"Yes.''

He still could not tell if that was true. If his life was actually stable.

Anna said, "I still like hearing you talk. Really I do.'' She stepped to him and kissed him on the cheek. It was a gesture that he'd once feared—feared even now in his mind—but in fact the kiss made him happy. Unambiguously so.

AT THE SAME MOMENT, a thousand yards to the southwest, Lloyd stood looking up at the steel tower rising a hundred feet already from the desert floor. The girders tapered toward the top and a man was climbing the open ladder-like stairway along one leg of it. At the top, carpenters were beginning to build the wooden platform where the bomb would rest. Lloyd smiled at the thought of those carpenters. He'd heard them talking together earlier. They were still awe-struck over the sturdy all-wood tower they'd built for the test blast. Even the comparatively pitiful blast of a hundred tons of TNT had totally obliterated the tower. Lloyd had almost butted in to laugh at their awe, to tell them about the unthinkable power that would soon be loosed in this same spot. But he had no interest in making them feel foolish. The time would come when they finally understood for themselves.

Lloyd folded his arms across his chest and enjoyed the rise of the tower, although it struck him as spindly. The upward girders were broken by seven horizontal girders and the three platform stations were no more than small triangular wedges of steel next to the open stairway. Between the horizontal girders were simple X-shapes of steel and it all gave an impression of instability, as if it might sway and fall in the wind. But the mid-day heat let Lloyd smell the steel and the tower did not move at all, though the wind gusted hard at times. And he was very satisfied with its height. He was certain that the theory they were testing was correct: exploding the bomb from a height would magnify the damage. The air blast would far exceed any potential for ground shock. This was an instrument of the air, not of the earth. And at the thought of the earth he looked to the northeast, to the distant excavation site.

He'd left Anna earlier and he knew she was planning to go

to the excavation. He felt the wind in his face and it carried a smell he couldn't quite identify. He thought of Anna's hair, what it must smell like. He thought of her hair brush and there was a crackling sound before him. He raised his eyes to the far distance, the mountains; the sky was dark there and then he saw a thin, sudden fissure and he waited for the sound to come, a deeper crackling this time. Lloyd looked up to the top of the tower and saw the carpenters standing, facing the east. There'd been no rain in the desert the past month. With the test date so close, Lloyd didn't like this storm. There was a drought still in Los Alamos and he wished these clouds would turn north.

The thunder called again and Lloyd expected to worry, but he did not. He felt, instead, that the storm had no power over the work he was doing. No storm could turn him away. The mountains were blurring now as the clouds moved over them and Lloyd smiled. He realized that something this strong could only be his ally.

He went to his car and drove off to the northeast. The tents grew before him, he saw people moving and he looked at the rain, a high gray tide rushing in. He guided his car onto the fringe of the camp, in sight of the dig, and he stopped.

The two young people were struggling with a large green covering, their arms jerking, their bodies angling, as they opened it up. Nearby Anna and the archaeologist stood, the man looking off to the east, his arms hanging loose; he was beaten by the rain. Anna was staring into the hole. She was near the archaeologist, but she was not touching him. She could raise her arm and reach him but she was not touching him. They had not heard Lloyd drive up. The thunder was very loud.

Lloyd opened the car door and stepped into the thick air that smelled the way he imagined her hair would smell. He waited for a stroke of thunder to fade and he said "Anna" in a loud voice. All four faces jerked to him and this made him smile.

"Anna," he said. "Looks like you're done here for today. I need you."

Anna and the pale-eyed man looked briefly at each other and her mouth moved but it didn't bother Lloyd because he felt the storm very near. He knew she would come, and she did.

THROUGH THE BLASTS OF thunder and the rush of the rain, Darrell thought of Lloyd Coulter's smile, the quick hard smile the man had as he stood by his car and called for Anna. I have to go now, she'd said to Darrell. I'll be back. And he remembered the kiss she'd given him earlier, in his tent, and then he thought of Anna's smile, the wry smile that nevertheless held an unmistakable pride as he described a life of professional ambition. All the confusion of that moment threatened to rush through him again, but he was instantly aware that whatever life he could choose for himself began with the excavation outside. Thunder cracked over his head and he leaped up. He crossed to the mouth of his tent and he watched the rain, felt its odd impotence; for all its rush and cry, it seemed to Darrell that its force should be far greater. The rain beat at the tarp but the slick skin did not yield.

After the rain, the air lay heavily against Darrell's body, clogging his pores, sealing the desert heat inside him. The excavation resumed and the large man, the King's rival, slowly emerged. Near dusk, all that remained inside the earth was his head. Thomas and Betty were visibly weary. They moved slowly, their bodies sagged.

"Go on and wash up now," Darrell said to them.

"Shall we put the tarp on?" Thomas asked.

"I'll call you when I need help."

The two went off and Darrell wiped at his face, though the press of moisture remained, inside his skin. He felt weary, too, but he could squeeze more from this day and he thought of bringing the kerosene lamps out here so he could work on, after dark. He felt the fear coming—the fear of the scientists to the south, the fear of running out of time—and he cursed silently, cursed all these extraneous concerns. He just wanted to dig in the earth. These people lying around him here were the companions he sought. He raised his trowel. The fine, hard blade was black in the shadows.

The earth fell away under his hands; his hands grew bold and then gentle and then bold again as they drew back the covering of earth from this face. Quickly. He could sense the rhythm of the skull: where the dirt was packed into open space and he could rush on, where the earth met the surface of bone and he grew gentle. The skull was rising from its long sleep quickly and Darrell felt the grace of his own skill, the tender hands of a midwife, pulling this face into the world.

Then in a thrust above the cheek, the trowel struck hard and unexpectedly and Darrell drew back. He looked at the spot of earth that had resisted. It was several centimeters too far to the side to be bone, unless the man's skull were badly deformed. Only the jaw, nose, eyes were uncovered. Above the eyes the balk of earth rose up. There might be something on his head; a headdress of some sort, he thought. Or a deformity. The man was unusual in his size, perhaps he was deformed as well.

These speculations gabbled in Darrell's mind as his hands worked on, cautious now but efficient still, and then the speculation vanished in the first glimpse of metal. Darrell gasped aloud and he bent near to the gash of earth that showed thin-hammered iron. He touched it with the tip of his finger. Not an Indian after all. Not an Indian.

His hands rushed on, gouging and flaking and brushing and the earth fell away from a scythe-shaped brim, eartabs still clutched around the skull, and then the high, thin comb on the crown. It was a morion. A Spanish helmet worn by the conquistadors. Darrell kept his mind from moving until the helmet lay brushed clean in the dim light and then he rose and took in the vision and he stumbled back. Buried in the King's tomb was a Spanish soldier. Buried in a carefully selected position, his hands and feet bound, his helmet on his head but wearing no other armor, naked perhaps when he was buried, naked perhaps when he was killed. The King had met the Spaniards— at least one of them—he'd met the very aliens the rumor of whom he'd been fleeing, and he'd killed. He'd overcome the new weapons, the horse, the armor, the command of the stranger's alienness and he'd killed him. And then he'd given the Spaniard an appropriate place in the sacred enclosure. The killing had instantly been made part of the ritual.

Darrell wondered what the King's exact purpose had been in taking the Spaniard along to the afterlife. As a slave for the trip? As captive bounty to offer God? Or did he take him along to ask God to explain what this creature was? But the violence—the new violence of the Spaniards that had once frightened the King, that had brought him first into the Death Cult and then a thousand miles into exile—the violence had finally found him and he had prevailed. Darrell felt the King's triumph. Not only did the King kill this man, he'd made him part of his own world order.

Darrell felt a rush of vicarious triumph. "Yes," he said and his hands leaped up before him. "Yes," he said again and in his mind the King spread his cape before the sun, triumphant. But then Darrell realized he could not see the Spaniard's face. The dark had come and he knew his own body was too large, alien here too; in the dark, the King could not recognize him as a friend. This was a foolish thought, a function of the long, difficult day, his mind asserted. But the King's power frightened him and it was dark and he scrambled out of the pit, out of the sacred circle.

UP IN THE JEMEZ Mountains, beyond the Los Alamos laboratories, a few dozen acres of timber were burning. The wind blew down and carried a scent of the fire and Lloyd looked up at the flames. Oppie had set the date. Less than a week

154

away, just before dawn on July 16. Lloyd frowned at the irony. Here at Los Alamos there had been no rain for weeks and there was none in sight. The Rio Grande had dried to a trickle and the forests were beginning to burn. But in the desert there were storms and Oppie was driving himself and everyone around him crazy over the weather forecasts for this final week. Lloyd looked up into the cloudless, mocking sky. He would have spit if he felt anyone was up there. But nature was more stupid than God, he thought. He missed the face of God that he and his colleagues had erased, because he could curse a face.

Lloyd spat on the ground instead and stepped into the lab. Slotin was there, who would do the critical core assembly at the Trinity site. Two assistants were with him, hunched over a table, and one of the assistants was waving a slide rule, making a point. Lloyd thought for a moment that the thing he sought was probably before them on the table. But then he looked across the lab at a small wooden crate on a work bench against the far wall, and he approached it. Inside was the high explosive lens.

The box was padded and the lens sat tightly inside, carefully shaped metal, the size of a large melon. This was the inner lens. Its two hemispheres were fitted together but he knew inside were the triangular facets that would focus the explosion into the plutonium core. Lloyd's own work at the betatron had dictated the shapes of those facets. He reached out and lifted the lens from the box.

He held it in his hands and spread his fingers wide. The surface was smooth and cool and he closed his eyes and he sensed the containment of the sphere, felt how the most violent heart of the bomb would be held for a time in suspension by this sphere, held tightly and preserving the silence. Then he sensed the sequence: the sphere would collapse inward—Lloyd stretched his hands wider—and the mass inside would become critical and all that was potential in the very center of things would come to pass. Lloyd began to swoon. He opened his eyes, shook his head. The sphere glinted in the light from a window. Lloyd smelled the fire outside. He too felt contained.

A CAR ARRIVED SOON after the tarp was off the excavation. Thomas and Betty were digging the remainder of the square that held the Spanish soldier and Darrell noticed that their shoulders were touching as they worked side by side. They did not look up, even when a car door slammed. The door seemed to echo in the mountains and that struck Darrell as very odd. Then he realized it was not an echo and the sound came again, a cluster of the sounds. Gunfire. The man who had gotten out of the car—a soldier—had paused and was peering off to the east. Then he looked toward Darrell and approached.

It was not the captain. It was a heavy-jowled sergeant with a handgun strapped at his side. "Couldn't the captain make it this time?" Darrell said.

"He's busy," the sergeant said.

Darrell glanced toward the mountains. The gunfire had stopped.

"He sends his regards," the sergeant said, seemingly without irony.

"What do you want?"

"He says anything you're interested in preserving has to be out of here by sundown tomorrow. All non-essential personnel will be removed from the desert by then."

Darrell stiffened. The sergeant had tucked a thumb into his belt, his jaw moved as if he were trying to dislodge a piece of food caught in a tooth. Darrell looked over at the Spanish soldier—stripped and trussed and killed—and that consoled him. But his anger did not dissipate; it squeezed into his voice and he said, "Get out of here now, sergeant."

The man straightened in surprise and Darrell said, "Get out of here."

The sergeant spun on his heel and walked off. Darrell turned to find Betty and Thomas looking not at the soldier but at him; and yet the fear he might expect them to have for the outsider was still in their faces. Darrell sensed they were afraid of him, and this made him angry.

"Didn't you hear what we're up against?" Darrell said sharply. "Get to work."

The two assistants recoiled at his rebuke.

"Hurry now," Darrell said, even more sharply and he felt his breathing grow jagged and his arms grow restless. He turned to look again at the Spanish soldier. He wondered why looking at him had been a consolation a moment ago. Because the King had dealt with a soldier who had opposed him, Darrell decided. And when the crisis had come, the King had known how to make it all part of the natural order. Even as that thought shaped itself, Darrell shook it off. The natural order. Those were just words. He stepped to the soldier. Words. Theories. "No," he said aloud. There was something else here. Some pattern that he hadn't found. The King was wrong, after all. These flat stones had not contained the world. The real boundaries had been larger. Darrell was trembling now in anger. He wished he'd had the guts to leap from this pit and confront the sergeant. Force the man to stop hinting and act. Darrell's body trembled in its desire for a resolution. And then he realized what was coursing in him: the urge to violence. He'd been caught up by the undercurrent he'd felt in all of his visitors from the south. Not just the soldiers. Even the scientists. He saw Coulter's smile again as the man drew Anna away. Darrell felt a pulse of fear for her. Perhaps prompted by the thought of her, the threat against the excavation grabbed him and jerked him around. He looked at the King, the thousands of shell beads, the four other bodies, and he knew how their relationships were still shaping. There were two squares to go. Two whole squares and it was all in peril. Sundown tomorrow.

There was a crackle of gunfire. Closer than the mountains, this time. For a moment Darrell thought they were coming to force him out now. He looked around the excavation again, trying to be rational. Could he move the bones? He'd delayed so long already. How big could this next explosion be? He'd just cover it all up. He heard the beat of a horse's hooves.

Darrell turned and he saw, across the desert to the east, a horseman heading this way. Beyond him were four other horses, and much farther, though advancing rapidly, were the dust swirls of two vehicles. The lead horse grew larger. It held a dark figure and Darrell did not know yet to be afraid; the clutter of the feelings of a few moments ago was only beginning to clear. The horseman grew and he wore a wide-brimmed hat and his figure was small and broad-shouldered and Darrell recognized the rancher who had come briefly on the day they'd finished removing the mound.

Now the first flush of fear came and Darrell turned to his assistant and said "Thomas . . ." but before he could tell them to run, the horse pounded into their camp and pulled up, leather creaked and there were footsteps—all this, even as Darrell was turning back to face this threat, his body moving slowly, as if he bore a great weight.

The deep-cut eyes and potsherd mouth loomed over Darrell and the man held a rifle in his left hand and waved a pistol in his right and there was a belt of cartridges draped over his shoulder and he said, "You two come over here."

Darrell could not move his arms, his body was as sluggish as in a bad dream; Betty and Thomas came beside him and he saw the rancher look over his shoulder at his pursuers. A shot cracked from out there and a thin track of wind raced past and the rancher looked across to the tents briefly and then jumped down into the pit.

"Drop that thing," the man said, pointing his pistol at Darrell's hand.

Darrell looked and saw his trowel and the rancher said "Toss it" and Darrell tossed it away and the rancher said "Get down or I'll kill you right now" and Betty and Thomas dropped down and Darrell moved more slowly, his body was still very heavy. He saw the rancher turn and in a single, clean movement stick the pistol into his holster, shift the rifle and put it to his shoulder and aim. The pursuing horses were only a hundred yards off now. The rancher fired and the lead rider flew off his horse and fell to the ground and the other horses veered away. Darrell's body finally gained momentum and he hit the earth and drew his legs in and he pressed against a balk.

The rancher kneeled and used the pit as a fox hole, propping his rifle on the upper surface of the ground and squeezing off more shots. Then he laughed a sudden, short laugh, like a spit of tobacco. He seemed to aim the rifle but he did not fire.

Darrell's legs ached and his thoughts had begun to gather speed. He shifted his body slightly and stretched his legs out to ease the pain. Without turning, the rancher said, "Don't try it. You'll be a dead man before you could move an inch."

"No one's trying anything," Darrell said.

Betty had begun to weep and Thomas hunched over her, holding her.

"Stop that woman," the rancher said.

Thomas shot a look over his shoulder at the stocky man and it surprised Darrell. He read an anger in Thomas's face that he had never seen before, had never even imagined was in him, and he wondered if Thomas would do something foolish.

Then, as if he felt the challenge, the rancher's head slowly turned, those deep, dark eyes came to bear on Thomas and the young man began to shush Betty, to beg her in a frantic, quavering voice to be quiet and Darrell looked away before he saw the tears that he knew were coming to Thomas as well.

"You people have already paid the price of four dead. Probably five," the rancher said.

"We're not part of them," Darrell said and he was surprised, when he heard his own voice, to find a calmness in himself. "I told you that already, the other time you came here."

"That's fine with me," the man said. "If you're not part of them maybe they'd be less willing to give up your lives to get at me."

"We're to be hostages, are we?"

"Don't like how you talk. You do talk like them out there."

Betty's weeping surged and Darrell watched the man's eyes

move slowly to her. The slowness of these eyes initiated a deep current of fear in Darrell. He sucked in air deeply and Betty was babbling in her tears and Darrell said, "Why don't you let her go. Keep the two of us." Darrell heard the tremor in his own voice and he felt ashamed. The man was not responding and Darrell said, "She's just going to be a pain in your neck."

As soon as the words were out, Darrell regretted them. If he convinced this man who'd already killed at least four times that Betty was a liability, he might accept the premise but carry out his own solution by killing her.

Darrell focused his attention on the man's right hand. It held the stock grip of the rifle and his forefinger was extended to the trigger. The hand was very still. Very still and Darrell waited; he tried to think of words to divert the man's mind from the idea that Darrell feared was shaping there, but no words came and the time stretched on and Betty whimpered desperately.

The rancher's hand moved and Darrell flinched but the man simply shifted his weight and looked out into the desert. "In a minute," he said. "Your people ain't in place quite yet."

For the first time since this had all begun, Darrell felt that he knew what the next few moments would bring. He shifted his legs and took a deep breath and there was a brief but unmistakable feeling of luxuriousness in him. How utterly and instantly relative are human pains and pleasures, Darrell thought, even as that sense of ease fled away.

"Do you really think it's fair for a man to be put off his land?" the rancher said.

"Of course not," Darrell said and now another pleasure coursed in him—a sense of his own logic, his own mental life as a scientist, a sense that this man, in his appeal to some standard of fairness, was at least a man, a reasoning animal. Darrell would reason him out of this rage. First, he would put himself on a common ground with the man. He said, "They're putting me off my land, too."

The rancher's eyes narrowed. "You try anything with me and I'll blow your fucking head off," he said.

Darrell felt himself gape and the rancher turned his attention back to the desert. Darrell nearly laughed. He nearly laughed out loud but he clenched his mouth shut and caught the sound in his chest and inside he laughed wildly at himself, at his own pretentions.

A voice came from the desert, hollow, amplified. "Klamper. You're surrounded, Klamper."

"If you sons-of-bitches come any closer on any side, I'm gonna kill the girl in here."

Betty began to sob and the voice in the desert did not answer. The rancher turned sharply on Thomas and Betty and he said, "If you don't keep her quiet, I'll kill her now."

Darrell felt a voiding in his limbs and his strength vanished and his head rang with a sound like a ricochet. He knew Betty would die. With an instinct as sure as the feel of bones in earth beneath his feet, he knew the man was going to kill her.

"Klamper," said the voice from the desert. Darrell recognized it this time as the voice of the security captain. "You can't win this thing."

The rancher shouted, "You sons-of-bitches took away my land. That land was my daddy's and his daddy's before him and you had no right. I didn't want to sell to you. I wanted to stay." The rancher's voice throbbed with passion now. "That land was mine. My daddy's buried there, you sons-of-bitches, and I don't care how many of you I kill, you're not gonna take it without a fight."

Darrell could not lift his arms. He heard the rancher talk of a father, of a burial, and the man finally became more than an animated clay effigy. Darrell sensed a heart in this man, just as a moment earlier he'd sensed a mind. But even as he did, he felt a thickening in the air, something rubbed up against him, something invisible, something slobbering in Darrell's face, making his listless limbs turn cold in spite of the mid-morning heat. The rancher had brought something with him.

Rage, Darrell thought. No. This was more self-contained than that. This was something larger.

The rancher had lowered his head and faced around. He was loading his rifle. It was a military rifle, Darrell saw. Taken off a dead man, he knew. But he remembered the throb in the rancher's voice, his concern for his father's grave.

"I understand your concern," Darrell said and the slow eyes turned on him. The eyes made Darrell stammer for a moment, but he said, "I, too, respect graves." And with a great effort he lifted an arm and vaguely gestured into the excavation.

The rancher looked out to where Darrell gestured and he raised his rifle and even as he fired, Darrell's head was turning and the sound jerked his head faster and he saw the skull of the King's third young woman explode, the bones splintering and flying, the jawbone rising high and tumbling and disappearing. A plume of dust dissipated in the air and Darrell's body emptied totally, he was scooped hollow and the voice from the desert called out, "Klamper. Don't do anything foolish."

Darrell's head turned, and into the vacuum of his body, the pit's thick, animated air flowed quickly. Darrell felt his arms grow strong, even as he sensed the movement of his own eyes, his own slow eyes.

The rancher had turned his back to deal with the men in the desert. "I know what I'm doing," he yelled. "Your girl here is still alive. But all three of these . . ." And though the rancher spoke on, Darrrell stopped listening. The voice was brittle and had a metallic twang to it and Darrell knew that listening to it would rush the feeling that had filled him, rush it too fast.

Darrell blocked off the voice and turned his eyes slowly into the pit, past the huddled assistants—Betty's weeping, Thomas's weeping—Darrell felt a flicker of contempt for their weakness and then the feeling passed as his eyes moved on. He saw his trowel lying on the floor of the pit. He looked back to the rancher who was craning his neck, and the voice in the desert was speaking. The rancher's rifle rose, the man was concentrating on his targets out there, and Darrell lifted up and moved quickly to the trowel.

He grasped the trowel and turned smoothly and his body was lithe and full of life and now the earlier impression vanished. This vigor was not from the air; it was his own. It had not come from outside, it burned within him, on the surface of his skin, in the muscles of his arms and legs, in the center of his chest, in the marrow of his bones. This sudden power was his own and nothing could stop the fulfillment of this and he was moving swiftly across the space to the rancher who heard something and began to turn but too slowly. Darrell had great power now and he drove the trowel into the man's lower back, just above the ilium, and it went in deep.

The sound from the rancher was like popping cartilage but it came from his throat and that made Darrell's breath stop, and he pulled back. The man's arms were swinging around, the rifle was coming around and Darrell let go of the trowel and stopped the rifle with one hand and pushed the man's face with the other and then the rifle fell and a grip came onto Darrell's throat. Hands, thick and hard, and Darrell's breath stopped altogether and his own hands knew where to go, his own hands grabbed the rancher's throat and squeezed hard and the man smelled of horses and sweat, he twisted around and fell back. From the sudden bulge that Darrell felt in the throat under his hands and from the release on his own throat, he knew the man had fallen on the trowel.

The body beneath Darrell jerked and a tremor went through it and then it lay still.

Darrell felt his own strength ebbing and he fought to keep it for a moment more. The trowel. The trowel. He pushed at the body, pushed hard at its bulk and rolled it onto its face. He grasped his trowel and pulled but it would not yield, his strength was waning. He bent and held the trowel with both hands and he heard himself whining now but he held the trowel tightly and put his foot on the man's back, the blood-slick back, and he pulled hard and the trowel came out and when he felt the fluid coming off the blade and onto his hands he sank down onto the ground and he had no strength and then he had no thoughts and then he had no sight and he fell beside the man he'd killed.

WHEN DARRELL WOKE, HE was lying on his back at the bottom of the pit and the security captain's face filled the sky above him.

"You were out for quite awhile," the captain said and even though Darrell's head swirled with a fine, dark mist, he recognized a change in this man, a solicitude, a gentle edge to his voice.

Darrell tried to sit up but he moved too quickly and the dark swirl thickened and the captain said, "Not too fast," and a hand went to Darrell's back to steady him.

Darrell sensed bustle in the excavation. He carefully turned his head and there were people moving around in the pit. "Don't touch anything," he said. His voice was small.

"I gave them strict orders. They won't move a single bone."

This concern for the bones linked to the shattered skull, the gunfire, and in his mind he was rushing across the space to the rancher again and Darrell remembered now that he had killed. His body convulsed and he cried out.

"It's okay," the captain said, low, gentle, his hands guiding Darrell back down into a reclining position. "It's all over," he said. "You did an outstanding job."

"Is he dead?" Even as he asked the question, Darrell knew the sham of this little mental trick—these were the last few seconds in which he would be able to suspend the full realization of what he'd done.

The captain smiled at him and placed his hand on his shoulder. "Thoroughly."

Darrell closed his eyes briefly, forced himself into stillness.

"I have to give you credit, Dr. Reeves," the captain said. "You're a man of real guts."

164

Darrell remembered his own hands, the draining of the blade. He became aware of his hands; they were dry now but he knew what stain was still there; he remembered the flow from the blade and this time the sensation had the opposite effect: his head cleared. He opened his eyes. He felt a frantic scrambling in his chest as he tried to sort out the events some other way, but he knew at once it was futile. He'd killed this man. Darrell sat up, though he kept his hands low. His senses were acute. The voices of men lurched behind him; he heard Betty's crying begin to snub to a stop; he felt the desert sun stretching his skin; he heard the whisk of a sand devil nearby.

The hands called him and he slowly raised them and they were clean. He felt his body stop, his eyes widen, and the captain's quiet voice said, "When the first one's messy, it's sometimes hard. I washed your hands."

Darrell turned to the captain. The man's eyes were gray and small and steady. Eyes were more mysterious to Darrell than bone in their expressiveness but he knew that this steady gaze was full of respect and warmth and the paternal concern of an officer for his favorite enlisted man.

"I misjudged you," the captain said. "As a man. My men and I owe you sincere thanks. And I owe you a personal apology."

Darrell felt a strong, tidal pull. This man respected what he'd done. This man honored him for it. This gentle-speaking, sensitive man who'd washed Darrell's unconscious hands. But as soon as Darrell lifted in this direction, the rancher twisted inside his head and the brittle, cracking sound came from his throat and Darrell felt a trembling begin in his chest.

"Please," Darrell said. "I need to be alone now."

"Of course," the captain said. He looked over his shoulder. "We're almost done here."

Darrell began to stumble to his feet and again the captain's hands were helping him, holding him up. He pulled away from the man's help, saying, "I'm all right now."

"Thanks again, Dr. Reeves," the captain said and his arm

swept toward all the strangers in uniforms moving around in the pit. "Some of my men here undoubtedly owe you their lives."

Darrell felt sluggish. His mind brushed away the words because he knew that these men had had no part whatsoever in his act. He climbed out of the pit and crossed to his tent and as he moved he wondered where they would bury the rancher. Not on his land, he knew. Not near his father. Darrell entered his tent and sat down on the rattan chair and he was suddenly very weary.

Not for those men out there. His mind was feeling its way along now. If he did not go forward, there was only the memory on his hands; there were only the rancher's throes, ceasing. Not for those men did he kill. He did not kill to save anyone's life. Not even Betty's. Not when he'd felt that Betty would die: not then did he rise up to kill. When? His hands lifted and fell back onto the arms of the chair. The rifle had barked and it was the bones. Darrell leaped up at this. A skull was shattered out there. The bones were splintered in the pit. The jaw lay somewhere—displaced. And Darrell stopped himself. Even now he was driven by the bones. It was the bones. He'd killed for bones.

No, his mind answered. These were people, Indians, out there in the pit, lying and waiting for his understanding. It was Darrell himself who'd exposed them to these dangers. The King needed protection. But then Darrell thought of the King's own killing. He'd had the Spanish soldier killed. He'd had the three women killed. The women had understood, his mind replied. And the soldier had been a threat. A threat. The rancher had been a threat. It had been the only thing to do, to kill. The captain was proud of Darrell. It was logical even, to kill in those circumstances. But logic had not driven Darrell. The threat: not even the threat had driven him. The threat had been there from the first moment the rancher had come. But Darrell had waited. Something had been shaping in him—like a child growing in a womb, quickly, a full gestation in a matter of minutes, and it had been born and had fitted its limbs into Darrell's and had carried him swiftly and with power. It had been someone else, Darrell cried. Someone inside his skin, his bones. It had been born and it had acted and it had died. But none of this made sense. It had been Darrell. It had been Darrell, who had no feelings for the Jews or his brother or the war out there or for Betty or the captain's men or the rancher and his father's bones, defiled by these soldiers, defiled by the same men who would defile the King's grave, defiled by that thick-armed man who had Anna in his power. And at this thought, Darrell grew angry. It rushed on him and made his arms flex with great power and Darrell knew that he had killed a man and he cried out aloud, a wordless noise.

He felt faint again, and he turned back to his chair. He sat down in time to hold back the creeping darkness in his eyes and he propped his head on his hand and for a time he could not think, his anguish grew dull and his feelings had again become instantly relative, for this state seemed a relief. He realized only after Thomas had called his name with loud insistence that he'd been less than fully conscious for a long while.

Darrell looked up at Thomas who stood before him. Thomas said, "I'm sorry to intrude." The young man's voice was hoarse.

"It's all right."

"The others left."

"Yes."

"Some time ago."

"What time is it now?" Darrell asked.

"Past noon."

Darrell nodded and he expected Thomas to go away, as if the reason he'd come in was to tell him the time.

Thomas said, "The captain left a man and a vehicle behind if we needed anything."

"Yes?"

"Betty's still . . . in a state."

"Go on now," Darrell said. The impulse had come unexpectedly but it began to elaborate itself in his mind and he
knew it was the best thing.

Thomas stood waiting. "Go on," Darrell said. "I've no
need for you now."

"Do you mean . . .?"

"You've done your duty for me. You and Betty pack your
things and go on." Darrell paused to rest his mind. He wondered at its being only noon. "It feels like noon *tomorrow*,"
he said and this clearly confused Thomas, who had made no
move to leave as he'd been told.

Darrell said, "I'll send your records up to the dean. I don't
need your help any longer." He began to understand more
clearly what he must do. He wanted to be utterly alone now
with the excavation. His priorities had been made clear to him
in the moment he'd picked up his trowel and turned to kill the
rancher. He wanted to be alone now with these bones, just as
his King had to face the sun alone, had to open his cape and
give himself to worship.

Thomas said, "Do you mean . . .?"

"You know what I mean, Thomas. You and Betty get your
things and go away. I thank you both for your help but this is
all done now."

After a wide-eyed pause, Thomas said, "Well . . . yessir.
Of course. I've appreciated . . ."

"Go on, Thomas," Darrell said firmly but gently. "Please
. . . You'll forgive me if I don't rise."

"Yessir, I . . ."

"Go."

Thomas nodded and turned and disappeared into the glare
from the tent flap.

Darrell closed his eyes against the sun and he sat very still
for a long time. He oscillated faintly between two feelings he
did not shape into words, even in his mind: grief that he was

168

the man he'd feared and relief that the grief itself made him feel a little more rational.

DARRELL DID NOT KNOW how much time had passed, though he had remained alert as he sat in his chair, and the killing settled into him, filled crevices in his limbs, in his throat, in his mind. Then he was left with the proof of his commitment to the bones outside. He knew that commitment had become exclusively personal now. The university, the discipline of archaeology, the perspectives of history, all the institutions, had vanished. The killing had rent the veil in the temple of his King; Darrell had been converted, as if from High Church ritual to Pentacostal personalism.

When he heard Anna's voice outside, he rose. "I'm in here," he said.

She appeared at the mouth of the tent in her Army uniform, her face tight with concern. He knew he could open his arms and her concern for him would bring her to his embrace. But even as the momentum of his desire for Anna gave him this certainty, he could not make himself raise his arms. He saw in her face that she might come to him and embrace him on her own and he sat down on the chair to preclude it. He didn't want to touch her with the hands that had killed. He could not glibly lay these two feelings against each other. And he feared that he'd already chosen a jealous god for his worship, an exclusive god that lay outside the tent and waited for his undivided attention, that offered in return to put this act of his within its sacred circle and give it its place in the order of things. The King understood why Darrell had killed. These thoughts pawed at him and he realized that Anna had drawn near him now.

"Are you all right?" she said.

"Yes."

She squatted before him to look into his lowered face. "What is it? Are you sure you're all right?"

He knew he had to act as he always had in order to have

169

her leave. "I'm sorry," he said and his voice sounded rational, calm, friendly. "I was just a little dizzy for a moment."

"You weren't hurt?"

"Not at all."

"As soon as I heard . . ." She broke off. She rose and went to the other chair and dragged it over to him and sat.

"I'm really all right, Anna," he said. "I just need some rest." He found that he was straining now to keep his distance from her. He looked into her solicitous eyes and he suddenly yearned to talk to her about what he'd done. But speaking the words would be like putting his hands on her. He felt he would soil her. He knew he had no way with women. And then he sensed a strain of self-pity in all this and he shook his head sharply to clear it away.

"What is it?" she said.

He thought, Killing a man has brought out the lesser sins in me as well—self-pity, callousness, passivity, irrationality. But he said, "Nothing."

Anna's eyes filled with tears. "You don't have to talk to me," she said. "But I've been very worried."

"I killed a man," he said and his voice quaked. He felt good declaring this to her, though he desperately desired not to break down before her.

"I know."

"I was thinking not long ago that the King was wrong."

"The King?"

Darrell looked toward the excavation and Anna said, "Oh yes. Him. I know."

Darrell said, "He thought that he knew what the boundary of the world was." He paused and Anna said nothing. She waited, her eyes staying unflinchingly on his. He knew she would wait just like this for as long as he wanted her to. He appreciated this and tried to get control of his voice. "Of course the boundary should have gone as far as Spain, at least. But we know even that was not far enough. There were lands the King had never even dreamed of."

Anna's head had cocked slightly and he felt her unspoken

challenge to come to a relevant point. He remembered her
challenge on Pompeii and he smiled. He wished he could touch
her but as soon as he thought to, the feeling of its being wrong
rushed back into him. This time it came bellowing, letting no
other thoughts be heard. He felt he would never be able to
touch her again. He felt the delicacy of her bones—as if she
were a caged finch that he could not hold in his hands without
killing—he felt he would inevitably hurt her and his mind lost
its focus, even as she charmed him with her unspoken demand,
even as he realized that these abstract, pedantic words were
the only way he could touch her now, even as he ached to do
at least that, at least talk to her. He squeezed hard at his mind.
"But I'm not really talking about the geographical boundaries,"
he said.

Her head straightened and she waited.

He said, "I had been too quick to pass over the killing of
the man out there. Even when I thought he was a rival of the
King. Then when the man turned out to be a Spanish soldier,
I thought . . . I felt . . ." Darrell had talked his way back to
a feeling that bothered him. He'd felt the King's victory as his
own. "It was clear that the King had known how to understand
what he had to do. He'd killed the man and buried him in such
a careful way . . ." Darrell's voice trailed off and he looked
out of the tent. The sunlight was still bright. The ground was
gouged open but he could not see in, from where he sat.

"What did you expect of him?" Anna said.

Darrell looked at her but could not speak.

"Your King," she said.

He still did not speak.

"Did you think he'd be above killing?"

She waited for him to reply, but only briefly. "He was just
a man," she said. "I think those three young women finally
saw him as he was. He was frail. A man, not a Sun King. He
wore shells on his back and commanded the lives of his tribe,
but the women saw that he was frail and they even saw that
he was frightened and they went with him."

Darrell looked outside again. The bones. Anna was talking

about the bones and he wished she would stop. And even as he thought this, she did. She said, "What are you going to do now?"

"Now?"

"The test is in just a couple of days."

"I let Thomas and Betty go," he said.

"You're alone here?"

"Yes."

There was a silence and his eyes stayed fixed on the sunlight outside, the void of earth. The King had known what Darrell felt, had done what Darrell had done. But the King knew where it all fit.

"Are you going to move the bones now?" Anna asked.

Darrell turned his face to her and he knew he must be very careful how he answered. No, he thought. It wasn't necessary to move the bones. How much bigger could this test possibly be? All the dire hints were foolishness. The Army had left the wooden planking behind, out near the equipment tent. He would dig here by himself for as long as he could and then he'd go into the pit and cover up the bones and himself and he'd just wait out the blast and then go on working. He had nothing else now. He had chosen earlier today. He'd killed for these bones and he could not move them now. But Anna would worry about him and he said, "I'll move them tonight."

"Find me, after the test. Please," she said.

"Yes."

"Or I'll find you. All right?"

"Yes. Of course." Tears bloomed just behind Darrell's eyes and he fought at them. He could not touch Anna. He could not.

LLOYD AND HALF A dozen other scientists stood around the perimeter of a table. Before them was a survey map of the hundred-mile square surrounding the test site. A scientist named Koonz held a large silver compass. He put one point on the desert, on the spot where the shot tower stood, and he paused.

Lloyd said, "Well, gentlemen, I want four justifiable scenarios, each at a different plateau of preparation. How far do we open the compass?"

There was silence for a moment. Lloyd waited. He would let the voices commit themselves before he spoke again.

"Are you in the pool?" someone said.

"What pool?" another said.

"The one-dollar pool on the bomb's yield."

"No."

"I'm in," said another voice.

"I didn't get in. Who's doing it?"

"See Oppie."

"I've got fifteen thousand tons of TNT," Koonz said.

"I've got ten thousand."

"A lot of the guesses have been running low."

"That's just a psychological hedge."

"Superstition."

"Fifteen thousand's okay."

"Where would that put us?" Koonz said, nodding at the compass.

"Within the ten thousand yard range."

"Fifteen thousand tons won't fry us in the bunkers."

"Teller bet forty-five thousand tons."

The voices fell silent. Lloyd knew why. Edward Teller had been in charge of considering the potential exotic effects of the bomb.

"At least he's not betting the bomb will incinerate the atmosphere," one of the voices said.

"Fermi bet that."

"What?"

"I heard Fermi bet that the state of New Mexico would disappear."

"How would he collect?"

The voices laughed.

Koonz opened the compass and put the second leg down.

"Forty-five thousand would give us real problems at our observation site."

"We'd never know what hit us," said a voice.

"Yes we would," said another. "The killing blast effects would fall short of our bunkers at forty-five thousand tons but our bone marrow would be garbage inside a month."

"Carrizozo would get a bad dose too."

"Carrizozo would undoubtedly get a big dose."

Koonz swung the compass leg over to the northeast. Out beyond it, beyond the Oscura Mountains was the little town of Carrizozo.

"It wouldn't need forty-five thousand. If the winds do to the big test what they did at the TNT test, the fallout would take Carrizozo easily."

"And if the fireball gets up over twenty thousand feet, that kind of wind would give Albuquerque or Amarillo real problems too."

"Their bones might take a year or two."

"Sooner probably."

"At twenty thousand feet?"

"Sure."

"How big a blast?"

"Oh, even your fifteen thousand."

"Glad we'll be downwind."

"Winds shift."

"Look out Tijuana."

The voices laughed.

'It'd cure more than it'd kill down there."

The voices laughed again.

"There's just so many variables for these scenarios."

"Can we keep a constant? Like wind?" The question came to Lloyd.

"Yes," Lloyd said.

"If the winds shift, we're not going to be around to answer for our mistake anyway," Koonz said, without humor. He was tracing a slow arc with the compass. The other voices tittered. Lloyd thought they were all damn fools.

"All right," a voice said. "I'd say with forty-five thousand we have to be prepared to evacuate Carrizozo and put every-body else on alert—out to and including Albuquerque and Amarillo.''

"Carrizozo would never have a chance.''

"Just for show then.''

"Okay,'' said Koonz. "That's one plateau.''

"Seventy-five thousand tons . . .'' The voice paused.

"It's all the same.''

"At that point just pack it in. It's out of our hands.''

"Evacuate the state.''

"Sure. And half of Texas.''

"I heard Fermi was giving odds on the chain reaction carrying into the atmosphere and the whole planet going up in flames.''

There was a brief pause.

"Wonder what the odds were.''

"I didn't hear.''

"Oppie bet Kistiakowsky ten bucks that the bomb would fizzle.''

Lloyd's fist slammed onto the table and the six men leaped and cried out. In the silence that followed, Lloyd said, "Then Oppenheimer is a damn fool.''

DARRELL MOVED TO THE opening of his tent and looked out. He was alone now. He could see the tableau of the excavation site. He took it in as a whole, without letting himself focus on any object, especially avoiding the third woman, even though he knew he'd have to face her soon.

The yellow light had grown pale and then in a stroke it turned gray. Clouds were coming in. There were still a few hours to work, but Darrell knew it might rain. Alone, he had to anticipate the rain by a wider margin. Handling the tarp would be awkward for him.

He had the sudden urge to dig. A strong urge. He always had some measure of this feeling but this was very strong.

Then he thought of his trowel and his breath caught. From where he stood, he could not see the floor of the pit, only the bodies and objects raised up on their pedestals. But he knew his trowel was somewhere inside there. The captain surely had not thought to wash the blade of his trowel as well.

Darrell nearly retreated into his tent to wait some more. But this problem would not yield to the passage of a little more time. He thought of waiting for the rain, but he didn't want the rain to touch the bones, and the digging would be slowed down after that. Though I've got plenty of time now, he thought.

Darrell could not leave the King exposed to a storm and he went outside. He moved to the edge of the pit and stepped in. He was on the opposite side from where the killing took place. The three women lay nearby. He was careful where he looked but he examined the safe areas to see if all the strangers had caused any damage or displacement. It seemed that the captain's men had been very disciplined—there was no trace of anyone having been there.

Then he let his eyes slowly move down the file of three pedestals and he saw the shards of bone scattered on the floor of the pit at the far end. The jawbone lay angled against a balk. He approached and he was conscious of the first woman and the second, their identical poses, their wide eyes, as he passed them. Then he saw the third woman and her head was gone—he knew it would be gone but it staggered him. He stopped and he was aware of his grief for her, aware that this grief had, for the moment, squeezed his guilt over the killing almost entirely out of him, and then his mind urged a guilt on him over that. And his feelings picked up this guilt, but gingerly, as he might handle the shattered jaw at his feet. He felt a delicate, rational guilt over the priorities of his life. And yet the wreckage of the third woman's skull made it possible at last to move around the pedestal and along the wall of the pit to the place where he'd killed the rancher.

The trowel was there, lying alone next to the now empty

space where the man had fallen. Darrell came to the trowel and he glanced at the blade and it was stained dark red and the stain had texture and he jerked his face up. He focused for a moment on the distant mountains. Then he bent and, without looking directly at the tool, he picked it up. He had to wash the blade clean. But not in water. He knew what to do to remove the stain. He would wash it in the earth. He would dig.

Darrell looked around. The square that held the Spanish soldier was nearly done. There would be nothing in the remaining fringe, he thought. The next square lay directly above the King. It was hard to say what was in there. He knew that he could dig for a long time without touching any bones or artifacts. That would be all right, once the quaking in him was entirely gone, once the lick of flame came and went and the physicists cleared out. But right now he wanted something certain. This need fit into a vague restlessness he'd had for a long time over the slow progress of the sacred circle. Now of all times he wanted to complete the circle. He wanted to be bound in, held tight; maybe the King was right after all about the boundary of the world. The real boundary. The boundary he'd made for himself. Neither the King nor Darrell now acknowledged anything else.

He climbed out of the pit and walked on the desert surface in the area of the upper left square. The evenly placed stones of the circle approached this square and disappeared into the earth and Darrell knew exactly where to dig. The trowel nagged at him and he held it far away from his body. He turned and looked at the sky. The clouds were still high and distant, though the sun had disappeared. He had time before the rain.

He knelt and plunged the trowel into the earth. There was a stone here, he knew, and his hands dug hard, making the trowel do the work that a shovel should. He felt the earth gripping and scraping the blade. When he reached the stone, he sat back and held the trowel before him and glanced tentatively at the blade—the first look since he picked it up—and then he fixed his eyes on it and it was clean. The blood was gone.

A vigor scrambled into Darrell. He jerked around and looked at the sky. The clouds had not moved. There would be no rain, he felt. He had another two hours of light. He had good lamps, gallons of kerosene. He felt strong. He would dig late into the night, as long as he had strength to move this blade.

He exposed the stone but left it at the bottom of its hole and he looked at the arc, judged the distance instantly, and went to the next spot. He wanted to uncover the rest of the circle before anything else. For the present it would be enough just to expose the stones to the air; but he wanted the circle complete.

He felt something akin to joy now. He felt strong. He was alone in the world with these Indians. No one else existed. This was the boundary, this circle of stones.

He went and got the short-handled shovel and he returned to the place of the next stone and he began to dig. Darrell savored the chuff of metal into the earth, the strain and heft and release as he lifted each shovel-full of earth away from the stone.

As he drew near, he slowed and switched to his trowel. His trowel had returned to him. His regard for this fine, supple instrument was even greater now, like the father's feeling at the return of the prodigal son. The blade dipped and parted the earth and then Darrell caught sight of bone and he gasped.

This was the very level of the sacred stone. The light was growing dim and Darrell bent near; he moved his face down to the earth to see if the sudden vision had been a trick of the light or a residue of the day's stress, a desert mirage. But it was bone. Unquestionably.

This was beyond speculation and his hands trembled into life and began to clear the dirt away. A rib. He looked over his shoulder at the sky. There'd be no rain but the light was growing very dim. He'd get the lamps soon. His body was clammy with sweat and his knees ached and this new body frightened him. He knew he should be exhilarated, but he was not. His hands felt frantic. He was driven to pull this next secret from the earth but he had no delight in the discovery. He heard a heavy scuffling at the edge of his mind, as if someone were dragging a body toward him. He wiped hard at his face and now he feared madness.

He rose up and went into the equipment tent and he carried two lamps out to the excavation. Then he went back in and carried out another two lamps. He brought two more and then he arranged the six lamps around the place where he was digging. But he did not light them. He paused and wiped away the sweat from his face. He took a deep breath and another and another, until he felt rational again. There was still a little natural light. He would conserve kerosene. He bent slowly down to the earth and began to dig.

He made a mistake. He turned earth quickly and there was a flash—something displaced—and he cursed himself, even before looking closely to see what it had been. He reached in—it had already been moved anyway—and his hand came out of the hole with the sharp-edged object. He knew what it was at first touch, even before seeing it. In his palm was a side-notched arrowhead.

He stared at the object for a moment without regard to its context. The notches were deep, to take a tight wrapping. The triangular tip was evenly flaked. Then Darrell realized where this stone point had been. Inside the rib cage of this body. This man had died—he assumed it was a man, as the target of an arrow—this man had died from this ounce of stone in Darrell's palm. Darrell's hand jerked out away from his body and dropped the arrowhead on the ground. He wiped his palm hard against his shirt even as he fought back this irrational surge. He fixed his mind on the archaeological facts. The man must have been a contemporary of the King. This could not have been a later, intrusive burial because the spot had been covered by the burial mound. But the sacred circle had been broken. The stone was not here, the stone that had to be here to preserve the circle; and the orientation of this man's rib cage would even put his body half inside, half outside the circle.

Darrell's hands felt the same urge to recoil that they had a moment ago. He could not let himself become frantic again. He clenched his hands and looked around and found a measured task for them. The day was almost gone and he began to light the kerosene lamps. He thought he heard a slithering near him but he kept working at the lamps. Any snakes would fear the light. His hands grew very efficient and he lit the six lamps in a circle around him. His own boundary. Inside his world now were only himself and the mystery of this man.

Darrell's hands were steady. The lamps bound him in and he felt very calm. He reached into the hole and began to carefully move dollops of earth. Soon he found another arrowhead, also inside the rib cage. The man had been hit twice, Darrell thought. Then he found a third arrowhead and then another and another. His hands began to move more rapidly but he kept his mind slow. The man's side had been shot full of arrows. Darrell continued to dig and there were more. And with each new sharp flake of stone his hands went faster, his body grew colder. He reached the top of the pelvis and there he found an arrowhead driven deep into the bone itself. He stopped.

He was trembling. From this chill that had come upon him. But from something else as well. The body beneath him spoke of rage, of a wild, passionate act of killing. And the passion went on even as the dead man was thrust into the earth—someone had broken the sacred circle in burying the body. But then the mound had been built over it. As if nothing unusual had happened. As if the circle were still intact and the mound marked a burial just like the ones these Indians had always done. Darrell could not understand. And he knew there would be nothing in the physical evidence that would give an answer. The six flames around him wavered like water. The maw of the night—impenetrably black now—lay beyond. He still trembled before this body full of arrowheads, but his circle of lamps bound in the dead man completely and Darrell didn't want to move into that emptiness beyond; and so he continued to dig. The pelvis began to emerge under his hands. He felt his nerves stretching very thin inside him; his hands pushing at the earth were as sensitive now as a bad tooth. The light rippled against the bones. The desert was silent. He could hear his own breath. Fragile. The earth was falling away from the pelvis and he had the feeling again, the sense of something in the air around him, something rubbing up against him, and then the sciatic notch was free and it gaped wide and Darrell leaped up, stumbled back. He knocked over a lamp and the smell of kerosene filled his lungs and he turned and ran away from the hole. The sciatic notch was wide. He ran into the dark a hundred yards and stopped, panting. This act of ancient rage had been worse than he'd thought. The victim had been a woman.

OUT AT THE RANCH house with the fieldstone fence, the assembly began of the active material. Lloyd stood as near as he could, but Slotin wanted distance and quiet. Lloyd was about ten feet away and to the side and he ached to get nearer. But if Slotin, of all people, wanted this buffer of space, then it must be necessary. Slotin who had nerves that Lloyd admired. Perhaps the only people with the right nerves in the whole community were in this room now, Lloyd thought. Only Slotin and Lloyd and half a dozen others. Oppie had been in briefly, but he'd gone out.

Slotin sat at a table cluttered with radiation counters except for a cleared space before him. In the space the two hemispheres of plutonium were attached to a rod. They were perhaps a yard apart, facing each other. With a screwdriver, Slotin began to slowly push the hemispheres together. The counters crackled faster and the needles quivered.

Slotin pushed first the hemisphere on his right a few centimeters, then the hemisphere on his left. Then he stopped and watched the dials. The sound of the counters filled the room. The chattering made Lloyd feel itchy. He concentrated on the

181

hemispheres. He imagined them touching. He imagined their pregnant completion, the roundness that would hold within it all the secrets that would soon be revealed.

One of the others in the room sidled near to Lloyd. The man—a young physicist whose name Lloyd could never remember—was sweating. Lloyd edged further away. He wanted to wave his arm and clear the room of everything but Slotin, the hemispheres, and himself.

The assembly process went on for a long while until the counter chatter was frantic. The hemispheres were only six inches apart now and Lloyd wondered how it would be if these two hands of plutonium were to clap suddenly together. A moment of blue light, Slotin would laugh, Lloyd would rush forward to put his own hands on the hemispheres, to hold them tightly together, to pour his own pitiful molecules into the process. He would hold the sphere together and wait, heavy steps on a stairway, familiar steps and Lloyd would rise to them and then all would suddenly be vapor. But there'd be no time for any of this. Not even the sound of the clap of the hemispheres would have time to cross the room.

Slotin leaned back and he made a noise like laughter. The sphere was nearly complete. Lloyd quivered like the counter needles, the chittering in the room was his own nerve ends laughing just like Slotin; Lloyd was conscious of his very bones.

Then Slotin leaned forward and he pushed the left hemisphere and the right hemisphere and then the left again and the assembly was done. The other voices in the room cheered. But Lloyd made no sound.

THE MORNING CAME AND Darrell awoke. He lay on his back on his cot. His arms were at his side; his legs were together; he lay as still as the King. Darrell's bones were fleshed only with air, his ribs clasped empty space, he was transparent except for his bones, he felt his father enter the tent and the man's eyes moved to the cot—slowly; slow eyes—and they saw only the son's bones.

Darrell sat up and shook off the clinging layer of dream like the dry, gray soil outside. He rose and dressed slowly and he thought of the woman full of arrows. He had come back last night and covered the excavation with the tarpaulin and now he had to decide what to do. The scientists would be evicting him today. He would do what he needed to do to keep the excavation intact. No other option entered his mind. He thought of Anna and stopped. His body stopped and he stood very still in the center of the tent and he yearned for her, for some way to touch her, but he had no strength. Even before he'd killed, he'd been unable to touch her. He yearned for her still, but there was nothing left to drive his limbs when he was near her. He found that having killed had gouged out and cast off possibilities in him. He felt drastically simplified.

The wood planking from the earlier blast was still piled outside. He'd leave the tarpaulin on and hope that the Army had better things to do than clear this area. He'd go off until night. Then he'd come back and put the planking on and wait beneath it with his King until the blast came and went. After that, there was the woman who broke the circle. Her shoulders and neck and head. Her legs and feet. He had enough energy to face the record of her pain. But no more than that.

Then he grew very calm. His mind began to work clearly. The return to the site would have to be done largely on foot, to avoid detection. He wouldn't be able to carry much with him. He finished dressing quickly and went outside. The sky was cloudy and the air was wet and thick. He opened the tarp at one empty corner and began piling lamps, food supplies and tools into the hole. He worked quickly, glancing often to the south. When he was nearly done he saw a car in the distance, racing this way. He pulled the tarp back over the opening and turned to wait. An Army sedan raced up and came to a stop before him. Two doors swung open. The captain emerged from the driver's side. The passenger was Anna.

Darrell's breath grew shallow as he watched the two approach. The captain had a faint, paternal smile. Anna looked frightened.

"Dr. Reeves," the captain said warmly, thrusting out his hand.

Darrell knew he had to pull himself up to his normal level of animation or these two would become concerned about him and try to interfere. He shook the captain's hand and constructed a natural-looking smile and said, "Captain."

"Darrell," Anna said, "are you all right?" She moved in front of the captain.

Darrell could smell her, could smell her hair and he thought of standing behind her in the plaza in Santa Fe as the dancers swirled in the dust. The memory seemed very old, as old as the memory of his wife, or even his father.

"I'm fine," Darrell said.

Anna's eyes narrowed. She studied his face.

Darrell lowered his voice, thickened it with a tone of sincerity. "Really," he said. "Don't worry about me, Anna."

The captain said, "Are the bones all gone now?"

Anna's eyes held Darrell fast. He could not even glance away from her. This was the keenest test of his stripped-down will and he gathered his strength and, even looking into Anna's wide, Indian-dark eyes, he said, "Yes. The bones are gone."

He heard Anna's breath catch. Her eyes groped around his face, focusing on his mouth, his eyes, his mouth again. Darrell waited to see if she would challenge this statement she knew to be a lie. But she said nothing.

The captain walked past the two of them and Darrell turned abruptly away from Anna to make sure the man didn't begin to pry.

"You've got a lot of gear that's not packed," the captain said.

"I'm not taking much of it."

The man faced Darrell. "It will be destroyed, you know."

"It's not worth our storing it up at the university."

"Very well."

"I'll pull the things together that I'm taking," Darrell said.

"Good."

Darrell moved off without looking back at Anna. He realized she knew he'd lied. She wanted him to go with her, become ambitious for her, win her. But he felt he had nothing to give. He also felt the pain his turning away caused her, felt it as a pressure on the nape of his neck, but he did not look back. He could not bear to see her.

The captain fell into step beside him and the man said, "You feel good today, do you?" The question sounded rhetorical and the captain went on at once. "It's tough, the first one. But when you've saved the lives of the men on your side, the next day it feels great."

Darrell barely could make denotative sense of these words.

"Am I right?" the captain said, stopping them both. "Am I right?"

"Yes," Darrell said, although it was impossible to put any life into the word. "Of course."

The captain smiled and nodded and cuffed Darrell on the arm. "You should be proud . . . And listen. This whole thing now is gonna go off without any hassles. I'll help you load up your car with whatever you're taking, and whatever you'd like us to store for you and send on later, we will. I know you haven't had a chance in the last twenty-four hours to get organized."

"Thanks," Darrell said.

The captain cuffed him again and they began to work together, taking down Darrell's tent, gathering up clothes and books. Darrell wondered if the man would ask about all the things being left behind. Or where the bones were packed. But the captain was true to his word. He caused no trouble, asked no questions. He helped Darrell load his Plymouth, the two men working hard for half an hour.

After a time, Darrell glanced toward the place where Anna had been standing when he'd left her. She was not there. It occurred to him that at some point she'd probably peeked under the tarp to confirm what she already knew was true. But she'd caused no trouble. At worst, he'd have to tell the captain that the site was being abandoned. The bones were unnecessary. That would arouse the man's deep suspicions, but the desert was big, the security would have to be very loose, and surely the man had more important things to worry about than Darrell's coming back.

Darrell paused a moment and looked harder and he saw Anna sitting in the car. Her face was invisible in the shadow, through the glass, from this distance, and he turned away, wondering if she'd seen him stop and look, if she'd smiled at him and he'd snubbed her unawares. He wondered if she'd mouthed "I love you" at him, and this wilder, irrational notion surprised him, worried him; he had to keep control. He realized his desire for her was roiling inside him and it seemed capable of causing sudden, extreme thoughts and he had to be on guard.

The captain stood beside him and said, "Is there anything else?"

"No," Darrell said. "How long until the blast?" The question came without premeditation and as soon as it was spoken, Darrell grew nervous. It was a vital question and he'd almost not thought to ask. What else was he overlooking? he wondered.

The captain said nothing.

Darrell had to know if he had time to come back and cover the King and himself with the protective planking. He cuffed the captain on the arm. "Just a general sense," he said.

The captain smiled and nodded before he spoke, as if someone had just made a persuasively logical argument to him. "Around dawn, Dr. Reeves. Just before dawn."

"Thanks, captain." There would be time enough, Darrell thought. Not much to spare, but time enough.

"Are you ready to go now?" the captain asked.

"Yes."

"You can follow me. We'll go just about due east. There's

a road this side of the San Andres that'll take you north to Bingham and Route 380.''

''Thanks.''

''Thank you,'' the captain said and he straightened and shot Darrell a crisp military salute. Then he turned and moved off toward his car.

Darrell's eyes followed him and he looked at Anna. He still could not make out her face. He had the urge to go over to the car, to speak to her, tell her good-bye, touch her hand.

The passenger door opened. Anna stepped out and stood there. Her face seemed blank. Her body was very still. Darrell felt his own face, his own body motionless in the same way. He and Anna were as blank and as similar as skeletons. The driver-side door slammed and it sounded like a rifle shot and Darrell started. His hands stirred and he turned away, breaking this distant connection with Anna. He went to his car and got in and put the key in the ignition and started the engine and waited, looking straight ahead.

Shortly the Army sedan swung out before him and Darrell followed the car across the desert, his eyes fixed on the back bumper. Darrell wanted to look into the window and see Anna's head but he just tightened his grip on the steering wheel.

The car in front stopped and Darrell jammed on his brakes and stopped too. A pup tent was set up with a soldier sitting at its mouth and another leaning into the car ahead, talking to the captain. Darrell noted the place and looked to the north and the south and could see nothing but unbroken desert. He felt that his suspicion had been confirmed. The security at this point, deep within the desert, was spread very thin.

The soldier who had been leaning into the captain's car was approaching Darrell now. He saluted and smiled and stuck out his hand. Darrell shook it through the window and the man said, ''I heard about what you did, sir. You're okay in my book.''

''Thanks,'' Darrell said, thinking that maybe they would trust him as a result, maybe they'd just let him drive on up this road by himself, maybe they wouldn't bother to phone ahead to whoever they had at the juncture of 380 to verify Darrell's leaving the desert.

"Do you know how to go from here?" the soldier said.

"I do."

"You can proceed then, sir," the man said, backing off.

Darrell nodded and up ahead the Army sedan was making a U-turn. But Anna was outside of the car and walking this way. He felt her lope in his own hips, the swing of her arms in his own arms. She bent to him and her hand came out and clutched the window frame.

"What are you doing?" she said.

"I'm leaving." His voice was very small.

"The bones are still there."

He said nothing.

"Aren't they," she said rhetorically.

"Anna, please."

"You can't go back in there."

"Anna, I wish things could have been different. I . . . lost control somewhere." He felt foolish. The words he spoke, the words he heard, were alien to him, meaningless.

"You'll die," she said. "You can't go back in there."

The Army sedan rolled up just behind Anna.

For a moment, Darrell thought he might try to find her when this was all over. But this idea was as strange to him as all these words. He thought of the woman in the pit, waiting to be drawn from the earth. As much as her pain distressed him, he felt comfortable at the thought of her. He'd chosen the bones. Yesterday and even now, even with Anna's hand very near, waiting for his hand to touch it.

"I have to go," Darrell said and he turned his face to the front.

He felt Anna back away. He heard the captain say, "Good luck, Dr. Reeves." Darrell gunned his engine, the wheels spun without gripping for a moment and then the car leaped forward and he turned north and raced along the road till he was out of sight of the security check-point.

He pulled the car off the road and left the engine idling as he stepped out. He looked back south and then to the north and there was no one. The desert was empty. He turned and looked to the east and the San Andres Mountains reared up above him. He looked at the foothills a mile off and there was an isolated knoll and he slid back into the seat. He put the car in gear and drove across the open surface to hide in the mountains until nightfall.

LLOYD AND OPPIE CLIMBED the open steel ladder, up the hundred feet along the leg of the tower, where the bomb waited. They paused at a platform wedge halfway up and Oppie leaned against the railing to catch his breath, one bony hand on his chest. He looked out to the west where the sky was growing dark. Lightning crackled there and Oppie looked to the top of the tower. Lloyd knew what the man was thinking and he, too, wondered what would happen if lightning struck the tower with the bomb there, its plutonium heart throbbing deep inside it, waiting.

Oppie looked back out to the west and then resumed his climb. The ladder was thin-barred but steady. The wind beat at the two men, lifted Oppie's tweed coat, fluttered Lloyd's shirt sleeves. They were up high now and Lloyd felt a little shaky but he kept his face turned upwards, focused on the highest platform.

Oppie did not stop again and they stood on the upper level. Two scientists and an armed guard met them. Good to see you, they said to Oppenheimer. Don't like the lightning. Me either. Come see Fat Man.

Lloyd cut off the babble. There was a galvanized metal shed in the center of the platform and he went to it and opened the door. The bomb crouched in the dark. Five dural segments bolted together to make a black sphere five feet across. The skin had been smooth at the end of the assembly but now racks and brackets and cables were tangled around it, detonators were clamped on its skin. All of these were the caresses of men but

Lloyd felt the life fully shaped, fully contained inside the dark skin, a life that pulsed impervious to the clutter outside, as aloof as a man of the mind. Lloyd felt calm before the bomb. Very calm.

Oppie's voice spoke low into Lloyd's ear. ''There's a passage in the Bhagavad-Gita. 'If the radiance of a thousand suns were to burst at once into the sky, that would be like the splendor of the Mighty One . . . I am become Death, the shatterer of worlds.' ''

Lloyd kept still. He didn't tell Oppie to go to hell. He didn't deflect them both into a technical discussion. He was calm now. The bomb was teaching Lloyd. He didn't jerk away and go down the ladder alone. The bomb was teaching him and he wanted to stand before the bomb and so he just said nothing in response to Oppie and Oppie said no more. Lloyd held his eyes on the bomb, but without focusing too narrowly; he took in all the sphere. He let his mind open like the bloom of atoms to come. He thought of Anna and that surprised him and pleased him. He knew that the time was drawing near for all of him to open up, mind and body. His calm thickened like the air. He thought: I'm ready.

WHEN LLOYD RETURNED TO the camp from the tower, he knew he should go to Anna. The twilight was gathering and he felt the time of day to be in concert with his calmness. Tonight he would find Anna and they would eat together and she would be with him working in the bunker until the dawn, until the bomb would reveal everything. He yearned for that light. He knew the light would be very great. The radiance of a thousand suns. Lloyd smiled at the irony of remembering Oppie's words. All right. Yes. Perhaps there was something to what he said.

Lloyd stood in the street and hesitated. He thought to go to her room. But he wanted first to wash his hands and his face. He wanted his body to be fresh. Perhaps they would go at once, after dawn, to get married. There was a chaplain in the camp. Lloyd would let Oppie be the witness and he'd marry Anna as his first act after the bomb.

He walked quickly to the quonset that held his room. He entered the central hallway and a figure rushed toward him. He stopped. It was Anna. He smiled, he lifted, he felt his joy swelling in his head, pressing out of his ears.

"Dr. Coulter," Anna said and he heard the anguish in her voice but his mind brushed it aside.

"Anna," he said. "I was going to find you."

"I have to talk to you."

"This is wonderful. Your being here."

"I'm very worried."

Lloyd was even happy at her distress. She needed him. She was open to him. He would put his mind to her problems, control them, bind her to him. "It's all right," he said.

"It's about . . ."

"Let's go into my room. You can tell me there." It was a good suggestion, he knew. She nodded and led him along the hall. It was a good suggestion. He'd close the door and they'd be contained. A leap of intuition: like two hemispheres of plutonium, brought slowly together. They wouldn't join yet, but soon. They'd approach now, in a contained space, test the multiplication of neutrons, the curve of energy.

Anna and Lloyd reached the room and he opened the door and followed her inside. He shut the door and turned and she was standing in the center of the floor. The light was very dim and she was starting to speak again. He shushed her gently and went to his dresser and switched on a lamp. He remembered the moments he'd spent in her room, a room that looked very much like this one. He remembered her rumpled bed and he looked at his own bed and it was tightly made. He smiled: it was more military than hers.

"You're not meant to be a soldier," he said.

She said, "I'm worried about Darrell."

At first Lloyd did not know who this was. Darrell.

She said, "I think he's doing something really crazy now."

Darrell. When Lloyd's mind made the link, it veered away instinctively. His mind protected itself and for a moment he was left blank.

"He really cares about those bones," she said. "They're important for his career."

Lloyd could hold it off no longer. She was talking about the pale-eyed man.

"But he's left them behind," she said.

She was talking intensely about the man.

"I'm afraid for him," she said.

Lloyd forced himself back to the bomb, to the moment of calm standing before the bomb. He had to recover his sense of containment. These words were making him stir.

"I think he's going back there," she said. "He doesn't realize what's going to happen."

Lloyd could not breathe.

"I couldn't get it across to him, that this . . ." She groped for a word.

Lloyd felt a pressure in his head.

". . . This thing," she said, "this bomb . . . was bigger."

The pressure at first seemed a relief. It pressed inwards. It squeezed the fretful surface feelings out, it squeezed even the pale eyes themselves out of Lloyd's head.

"How *much* bigger is it really going to be, Dr. Coulter?" Anna asked with a surge in her voice, with her hands fluttering out toward him.

The pressure increased and there was a moment of balance, there was a moment of calm again as the pressure spread out of his mind and into his chest and into his arms and even into his groin, even there, and the calm held for one breath—one easy breath—and another.

"I'm afraid he's going back there. Darrell's going back to the excavation site before the bomb goes off."

Darrell. Her voice was full of feeling, full of passion for this name.

She said, "He left only that covering on the pit and he's got to protect the bones."

Anna's face was twisted in fear and Lloyd wanted to turn his eyes away but he couldn't, Anna was in this other man's control.

"He doesn't know the danger," she said. "Help him."

Then Lloyd felt his body contract in a flash of strength, his body collapsed into a tiny point that was first in his chest—just long enough for him to be conscious of all this, of his own power, of the sudden simplicity of things; she was before him, wavering, weak, full of fear, she invited him, he had the power, the vast power—and then the centerpoint lunged from his chest into his groin and she was in his arms and her face widened and its words stopped and his own face came forward and pressed against this skin and his hands moved, he twisted and fell and he was stretched out flat against her, she was on his cot, the covers were rumpled beside her face, he noticed, and he felt the pressure now bloating him up, filling his body, every part, his hands were moving and he heard her voice begin, wordless, a foolish sound and there was something in his hand from where he'd taken it, cloth, a lump of cloth, he remembered the drawer of her dresser calling him, not the hard objects from the top this time but the soft things in the drawer, in his hand now and he stuffed the thing into her open mouth and the wailing stopped and he felt the thick air, the moist air on his body, his hands were moving, flaring and tearing away the layers that held him back and she was quiet and she was still and she was his and he was inside her and he bloomed, he bloomed, he felt the atoms of his body fly apart and he bloomed and she was his. He beat against her even after the blooming had begun to fade, he beat against her, beat her, inside her, beat her and she shivered and shivered and he felt a sound in his throat, a hard sound, and she was his and he felt angry still, angry so he beat at her, his hands quiet, pressed flat on each side of her face, the fingers splayed, he beat at her until he grew weary and he stopped. And then he tried to catch his breath; he was empty and he tried to fill his lungs. He shuddered.

Now he saw her face. It was turned to the side. The eyes

were closed, the face was still. He thought she was dead and he felt a terrible clutching in his chest. The face was so fragile. It must be dead. And then he saw tears coming from her eyes, rolling away, streaming from her eyes and he felt happy that she was alive but very sad for her, that she should be crying.

He grew conscious of the awkward position he was in. He feared his weight was hurting her but when he started to move he knew that he was inside her body. He didn't quite know how to withdraw. A simple matter of vectors, he thought. A simple angle. Force, direction, resistance, he moved and was free and he rose and began to dress, keeping his back to Anna. He wanted to cover himself quickly but his body felt balky, heavy now, and his mind began to shape thoughts again and when his body was covered he stopped still.

What is it? Lloyd thought. What's happened? What is it? he thought, and he turned slowly. Anna was curled like a fetus on the bed and she was shaking, her limbs were drawn into her and she was making a terrible sound, a tiny peeping sound deep inside her and Lloyd thought, What? What is it? But he knew. He realized now and he felt the anger again roll through him, like a shock wave after a bomb blast, it rolled through him and he staggered before it and he was angry at the pale-eyed man, very angry. But the man couldn't hurt him, he knew. Lloyd had taken control of these forces. It was all beyond the pale-eyed man's touch now. Not even with that blade he held could he touch Anna or Lloyd, he could not interfere.

But Anna still made that sound. She still made that deep, flesh-packed sound inside her and he took a step forward. She opened her eyes suddenly and her face jerked up to him and Lloyd recoiled from it. The eyes—those eyes that made him yearn—the eyes grew wide and this was no longer awe, this was no longer Anna's gaze at the bomb, this was more, far more, Lloyd couldn't bear these eyes, he stumbled backward against the dresser and these eyes did not move, they leaped through his own eyes and inside his head they burned, they burned.

Anna was rising and he couldn't move. Her hand went up

and took the lump of cloth from her mouth and he couldn't move. She only gasped, only breathed, gasping. No, he shouted in his mind. Not those eyes. Not that look. This was not the look he wanted. And she was gone. The door was open and she was gone and he could not move.

WITH HIS HEADLIGHTS TURNED off, Darrell drove his Plymouth in low gear along the road that followed the Jemez Mountains. The night was very dark and still and in the beam of his flashlight he watched his odometer carefully. He drove three miles exactly—the distance he'd estimated on the trip out this afternoon. Then he stopped the car and removed his compass from the glove compartment and leaned down under the dashboard where the beam from the flashlight could not be seen from outside.

He reckoned the angle off the road to find the excavation. But the night was so dark that when he peered out into the desert he could see nothing. There'd be no reference point to key on, to keep him moving in the right direction. Not easily. He'd have to keep his eyes fixed solely on the compass. That meant he'd have to leave the car here. And it would be even slower going on foot, with no reference points.

He put his watch under the beam of light. He had perhaps eight hours, perhaps less, before the bomb blast. The planking would be heavy. And now it looked as if at least two of those hours would be spent in walking from this road to the excavation site, even if he didn't miss the site and waste time backtracking.

Darrell eased the car door open and got out. He realized that he'd have to keep his flashlight lit almost constantly, to watch the compass. It was a risk he could not avoid. He started off into the dark, walking as fast as he could on the rocky desert floor. He was watching the needle, keeping it steady, and he strode into a low mesquite bush and sprawled forward onto the ground.

He felt disarranged but unhurt. He got slowly to his feet and a weltering began in him, starting in his chest, threatening to rise into his head. He fought at it. He would have time. He would have time. He'd slow his pace and be very steady and he'd still have four or five hours to prepare for the blast.

Darrell picked up his flashlight. His compass was still clutched tightly in his left palm. He took a deep breath to steady himself. He felt calmer. He listened to the thick silence of the desert and he lifted his eyes and he looked before him—far ahead, in the direction he was moving—and he saw a column of white light. It was very distant but very clear—a klieg light, and then a second one—and the two columns of light played against the low clouds and then lowered and converged and held steady.

Darrell blinked hard and strained to see if the lights were real and they were. They fidgeted slightly, but they did not vanish. They fixed on some point, far off in the desert, and Darrell checked his compass again and the direction was precise. He had a brief pulse of fear that these lights were indeed set up at the excavation. But then he remembered the blast site. It was southwest of where Darrell had been digging. These lights were illuminating the blast site, where the last preparations were no doubt being made. The King was lying directly between those lights and Darrell, waiting. Darrell laughed silently. The scientists had given him a beacon in the darkness to find his way home.

DARRELL SAW THE SHAPES of the tents up ahead. If the tents were still standing, the rest of the excavation would be untouched too, he reasoned. The klieg lights held their beams on a spot just a thousand yards off now. Darrell thought he could see something there—a spike in the silver beams—but he lowered his eyes. It only made him anxious over all he had to do yet. He switched on his flashlight very briefly, shielding it from the blast site with his body and he looked at his watch. Time was growing very short. If the explosives were set to be

196

detonated very much before dawn, he could have only five hours or even less.

Darrell hurried on. He entered his camp boldly, satisfied that nothing had been changed. There were some patches of night sky and starlight overhead and he could see better than he'd expected. His assumption seemed correct. The tarpaulin was in place. Not even a portion of the pit was exposed.

He rolled the tarp back at the corner that held his supplies. He'd cover the whole pit with the planking and save this corner for last; he'd enter the pit here and pull the wooden planks over it from inside. He'd crawl into the center, next to the King, and he'd wait. The flow of this plan in his mind thrilled him. He realized how strongly he desired these coming hours, burying his King once more, lying in the grave with him, alone, waiting for the foolishness of these men to sweep overhead, and he knew he'd be all right after that. Darrell would have met these outside enemies and met the forces in himself and he would have made them all part of a new ritual. "Yes," he said aloud. This was what his mind had been shaping for him. Only now did he understand. Oppenheimer, Coulter, the captain, the rancher, Darrell's own violence, his trowel, the pit, the three women, the shattered skull, the Spanish soldier, the weeping eyes, all the world, Darrell's wife and his father and his brother, they would all go into the pit with him, the slickness of his hands, this memory in his skin of the draining from the blade, the woman with her body full of arrowheads. Darrell was gasping aloud now, his chest was heaving. All this would go into the pit with him and the scientists' ball of flame would rise up and rush over them and then it would be all right. He would move the planking away and come out of the grave and he'd be able to do his work again.

Then he thought of Anna. He would take her memory into the grave with him as well, the memory of her kiss. This made him stop. This began to gnaw at his satisfaction. Anna was not contained by the circle he'd drawn for himself. The memory of her was not enough now. He clenched in anger at himself for not touching her hand as she leaned near his car trying to tell him good-bye. She had been afraid for him. He looked to the southwest, at the two tracks of silver light, and they were blotted out, a shadow, movement, a figure coming at him. Darrell cried out and stumbled back.

"It's me," a voice said, a woman's voice, Anna, and Darrell thought he had lost control of his mind, he was hallucinating. He stumbled farther back, prepared to turn and run. This voice, this figure, were dislodged from some crevice of his mind, just like the impulse to pick up the trowel and plunge it into the rancher's back.

"Please," Anna's voice said and it was jagged with pain.

Darrell stopped and he knew Anna was there before him in the dark. The figure approached and he could make out her face. He saw her eyes, wide and black, and he said, "Anna."

Time passed with no words, no movement, and then Darrell opened his arms, knowing that at that very moment she would come to him and she did, her body pressed up against him, trembling, but as soon as his arms began to settle on her, he felt a spasm rush through her and she pulled away.

"What is it?" he said.

She had moved off. He followed her, but he did not try to touch her. She was weeping.

"What is it?" he said.

She didn't speak for a moment and then her weeping squeezed to a stop and she said, "I . . . I was worried about you."

Darrell sensed that was not the full truth, but he did not press her. "How did you get out here?" he said.

"I hid in a truck that went to the test site. Then I walked across the desert."

"You knew I was coming back."

"Yes."

Darrell wondered if he should try to hold her again. But he sensed a movement of light and he looked to the southwest and saw one of the klieg lights angled up to the sky. He knew he had to begin his work. "Have you come to make me go back with you?" He sensed her shudder. He said, "I still intend to protect these bones," though even as he said it, he felt a quickening because of her, he felt his yearning for her separate from the act he'd committed. He decided his feelings for her were clarifying because he understood the meaning of these coming few hours. "There's nothing you can say to make me go. I'm determined to stay until this damn fool thing is over," he said.

Anna turned to him. He wished he had better light so that he could read these eyes that registered in the dark only as large and black. He wanted to see the regard there, her feelings for him, her fear for his safety.

"All right," she said. "I'll stay with you."

Darrell took a breath that lifted him up onto his toes. His arms grew very strong. He rushed to the planking to begin to prepare a place for Anna and himself in the King's grave.

LLOYD KNEW WHAT HE'D done. He knew he'd raped Anna. After awhile he went out into the street and cars were whining past, people were scurrying around. Scientists were arriving down from Los Alamos and they were being sorted out by the security men, taken to trenches that had been dug for them around the camp.

Lloyd stood in the street and expected one of the security men to notice him and come over, gun drawn, and arrest him. Lloyd thought that Anna would certainly have gone off to tell the authorities what had happened. He felt no anger at this. No fear, either. He felt spent. He wondered if it was always like this, even if the woman was willing. There was a languor in his limbs, in his mind too. He thought of Anna's face. The look had hurt him; he pitied her still, the face seemed as if a layer had been burned away and the raw level beneath ached even at the touch of the air. He wanted to reach out to it—but he could not put his hands on it. That's what hurt him the most. The face was too raw. His power gave him no way to touch this face, this face that was left even after he'd been unleashed; his power had not been enough, it had not won her. Now he was poised again between the pull of two feelings: anger at his failure to do what he'd wanted to do and pity at her pain. But he felt no remorse. He noticed that. He had no remorse because what he'd done had been done with the logic of verifiable natural laws. The links of cause and action, cause and action, were as inexorable as the collision of neutron and nucleus, neutron and nucleus.

A car honked and Lloyd jumped back and it sped by in the dark. A voice over a loudspeaker said, "A-Team to control bunker, please. A-Team please go to control bunker."

Lloyd moved off along the edge of the road. He concentrated on the path, putting one foot in front of another, keeping out of the way of the vehicles and the bodies that careened past him. He approached the control bunker on the northern edge of the site. He went down three steps and into the central room.

The place bustled with scientists, the walls were cluttered with banks of dials and fuse panels and monitor screens and they flashed with spots of red and green and yellow. Lloyd waited in the doorway to be seized. The security men would be waiting for him here. But no one took notice of him. Then Oppie came up.

"Lloyd, troubleshoot all the instrumentation for the next couple of hours," Oppie said. "Keep us out of trouble."

Lloyd nodded. Oppie disappeared and Lloyd knew she'd said nothing. Another tension of two possibilities: perhaps she was prepared to accept him; perhaps she'd done something to harm herself. She'd been given a clearance for the control bunker. If the first of those two possibilities were true, she'd appear in this room at last. Until then, Lloyd had his work to do. She'd appear and they'd watch the bomb together, its light would fill their two minds, side by side, their minds would be cleared and they'd be fused together, and the heat from the bomb would burn that layer of Anna's face away, the layer that Lloyd had seen in his room. They'd both be wiped clean and she would see what it was that he'd done with his hands, this vast bloom in the desert, and she'd even understand the forces that had driven him to take her body against his prematurely. It had been as if Slotin's screwdriver had slipped and the hemispheres had clapped together: the event would have been the same, it would simply have been premature.

So Lloyd plunged into the room and helped the group leaders at their control panels. And the pregnancy of the night, the promise of the atom bomb, held him for a long time, until he paused behind Joe McKibben at the firing console, and watched the man tapping his forefinger on the Lucite cover over the automatic timer.

McKibben looked at his watch and glanced up at Lloyd. "The next hour's going to be the hard part," he said.

Lloyd turned and looked at the clock on the back wall. It was nearly four-thirty. One hour to go.

Suddenly he thought of Anna. She'd not arrived yet. He had a vision of her dead. Anna dead. He saw her face turned to the side, lying on his cot, the face seemed dead. He'd raped her and driven her to her death in shame. He saw his mother's head bounce against the floor. Why this rush? his mind protested. Why this? He was in the control room. From here the bomb would be pressed into life. It would spread. It would rush over this very spot. Why should he care about this woman? But he did. He knew she hadn't forgiven him. He knew she'd wanted to die.

Lloyd crossed the room—much too slowly, his body would not hurry the way he was hurrying inside. Then he was in the night and he had to find her. He cursed himself silently for letting these last few hours pass. She was dead already, he feared.

He ran down the road, dodging a car as he cut across, the horn honking, a voice shouting. Lloyd ran hard down to the quonsets and went to her room and he broke the door open and groped in the dark to find the light. An object clattered to the floor from the dresser-top and he found the light and switched it on. The room was empty. The hairbrush had fallen to the floor. The thin wisps of her hair. Tears filled his eyes. He didn't know where to go. He bent to pick up the brush. He remembered wondering if his mother was dead after she fell, after his father had hit her.

Lloyd touched the brush and he heard Anna's words in his head. She was afraid for that pale-eyed man. She loved him. She was afraid the man was coming back to his excavation. Lloyd's hand snapped away from the brush. He straightened up. He felt strong. He did not know how his power would focus itself, but he felt strong.

He looked at his watch. Fifty-five minutes to the blast. There were twenty-five minutes before the vehicles would be called in from the desert. He plunged out of the room and into the night. He ran to his quonset and got into his car and he started the engine. He turned into the street and followed a deuce-and-a-half full of scientists in ties and suits—he could see them in his headlights, sitting on the troop benches in the back of the truck. Lloyd didn't like the slow pace but in a moment he was able to turn onto the north desert path. He raced off in the direction of the archaeologist's camp.

THE LAST PIECE OF wooden planking was ready. There was a space for Darrell and Anna to enter the grave and he turned to her. She was sitting on the ground nearby. She'd been waiting in silence all this time while he worked, without even looking at him. He crossed to her and sat down beside her, feeling weary and sore from the exertions of covering the pit. She still said nothing.

"What's wrong?" he asked.

She did not reply.

"It's more than your fear over my safety," he said.

She began to cry and Darrell hesitated for a moment, afraid to act; afraid, he realized, of himself. But he lifted an arm and placed it around her shoulders and pulled her gently against him. She held back at first but then yielded. She turned her head into his chest and drew her hands up and curled into him and she cried.

They sat like that for a long while. She wept and he felt blank in his ignorance of her pain but calm and focused in her touch. Then her weeping ebbed and she said, "I was very afraid for you . . . I found I . . . cared for you very much." She began to cry again and Darrell closed his eyes in joy.

Anna struggled with her tears and said, "So I went for . . . help . . . I wanted to help you." Her voice cracked and dissolved into sobs. Darrell rocked slightly back and forth with her and his first rush of pleasure was beginning to change into a dread at what was causing this pain.

"I just want to be with you." Her words leaped from the tears and she said no more.

Darrell could not accept this. He knew there would have been a time when he'd just take what it was that he needed— this profession of her devotion—and he'd let the rest resolve itself. If she didn't speak it, then it didn't concern him. But now that wasn't possible. He said, "What is it, Anna? You have to tell me what's wrong."

She shook her head in protest and went on crying.

"I can't bear to see you like this," he said.

He felt her body coil and harden and she snubbed her tears into silence. She said, "You said nothing would take you away from this place. I want to be here too."

"I thought there was nothing else," Darrell said, and even as he spoke the words he felt the rise and fall of Anna's breathing in the bend of his arm, he felt her head against his chest. To support this conclusion, his mind propped up the rancher before him—the face turning at the sound of Darrell, the back broad and vulnerable—and then Darrell heard the chuff of the trowel sinking into the man's back—a chuff like the cutting of earth—but the man's throat gagged at the pain and he died, he died. A shudder passed through Anna, as if she'd been linked to this thought. Darrell's mind said to itself: So you understand now; there's nothing else; even this pit holds a woman, perhaps like Anna, and she is full of the artifacts of a rage that is like your own. Anna began to cry softly once more and the sound sprinkled darkly against Darrell's mind, covered his thoughts with dust, covered them over and he heard only Anna. He held her more tightly against him and then he heard the sound of an engine.

He looked out into the desert to the south and he heard a car but he saw no lights. He thought for a moment that the sound was in his mind, a memory ill-formed, but Anna's head rose. She heard it too.

Then two lights leaped on—about two hundred yards away— they were rushing toward them—and the lights went off, the engine roared, the car was hurtling this way, invisible now, and Darrell and Anna jumped up. The car raced into the camp-site, a shadow, and swerved to a stop and a door creaked and there was a form rushing around the car, running up, Darrell took a step back and braced himself. The form approached and it was Coulter, and Darrell knew that Anna's pain had some-thing to do with him.

Lloyd stopped before Darrell and the two men straightened, hardened. Lloyd looked at Anna cowering behind this man whose pale eyes were almost invisible in the darkness and Lloyd was very glad she was not dead. He wanted to stroke her hair, make it all right, but this man was in the way. Even physically now, he was in the way, and Lloyd felt a rush of power and he lunged into Darrell and they both fell backwards onto the earth, their minds and feelings emptied instantly and their limbs entwined, squeezing hard, their hands pummeled at head, shoulder, side, they rolled on the ground and Lloyd freed an arm and hooked it around Darrell's head and twisted a deep pain into Darrell's neck that ran across his shoulder and down his arm and he had an arm himself that was free from the elbow and he could just reach Lloyd's throat and he grabbed at it, he dug his fingers deep into the throat. Lloyd gagged and his grip loosened and they rolled again, onto wood, the planking, they were over the pit now and they were immobile against each other, straining hard, hurting. They rolled farther and stopped and strained, the pain equal in both, the pain coursing through face and neck and arms and chest and for the first time since they began, a thin trickle of thought returned to each of them, like the blood from Darrell's mouth, Lloyd's nose. They both heard Anna crying and they each grew angry at this, angry at this man who had caused the pain, and Lloyd felt how bony this man was, unusually strong but bony, breakable, and Lloyd squeezed at his own will and hardened and he moved his legs and he was grasping Darrell across the chest, he could lift him if he only stood up and Lloyd's legs moved and he slowly got to his feet, Darrell feeling a new strength in this man who held him even as his own strength faded.

Darrell's legs moved, tried to tangle Lloyd. Lloyd slipped and the planking shifted and Lloyd yanked Darrell back and forth like a dog killing a rat in his jaws and Darrell cried out in pain and his strength vanished and Lloyd stood up, grasping this bony man. He stumbled and his foot caught in a seam of the planking and his weight went down, the planking opened, slipped, tilted, the two men fell, but not far. Darrell felt knobs of bone, heard cracking, he knew they were on one of the pedestals, a skeleton, then they rolled off; the planking crashed and they dropped to the pit floor, landing hard on their sides, the breath of both men yanked away. They gasped but Lloyd still had his strength even as he gasped. Lloyd jerked around onto the top of Darrell and he lifted his own torso, freed his hands and took hold of Darrell's throat.

Another moment of thought came to them both. Darrell could not move, his arms were pinned under Lloyd's weight, his legs had no strength, he had no body now, only his face and his exposed throat, seized by thick hands and then he could not breathe. He thought simply that he would die. He felt a bone next to his face, the slick surface of a bone. Lloyd felt all his strength rush into his hands and he began to squeeze this thin neck, this stalk he'd long wanted to snap, but his mind worked in this motionless moment and he looked for the logic of all this; he was a man of the mind, after all, and then he heard Anna crying out, "Oh God, oh God," and Lloyd had a sense of women, a sense of gentle hands, his mother's hands, the fingers of his mother's hands on his face, the fingers of her hands lying as still as her face on the kitchen floor. He was killing this man beneath him, he knew, and his hands paused.

Then a pain bloomed on the side of Lloyd's head, a vexing pain but he did not yield. He heard Anna's voice, very near, saying, "No, no, stop," and another pain flashed against his shoulder. He turned and Anna's arm was rising. There was something hard in her hand and he let go of the man in the pit and Lloyd rose up smoothly in time to stop the falling hand and his own right hand turned hard and it came out fast and he felt Anna's face briefly and she flew back into the dark.

There was a moment of suspension. There was no movement in the pit, no sound. Lloyd thought he'd killed them both and he began to tremble. His strength left him and he could not stop trembling and he feared he'd killed her, he'd killed her again, once on his cot, now here in this pit, and this was not what he wanted for himself, there'd been too much of this, his mind had not kept these things out, never could. There was a stirring behind him. Lloyd turned. The man was not dead. He was alive and Lloyd felt a rush of joy at that. But Anna. Anna was dead. He'd broken his word. He loved her and now he'd killed her. He turned back to the darkness where she'd disappeared and he stepped into it and even as he saw her there, saw her limbs moving, and even as his chest lifted in joy, an arm yanked across his throat and he could not breathe. He felt a hard bone against his throat and it took away his breath and he grabbed at the arm but it held fast and Lloyd stumbled and fell down and Darrell was filled with a great strength, a great strength, and he knew he could kill again and Lloyd knew he would die and he struggled to his knees. Darrell clung tightly to the man and strained hard at his arm, radius against larynx, and Lloyd tried to crawl away from this. He did not want to kill this man now, he did not want to kill and he tried to crawl away, he crawled over the angled planks, into a cleared space, but the weight on his back went with him, the pain went with him, the breath would not return. Lloyd fell and rolled and there were objects clattering around, lamps, shovels, he was growing weak and Darrell would not let go, even though he saw the rancher's face. He knew this man would die like the rancher and then Darrell heard Anna crying into his ear, "Please no, please stop," and Darrell felt Anna's hand on his arm, tugging at him and Darrell felt the slickness on his hands and he let go. All the strength flowed out of Darrell like blood from an open vein and he lay against the cool earth and Lloyd could breathe again and he was happy at that, happy he had not killed, and the two men lay still for a time.

Darrell felt a hand on him, on his face, a soft hand, lips then. Anna was touching him, kissing him, and he tried to move, but for a moment he could not. Then he lifted his arm and he held her hand. Lloyd, too, was stirring. He raised his head and he saw the two figures there, close together, bending against each other like a married couple, and he was glad they were both still alive, he felt gentle toward them. Then he thought of where they all lay.

Lloyd sat up. "You have to go quickly," he said.

Darrell lifted himself at the man's voice; he sat up expecting another assault, but then the tone of Lloyd's voice registered in him and it was urgent, protective even.

Lloyd said, "You don't have much time."

Anna began to weep again and at first it surprised both men. But then Darrell recalled that she had a pain that was still a mystery to him and Lloyd understood the tears. Lloyd grew angry. At himself now. At the forces that had come into him. He was very angry and clenched his fists and when Darrell saw it, he thought the struggle would begin again.

But Lloyd said, "Forgive me, Anna. Please," and the voice quaked like a child's.

Anna wept on.

"Please," Lloyd said.

"What is it?" Darrell said.

"I don't care anymore," Anna said to Darrell. "We can stay if you want."

Lloyd said, "Please. Don't. You'll die. You'll both die."

Darrell turned on Lloyd. "You men are fools. You've been trying to . . ."

"You're the fool," Lloyd said, but softly.

"How many tons of explosives could you possibly . . ."

"This is different," Lloyd said. "It's a new bomb altogether."

Darrell had no answer to this. He believed the man at once. A new kind of bomb. He had no reason to doubt it. He was chilled by the danger he'd put himself in—himself and Anna—and he wondered why he'd been so muddled in his thinking on this.

"It's called an atomic bomb," Lloyd said. "These are new forces we're dealing with."

The rancher, the killing, Darrell thought. Had I wanted to die?

"You've got very little time," Lloyd said. "You have to go."

Darrell rose, his bones quivering in pain. But as he stood, Anna's weeping began again. "What is it?" Darrell said. Then sharply, "Tell me."

Anna cried, "You won't love me. You won't be able to touch me.

"Tell me," Darrell said.

"He raped me," she said.

Darrell felt oddly calm. He turned and they were among his tools and in the dimness he saw a short-handled shovel with a heavy iron blade on the floor of the pit. Darrell reached down, slowly, and he was still calm and there was no other movement in the grave, no sound. He picked up the shovel and stepped to Lloyd and he felt a strength in his arm, but he was still distant from it and he looked at the man who'd raped Anna. Darrell waited for the man to raise his fists, to lunge. Darrell waited for the thickening of the air, the presence he'd felt before he'd killed the rancher. But Lloyd Coulter opened his arms and inclined his head upwards and waited. Darrell could see, even in the dimness of the grave, that there were tears in Lloyd's eyes. The man waited for Darrell to hit him, to kill him, and Darrell felt no impulse now, no strength, he could not even hold the shovel aloft and he let it fall, let it drop from his hand.

At that moment Lloyd felt the tears flow out of his eyes and he understood that he was forgiven, that he was sorry and he was forgiven, a very simple little linking of cause and effect, nothing splitting off, no chain, no bloom. This man standing above him turned and Lloyd heard him say to Anna, "I love you." There was a movement and Lloyd knew the man and woman were embracing and he felt happy. Then he knew what he had to do. The next chain of cause and effect would not stop; there'd be no forgiveness, and he had to prevent that. He rose up and took his car keys out of his pocket.

"Here," Lloyd said, pulling at Darrell's arm. "Here."

Darrell turned and took the keys. "What about you?" he said.

"I'm going over to the shot tower," Lloyd said. "I have time but you don't. You go quickly now. Drive east. Fast. Don't stop at any bunker. They'll all be wiped away. Go to the mountains. The blast is going to be big, but no one knows exactly how big. And don't look back. Don't look back." Just in case I fail, Lloyd thought. But I can't. I won't.

The three stood motionless for a brief moment and then they broke from each other. Lloyd went up, out of the pit, and he looked to the southwest. The klieg lights were still on the tower. They would remain there even up to the moment of the blast. Lloyd was tempted to glance at his watch but he did not. He would work as fast as he could to disconnect the bomb and the time didn't matter. It would only make him panic. He began to run, out of the camp, onto the open desert. He ran toward the shot tower.

Darrell put his arm around Anna and helped her out of the pit. Before he himself climbed out, he paused and looked back. They had fallen, in their fight, into the center of the pit. Darrell stepped to the King. The King's bones were separated and scattered, his skull was angled off his neck, the jaw gaped. Bones. There was nothing here but bones. Darrell looked at the pedestal next to the King. One of the gorgets—the spider— was missing.

"Darrell," Anna said, her voice thick with urgency.

He reached and took up the weeping face gorget and put it into his pocket and turned. Anna waited outside the pit and he strode across to the balk and lifted himself out and they both ran to the car.

Behind the wheel, Darrell had a suddenly acute awareness of the casing of steel around him. He had a vision of himself locked inside the bomb and a scrambling began just behind his eyes, blurring his vision; panic, he knew, panic and he fought it. He fumbled the key into the ignition—how long did they have?—and he started the engine and Anna slid closer to him. That let him focus his eyes again but the scrambling went on his head. He squeezed hard at the steering wheel and he turned around to see the klieg lights, to get his bearings. The mountains were visible before him only as a deepening of the dark and when he switched on his headlights they disappeared entirely in the glare. Now Anna's nearness sharpened his panic: her very life was in danger.

Darrell floored the accelerator and the wheels spun wildly in the dust for a moment and then the car leaped forward. They bounced hard over rocks, the car frame screeching, and then they were running on smooth ground and the flutter in Darrell's head slowed. He felt the speed, he leaned into the wheel, yearned for more, the car ran very fast and then it hit uneven ground and it swerved and Darrell felt weightless, Anna screamed and he let up on the accelerator, he fought the wheel, the car spun back around and whined down and Darrell was shaking. He did not stop the car but he had to drive slowly for a few moments to see clearly again.

"We have to be careful," Anna said, low.

Darrell nodded and she pressed nearer to him and a cactus as tall as a man leaped into the headlights and he steered around it, an arm of the cactus scraping against the door, then the back fender. He knew if they'd been going any faster they would have hit the cactus.

"This is as fast as we can safely go at night without a road," he said.

Anna put her head against his shoulder. He felt the urge to speed up again, go fast, get her away from this coming fire, but he held back. To go fast now would be to lose the car and then they would certainly be doomed. He wondered how much time they had.

Lloyd wondered that, too, but he still did not look at his watch. Whatever it said, he could run no harder. His chest was pinched tight in pain as it was. But the tower was very near now, near enough that Lloyd even slowed instinctively, in case there was someone there. As soon as he considered this possibility, though, he rejected it. The blast was much too close. There was no one within ten thousand yards of this spot now. Except him. And the couple he'd sent on their way, the married couple—he knew they would marry—he wondered if they were touching now, leaning into each other. This thought made him smile and it began the pumping of his legs again. He ran another hundred yards and stopped before the tower.

The converging columns of light made the metal frame glow as if it were covered with frost, as if it were very cold. There was a sharp line between the light and the darkness where he stood and he hesitated. There was only one way to the top— the open ladder up the southwest leg. He would be exposed all the way up. He wondered if they were watching the tower through a high-powered scope. He tried to remember the details of the security plan—he'd heard it at some point—but he could not. He didn't want them to stop the countdown and come and pull him off the tower. Already he had a plan. He'd do more than disconnect the bomb. He'd get into the firing unit, into the informer device that was the final connection for the detonators that clung to the bomb's skin. He knew how to adjust the impulse to induce a fizzle. The plutonium would be lost, the bomb would fail, the whole project would be aborted, he'd escape into the night. He lifted up onto his toes. He could break this chain. He tried hard to remember the security arrangement. He had no recollection of a plan to keep eyes on the tower. His colleagues were all nearly six miles away. At most, they'd watch the tower in its larger outline. If he moved carefully, he'd have the access he needed.

Lloyd crept into the light, lowering himself near to the ground. He approached the ladder and straightened up, squinting against the glare of the klieg beams. He grasped the ladder rungs above his head, still expecting them to feel cold. They did not. He felt a faint vibration in them. From what, he didn't know. He looked up the hundred feet to the top and he realized that at any moment McKibben could send the firing signal, the detonators would flare, the explosives would ignite, the shock would be caught and focused by Lloyd's own lens, the plutonium core would implode and the process would begin. He would vanish; if it came at this moment even Anna and the man would vanish. No. It would be worse for them. They'd burn. Lloyd began to climb as Darrell swerved the car.

"What is it?" Anna cried, her head snapping off Darrell's shoulder.

"The security tent," Darrell said as they went past.

Anna turned around in the seat to look. "It's abandoned."

"Of course. We've only come three miles."

He heard Anna suck air in deep in fear and stop. She pressed closer to him and let out her breath. Darrell pushed a little more on the accelerator, then they crossed the desert road that had taken Darrell into hiding earlier today. He wondered if he should turn onto it, travel faster. But they'd be forced to stay in the open. Coulter had said to go straight to the mountains.

They bumped off the road, went down an incline, the rear wheels spinning loosely, sliding. Darrell gasped. Don't stop. "Don't stop," he said aloud. The car straightened and moved on, but a banging began, like hail, rocks jumping up into the underframe, kicked up by the wheels, banging, ringing in his head. Anna put her hands over her ears. The rocks banged and Darrell had to force the car faster. He felt the time rushing away. He felt the blast coming any moment. He had to press the car, they went faster and the stones stormed in Darrell's ears and Lloyd looked up the tower. He would not look down. Lloyd felt faint. He paused to catch his breath and he clung to the thin bars. He waited only a moment, seeing in his mind the bomb as it squatted, ready to awaken. He was breathless still and weak but when he saw the fat black sphere a shock of energy surged in him; he could not pause again. He grasped a high bar and climbed, faster, faster, his feet pounded at each step and then his foot missed a rung and his body jerked to the side, his other foot twisted and slipped off and he caught hard with his right hand and he dangled there, his left hand groping for a hold, his right arm extended and quivering, he could not fall. Then he caught a rung with his left hand and his feet found holds and he was firmly on the ladder again. He did not hestitate a moment after this, but started to climb once more, though slowly, steadily, and Darrell saw on the odometer that they'd come five miles now from the camp. The rocks had cleared, but he could feel the rutted surface clutching at the tires, twisting the wheels. They'd begun to climb; Darrell had to slow down more and more.

"Can't we go faster?" Anna said, her voice tiny, insistent.

"This is all alluvial detritus. We can't." And the car thumped hard into a hole, swerved, Darrell pressed at the accelerator but the car lurched to a stop. He ran the engine hard but the wheels just raced and the car did not move.

"Darrell," Anna said and she clutched at his arm.

"Come on," he said and he opened the door. They scrambled out and they did not look the way they'd come but instantly began to run up the incline. The sediment shifted and cascaded

under their feet. Anna fell with a little cry and Darrell helped
her up and they began to run again and Lloyd was still twenty
feet from the top of the tower. He was climbing faster now.
Lloyd was grasping as high as he could each time, letting his
arms pull him up, his legs were pushing off with great force
and he glanced up to see the top platform and his foot slipped,
the other foot missed, he was holding again with his right hand,
reaching with the other and then he felt his grip slipping. Sweat,
he reasoned. And he was free, he fell, fell, but he never reached
the earth and Darrell was straining up the incline when the
mountains leaped at him, he saw them briefly but the light that
rushed into him was so bright he could see nothing for a moment and then he saw the mountains again, white as bone,
rearing high above him into a black sky, as if this were the
surface of the moon, without atmosphere, dead, the mountains
vivid before a bright sun but the sky black, and he straightened
up. Anna gasped and Darrell saw her turn around to look. He
remembered Lloyd's warning not to look back but Anna's eyes
widened, her mouth opened and he himself had to look. He
turned and he was battered by air, he flew back and fell from
a shock wave and he sat up and there was a great sound and
before him a vast dome of white flame broiled, convoluted,
sutured like a skull, a burning skull that was squeezing up
from deep inside the earth, filling the desert and it began to
rise and every bush, every rock, every crevice, in the desert
was sharply limned in the light. This light clawed at Darrell's
eyes but he could not look away, the skull darkened with the
earth it was gouging up, it was pulling all the dead from the
earth like an act of memory, all the dead darkened this skull
and it rose, a featureless face there and it spoke, its voice roared
and filled the desert and Darrell backed away as he grew conscious of the sound and it did not stop but roared on and Darrell
wanted the mountain behind him to fall, to bury him, to hide
him from this thing that rose on a black neck of earth and it
cracked through the clouds but did not disappear. It burned
brightly through the clouds, as if they were transparent, and

it was changing in color as it stretched up, churning from yellow to green to orange to red—Darrell knew this color, he knew the memory in this skull was of more than bone, but also of blood; the flesh shaped back onto all the bones it had recalled from the earth and the blood flowed anew. Darrell felt as if his own blood was being sucked from him, drawn into the body of this thing, sucked up high into the mind there, and the voice roared on and the skull turned purple eight miles up in the sky. Then the roaring faded and ceased and there was a ringing silence, a silence that shaped in the center of Darrell's chest and hung there like the shape before his eyes. The ambient light began to fade and he thought of Anna. She'd been wiped from his mind for a time. She was one person only, as was he. This thing filling the desert comprehended nations, races, worlds. But he felt he'd been noticed by it, noticed in a personal way. He and Anna had defied the warning. They'd looked back. Darrell turned to Anna, expecting to find her dead, or changed into a pillar of salt, but she was there still and he felt the silence in his chest dissipate. He took her hand and her face turned to him and it was blank, benumbed, as if she'd just been raped.

DARELL CROSSED THE HOTEL room in the dark. There was a drone of noise outside with spikes of whistles and horns and nearby laughter. He didn't know why he moved to the sound or opened a crack in the curtains, for the celebration made him uneasy. He couldn't explain that, either. The war had ended today. He was married to Anna. She was on furlough and he'd brought her this morning to New York City and she would be mustered out of the Army soon. She slept quietly in this room, even now, safe. But the sounds of joy from outside lay without warmth against him, like the red neon of the hotel sign.

Still he did not draw away. He angled his head and looked out through the welter of city lights toward Times Square. Near the ground, behind the points of light, the darkness had texture and it roiled. People, he knew. Down in the street before the hotel, he could see the parts, the individuals, forming the crowd. In the center of its mass was a linking of bodies, a chain, doing a rhumba, curling through the crowd, gathering bodies as it went, the chain growing quickly, seeming to gather a sentience that shaped its movement. Darrell let the curtain fall shut.

He turned and faced into the dark of the room, where Anna lay sleeping. For these first few days of their marriage they'd touched each other very carefully, as if they were uncovering fragile bones in hard earth. But tonight at last they'd clung easily, comfortably, and Darrell listened to the deep silence of her rest.

Then he felt a faint tugging—first in his chest, then in his mind. He thought of the object that lay buried in a cloth in his suitcase on the floor of the closet: the weeping-face gorget he'd taken from the excavation before he'd climbed from the pit on that final night.

He crossed the room and found the closet doorknob in the dark. He turned it gently and opened the door. The hinge squeaked. He heard Anna shift in the bed and he paused. There was no further sound in the room, just voices from the street lifting a fragment of song that dissolved into laughter. Darrell entered the closet and his hands moved into the suitcase, through layers of cloth, down to a fine, hard center, the gorget. He unwrapped it where it lay and pulled it out, the stone cool and dense in his hands. Then the weeping face leaped from the dark. The light was on in the room.

Anna's voice said, "Darrell?"

He thought to hide the gorget again, but instead he stepped out of the closet. Anna lay propped up, her hair scattered against the pillow, her dark Indian eyes steady before him.

"What is it?" she said.

He crossed to her and sat and opened his hands. He looked with her at the stone face, simple, wide-eyed, the tears running in hard, jagged lines down the cheeks.

Anna's hand came forward, her fingertips touched the tears. "You saved it," she said.

"Yes."

"I'm glad."

Darrell looked at the face. The symbol of the death cult. The tears of the ancient Indians. The tears of men. His mind offered the accepted reason: the eyes wept from fear and from awe. "He's afraid," Darrell said. But it sounded wrong, this explanation.

Anna's fingers traced the path of the tears. Then she said, "No. It's not from fear."

Darrell looked hard at the face. "No," he repeated.

She spoke the words, but Darrell knew them already. "It's grief," she said. "At what men can do."

They did not move for a time. Then Darrell placed the gorget on the nightstand and he turned off the light.

They lay beside each other in the dark, stretched flat, their hands clutched together, the sounds in the street sharpening Darrell's sense of their separateness.

"You'll do your work again," she said.

"Yes," he said. "The past, at least, knew to weep."

They did not speak for a time and then Anna turned her face to him. "Is the thing still in your dreams?"

"Not anymore."

"For me either."

"That's good," Darrell said, low, a reflex.

Laughter rose from the street, and a car horn.

He did not know the reason, but Darrell felt the urge to say he was sorry.

ABOUT THE AUTHOR

ROBERT OLEN BUTLER is the author of seven critically acclaimed novels—*The Alleys of Eden, Sun Dogs, Countrymen of Bones, On Distant Ground, Wabash, The Deuce,* and *They Whisper*— and a collection of short stories, *A Good Scent from a Strange Mountain,* winner of the 1993 Richard and Hinda Rosenthal Foundation Award from the American Academy of Arts and Letters as well as the 1993 Pulitzer Prize for Fiction. He lives in Lake Charles, Louisiana, where he teaches creative writing at McNeese State University.